VANITY KILLED

J. A. WINRICH

Writer Jaw Books, P. O. Box 356, Ukiah, CA 95482
www.writerjaw.com

Copyright © 2015 J. A. WINRICH

Cover design by Debora Lewis, www.arenapublishing.org

ISBN: 0989565025
ISBN-13:978-0-9895650-2-8

DEDICATION

For Kären, Ruthann, Jan, Mimi,
Michelle,
Mariah and Angelica

ACKNOWLEDGMENTS

Thanks to my family and friends for their support, my critique groups for their insights, to my editor Ana Manwaring of JAM Manuscript Consulting, to my favorite grammar diva, Arlene Miller, M.A. at www.bigwords101.com, and to my book cover designer Debora Lewis, www.arenapublishing.org

Chapter 1

Today, the prized possession dies.

I hide behind the brocade drapes and peer through the sheer curtains at the front parlor window. Everything looks distorted.

My heart races. Blood rushes through my veins. Chills shoot along my spine and I shudder from the rush. I have to kill again.

The window stands ajar. Sarah Hudson's heels staccato-click on the brick walkway outside. Carsonville's foghorn blasts its eerie warning. The clicking halts. Sarah tilts her head. She abhors that warning of imminent grayness closing in just as I do. We detest the cloying salt sea odor that mixes with the acrid stench from the pulp mill. That mill spews its odors, but will soon be shut down.

The minute I learn she wants away from her Northern California hometown, I set my plan in motion. Sarah Hudson will spend eternity here.

The young woman gathers her full-length, fake sable coat tighter around her. A vain attempt to keep the bone-chilling summer fog from engulfing her as it does her surroundings. She glances about, and then weaves up the steps toward the porch.

She drank the champagne that I sent to the salon for her.

When she disappears from sight, I rush across the carpet to the parlor doors and peek through the crack I left there earlier.

It doesn't take long before one of the mahogany double doors flies open as if the wind had seized it. The door bangs against the shiny brass stop. With her arm still outstretched from pushing open the door, Sarah steps across the threshold into the foyer. She moves to the side, and then stands still. She folds her arms in front of her, probably expecting the butler to close the door.

The sound of her toe-tapping on the black marble floor resounds throughout the quiet house. I watch, although yelling, "Quit it!" overwhelms me. The fever builds inside me.

Her coat slides from her shoulders and travels down her slender body to a heap on the shiny floor. Sarah—some prized possession. Because of the way she treats her coat I dub it a good thing she refuses real fur. She says she can't wear something they murdered. But that doesn't stop her from wearing real leather shoes or jackets.

Sarah wraps her arms around her chartreuse Yves Saint Laurent dress. Sounding a tad tipsy, she calls, "James? James, come close this door." After a few seconds tick by, she giggles and stumbles over to the door. She slams it shut.

I take in a deep breath. My mouth drops open. I never spy on her this way and her actions are unexpected. Sarah turns her head, staring in the direction of the parlor door. I ease back, pressing against the wall, and hold my breath. It demands to be released. Ignoring my pounding heartbeat, I wait. Did she see me?

When she looks toward me, I notice a twinkle in her blue eyes. I have not seen those eyes so bright in a long time. Too bad this house has gotten the better of her. Or is it the people?

I peer through the crack. Sarah gazes toward the oak sidebar. She snakes her way over to it and fondles the bottle of Brut champagne I left in a silver ice bucket. I want her to drink more alcohol. It will make it easier for me in the end.

Instead of drinking, she rifles through the mail lying in the cut crystal bowl next to the bucket. "Cash, Cash, Cash," she mumbles. "He always gets mail. Don't I ever get any?"

Sarah talks aloud to herself now, an annoying habit. But I won't have to put up with it for much longer. No one will.

A gold-edged mirror hangs above the sidebar. Sarah moves to within inches of it and examines herself. How vain can she get? She brushes back a stray, shoulder-length strand of blond hair. Her tongue darts out to lick her full red lips, giving them a sensual, wet look.

Sarah steps back and turns sideways, with her gaze still glued to her reflection. I admire her sleek model-perfect frame.

"James, where are you?" Sarah yells, glancing back at the dark pile lying on the marble floor. She doesn't give that coat any further consideration than if it is a speck of dirt. She has grown dependent on the staff, expects them to cater to her. A pity she changed in the last two years—became so vain.

Sarah started out so perfect, a loving companion, full of

energy and kindness. She thought about others. Helped bring glory to this house. But I cannot tolerate the vanity.

"James, are you going to open this champagne for me?" Sarah hollers. After three seconds, she reaches for the bottle. When she pops the top off and the cork hits a gilt-framed picture, she laughs. Instead of using the etched-glass flute I set out, she swills the champagne from the bottle.

This amazes me. No one drinks champagne this way. Will it bubble out her nose?

The telephone rings. She sets the bottle down. "James?" The phone jingles. "Somebody get that," she yells again.

She tugs off her calfskin gloves and throws them on top of the mail. Sarah studies her hands. She went to Headline International to get dolled up. Even had her nails done. Perhaps that's why she does not answer the phone. Doesn't want to ruin her manicure.

The telephone shrills one more time.

Sarah yanks the receiver from its cradle. "Hello."

The mirror reflects Sarah's smile. "Rocky!" Her voice— ecstatic. "Oh, God, you're psychic. Are you calling because of my letter?" While she listens, she gulps some more of her favorite champagne. "You didn't get it yet? Oh, well, I've been so depressed lately." Sarah's sigh hisses like a leaky tire. "You *have* to come visit me. I must get away from this place or I'll… I'll kill myself."

Upon hearing those words, I grin. *'Perfect.'*

That statement seals my plans.

"Where are you and Perry headed?" Sarah asks. "You must come see me. This place has changed me so much. I hate myself. It's not me anymore. You can't imagine what it's like being part of someone's collection of beautiful treasures."

She sips some champagne. Then she glances over to the fake coat and shrugs. "I should have never come back to Carsonville. Help me get out of here."

"No," Sarah says after listening. "My letter explains everything. Yeah, I know I'm original, not a reproduction as you said some of his stuff is. I don't think Cash knows I'm aware they're copies. Wonder what he'd do if he did?

"Anyway, I want the old me back, get away from Carsonville. One way or the other, I'm leaving Cash. But, I know I won't be able to do it without you."

Sarah listens for a second, and then says, "Well, if you're coming, I'll try and hang on 'til you arrive. Where can I reach you?" After a brief pause, she screams, "What do you mean I can't?"

Sarah downs more champagne. "Oh, that's all right. No, no, no. Perry needs you. I'm sorry his boyfriend died. This is so you. Sometimes I get jealous and depressed that you two are so close. That used to be us. How I miss seeing you."

I notice her words are slurry. She's swaying on her feet.

"But," Sarah says, "if that's the way it has to be… Oh, Rocky, I don't know if I can survive until you get here."

Sarah—so full of herself—a drama queen. I stare at her. She sighs again, noticing her reflection in the mirror. She sets the bottle down and straightens a loose strand of hair.

You cannot stop admiring yourself, can you? I click my tongue.

Sarah whispers, "Ssh! I think someone's listening." She puts the phone on the sidebar and steps toward the parlor doors.

My heart races. I inhale a shallow breath.

After taking another step, yelling comes from the phone receiver.

Sarah runs back and snatches the phone up. "What? I don't see anyone. Probably my imagination. No, I don't need to call the police. Oh, that reminds me; guess who I ran into a couple of weeks ago?"

My eyes widen. I lean forward, waiting to hear her answer.

"Oh, all right," Sarah says. "Go catch your flight. I have to go to a party. I'll be busy this weekend anyway. See you Tuesday. Bye. Take care."

Too bad Sarah wants to move on. I can't allow that. If only—no, she is too vain. Why do women have to realize they're beautiful? How come they cannot remain innocent and unaware? They are so much more attractive when they don't acknowledge it. Beautiful things, including women, are objects of art—to be admired, and acquired.

Sarah gazes into the mirror. Her reflection shows a smile, but gradually it transforms into a taut line. "So I talk to myself. Big deal. That doesn't make me nuts. Besides, top models can do anything."

I chuckle aloud at that one.

Sarah turns to look at the parlor door. Did she hear me? I draw back. Every muscle in my body feels rigid. I shift my weight. The old wooden floor squeaks beneath my feet. I count to ten and sneak a look through the crack. Sarah is staring into the mirror and muttering, "Wait 'til Rocky finds out about Steve. Imagine Cash and him becoming close friends. Oh, Rocky, hurry, I need you."

So do I. My mind works like a movie projector. An idea forms. Not paying attention, I shift my weight again. The floor protests.

Sarah jerks her head to the left and leans back from gazing in the mirror. She places her hand over her heart. "Oh, Marie, you scared me. How long have you been standing there? Did you hear the phone ring?"

The maid saunters up to Sarah, looking her up and down. "I heard it. I just came over for more ice for the

Martins' party. I almost answered the phone in the other room, but you picked it up."

"You shouldn't eavesdrop on my conversations." Sarah snaps each word out. Then she picks up the champagne bottle and takes another sip.

Marie straightens to her full height and throws her shoulders back. Her face appears like a mask set in stone.

Sarah dabs at the corners of her mouth with her fingertips. "Oh, God, do I sound like a shrew? These past few days... not me... it's been rough."

Sarah rubs her temple. Perhaps she's getting another one of her famous headaches. The way she imbibes the champagne won't help.

Marie strolls over to the foyer. She picks up Sarah's coat from where it lies on the floor and returns to stand in front of the mirror beside Sarah.

Sarah puts on her best sympathy face and pouts. That look disturbs me. "Marie," she says, "your loyalty is with Mr. Lancaster. But please, James, Steve... they're helping me come up with a plan to talk with Cash so I won't hurt his feelings. Don't say anything."

Marie curtsies, something she never does. "Okey, dokey, ma'am," she says in a fake Southern drawl. "Lil' ole me done come over for some ice. You best get ready to go to the party next door now, missy."

"Thank you." Sarah nods. "I'll come over to the Martins' bash in a little bit."

Marie shakes her head and drops the coat on the table beside the mail. She spins around and hurries down the hall. Laughter echoes through the house.

A door slams.

Time stands still. I lean against the door, watching and waiting.

Sarah gazes into the hall mirror one last time before she

approaches the carpeted stairs. Resting one hand along the well-polished mahogany banister, she trudges upward. At the top of the stairs, she turns left and heads to the master suite.

I linger a few minutes. Out in the hallway, I grab the bottle of champagne from the ice bucket. Tiptoeing to the staircase, I climb the steps, wondering if Sarah senses anyone's presence. Or does she believe the maid left?

I creep up to the open bedroom door. A risk peeking into the room, but I have to know if she drinks more bubbly. She loves Brut more than the expensive champagne. For the drug to work as I plan, she needs to imbibe lots of alcohol.

The four-poster mahogany bed is in the center of the great room. It has a red and gold canopy, fringed with gold tassels. As Sarah walks by, she swats at a tassel. It sways back and forth. I hate that canopy. It reminds me of a brothel.

I can walk around in this room with my eyes closed and not bump into furniture. A black dust ruffle skirts the bed. A multi-colored Persian carpet covers most of the hardwood floor, muffling the clacking of Sarah's heels.

She reaches for the closed, gold heavy drapes. The chandelier that I helped pick out radiates the light in the room. In one motion, Sarah parts the curtains. The antique cream-colored lace drapes tall, slender windows. Fog surrounds the house with grayness.

When I move to get a better look, the floor squeaks. *Damn these wood floors.*

Sarah spins around, glancing about the room. If she hears me and does not drink the champagne, I will enact another plan. I press against the hallway's wall and freeze. The old house creaks again in protest.

I draw enough courage to spy again. Instead of

advancing toward the door, Sarah kicks off her white leather shoe toward the large Honduras armoire. The stiletto heel bangs against the door, denting the mahogany finish. She giggles. "Oh well, James will fix it," she says aloud, and shrugs. Her foot slides out of the other shoe. "He can fix anything, do everything."

Her words—more slurry than before. I smile. Relief floods me. She thinks only about herself. Pays no attention to the noises in the house.

In her stocking feet, Sarah reminds me of a Lipizzaner horse as she prances across the carpet. She snatches the golden amber orb from atop her dresser, and gazes at the beetle trapped within, millions of years ago. She kisses the rock and sets it back down, exactly where it had been. Patting the amber, I hear her mutter, "I understand how you feel."

Vanity brings her back to the mirror. From where I watch, I make out her reflection, but I don't think she can see me. Although she stares at herself, her eyes look vacant, miles away. Does she know her hand rests on the silver-framed picture of herself and her friend Amber Rockwell? Why does she always call Amber "Rocky"? It's a strong, unfeminine name, and I do not care for it. That has to change.

A silver tray, placed on the nightstand, contains a champagne flute which is situated by an ice bucket with another bottle of her favorite Brut champagne floating in melting ice. She pours some champagne into the glass. I can't believe she prefers the inexpensive champagne when she has so many different ones to choose from. Her other tastes run toward the expensive.

Sarah shoves the bottle in the bucket. Water sloshes and ice rattles. Her hand freezes.

If she sees the pill bottle, my plan is thwarted again.

Sarah drinks from the glass. I grin and clasp both hands together in anticipation. Soon all Sarah's troubles will disappear. And, it sounds like her friend Amber arrives on Tuesday. This fits perfectly into my new plan.

Amber—the next most prized possession in the collection.

CHAPTER 2

Amber settled into the window seat beside her friend Perry Cole. He adjusted his seat belt and said, "You did it. You actually got me on this plane."

"You had doubts, boss?" Amber used her *I'm shocked* tone and followed it with a warm smile. "You deserved a break. Tom can mind the shop without us. He knows antiques as well as we do. You haven't had a vacation in over a year."

Perry squirmed in his seat and rubbed his neck.

"Are you comfortable?" Amber asked. "Would you rather sit by the window?"

"I may appear fragile, too thin, and overworked, but don't coddle me." Perry clasped Amber's hand, squeezing gently with his long fingers. "I'm fine."

"Good." Leaning her head back against the seat, Amber thought about her phone call. "Sarah sounded really depressed. After we take off, I'll call her again."

"What, she broke a fingernail?"

"Don't be catty."

The engine's roar drowned out conversation and the

plane's shuddering alerted Amber to their imminent takeoff. To blot out images of explosions and body parts flying through the air, she needed to concentrate on something. She removed her wallet from her purse and opened it. She stared at the photo taken back in high school.

Her best friend stood next to her in the picture. Sarah was a half-inch taller at 5'10", but reed thin. Amber, who was so much thinner now than when she'd been in high school, carried an ample bosom over a slightly rounded belly. Sarah told her, "Rocky, you're just as beautiful as I am and could be a model, too. Redheads are in." Of course, Amber never believed Sarah, but never disagreed with her, knowing it pointless to argue.

Amber smiled. Sarah nicknamed her "Rocky" the first time they met in the Carsonville grade school. Sarah called her that name until they graduated and moved to New York. Sometimes, when Sarah used "Amber," Amber would look over her shoulder to see who Sarah was talking to. She would have to get used to the name "Rocky" again, as that's all she'd be hearing from Sarah.

"We're in the air now." Perry reached over and tapped the photo. "Stop looking at that picture and chewing on your hair."

Amber blushed, wishing she could get rid of her bad habit whenever she grew nervous. "Okay. I really miss having Sarah around. Oh, we talk every week, but it's not the same as being together." Amber stuffed the photograph back in her wallet.

Perry patted her hand. "I know. After our meeting in L.A., we'll join her in Carsonville. I'm anxious to meet the famous Cassius Robert Lancaster you've heard so much about. Do you suppose they call him Cash as a nickname, or because he's rich?"

"I don't know." Amber gazed at her boss. His light brown eyes lacked luster, and his trademark sparkle no longer existed. She missed his spunky attitude and was determined to help get that twinkle back.

He'd be upset when they didn't disembark in L.A. They were flying on to San Francisco. She'd planned the getaway weekend for Perry and hadn't even let Tom in on their real destination. The assistant could run the antique shop without them. She'd have to do some fast-talking so Perry wouldn't call Tom to let him know where they were staying in the city. If nothing else, she would confiscate the cell phones and turn them off for the weekend.

Amber studied Perry from the corner of her eye. He appeared much older than his sixty-eight years. She wished he'd let his short, brown hair grow out a little. He'd kept it shaved when Mark was so sick. Thinking of Perry's loss made her more aware of not having seen Sarah in a few years. Chatting on the phone, emailing and writing wasn't the same.

"After the pilot announces the all-clear for phone usage, I think I should call Sarah."

"Thought you said she was heading to a party. Besides, why bother? From what you've told me, you know how she exaggerates. Don't worry so much about her. What could possibly happen to her?"

Perry and Amber's long weekend was like a magenta sunrise over water—beautiful and serene. Tuesday, after wine tasting in Napa, Amber let Perry drive North on Highway 101. He maneuvered the rented Ford Mustang convertible on the narrow, scenic highway that meandered through Richardson's Grove. Large peeling-barked redwood trees towered with boughs reaching heavenward, blotting out the spotty sunshine that attempted to touch the red-needled earth below. The scent of pine wafted past.

"Perry, quit daydreaming. Drive faster. I can't wait to see Sarah."

"You're the one who dallied yesterday at all those wineries. I could have left for Carsonville after San Francisco."

"But you love Merlot and Cabernet," Amber said. "I showed you where they make some of the best wines in California, maybe in the world!"

"And I savored tasting each one. However, after those six champagnes we tasted, you bought Sarah a cheapie. Some friend you are."

"Brut's her favorite. She'll love it."

"She can't resist the bubbly, can she? I must confess, I've enjoyed this trip. Thank you."

Amber winked at her boss. "You're welcome. If not for your stubbornness, you would have had this vacation earlier. Now step on it. We're supposed to arrive today, not tomorrow."

"I got to have friends." Perry sang along with the song blasting from the oldies radio station. His off-key voice made Amber smile.

The song reminded her of Sarah. "Odd I haven't been able to reach anyone at Lancaster's place today. I shouldn't have insisted we turn off our cell phones until now."

"No reception on this road anyway," Perry said. "Quit worrying."

"I told Sarah we'd arrive on Tuesday," Amber said. "Where is everyone? At least some staff member should answer." Amber looked at Perry as if he could explain.

He stopped singing and glanced over. His eyes twinkled. "What staff members?"

"Cash Lancaster's. How come they haven't answered the phone?"

"You telephoned once from a gas station pay phone and received no answer." Perry chuckled. "Possibly when they discovered you were bringing an old gay guy to their Carsonville abode, they all flew the coop."

"Don't be silly. You're adorable."

"You and I know that, but aren't we heading for a macho, redneck town where others might have different ideas?"

Amber laughed, appreciating her boss's sense of humor. "I doubt Sarah would have a boyfriend like that. Cash doesn't sound the redneck type. Bet there's an explanation for no one answering. I should have tried calling this weekend."

CHAPTER 3

Perry and Amber passed the flag pole at Fields Landing where, when the flag was up, they had fresh crab. Amber's heart raced. Carsonville loomed ahead. A year—too long not to see Sarah, but she couldn't find time away from her job. She dug deep inside herself. She realized she hadn't returned to this town because she hated the fog and the depression she felt when here. Even her best friend hadn't been enough to pull her back, until now.

Carsonville was filled with beautiful, Victorian homes. But sometimes, when she drove by those old houses, she'd picture Dracula's mansion with dying plants and black birds flying about. She rubbed her arms, feeling the goose bumps.

Sarah told her all of the details of her life. They were still as close as a hermit crab to its shell.

"I can't believe it's quarter to four," Amber said as Perry pulled the car into a circular driveway. It was one of a kind in this neighborhood littered with two-story Victorian homes. They stopped behind a catering truck.

"Looks like Sarah's gone all out for you, Amber. A party. Unless, we're at the wrong place."

The caterer grabbed a large bowl from the vehicle and shoved the doors closed with his elbow.

At their last stop for gas, Perry put the top up to ward off the damp coastal chill. He rolled down the window, and called out, "Is this the Lancaster residence?"

The young man walked back to the car and glanced at his watch. "Yeah, but I didn't expect anyone this early. It's not time yet. I'm not quite set up."

"Is anyone home?" Amber asked.

"No one's back yet." The caterer leaned down, looking across to her, and creased his brow. "Weren't you at the funeral?"

Amber inhaled sharply, feeling an icy numbness wash over her. "No. Who died?"

After checking his watch again, the caterer said, "Some lady. Services were at three, with a grave side address after."

The blood drained from Amber's face. Her ears buzzed. She barely heard Perry as he asked, "Where?"

"I suspect they'd be at Ocean View Cemetery-Sunset Memorial Park over on South Broadway by now. It's right off 101. You can't miss it."

Perry jammed the car in reverse and peeled out. "Don't think. It's not Sarah. Just give me directions."

The cemetery graced the hillside overlooking the bay. Gray headstones dotted the luscious green lawn like so many soldiers ready for battle.

Seeing cars and a cluster of people, Amber directed Perry to the site where two tall pillars guarded over the graves. She recognized those columns. They marked Sarah's grandparents and the Hudson family plot. They drove slowly through the narrow alleyways separating tracts of headstones. A black limousine, along with a few other cars, pulled away from the site.

Perry maneuvered the car into the limo's vacated spot and parked behind another one. He jumped out and hurried around to the passenger side. After opening the door, he reached in. Amber grabbed his hand, but could hardly breathe. Could this be Sarah's funeral? Sarah's mother?

Amber let Perry help her from the car. Fear reduced her to Jell-O. She took a few tentative steps and stopped. She searched for Sarah and Sarah's parents.

People surrounded a mound of green Astroturf where a shiny black casket sat atop metal braces ready to lower the box into the freshly dug hole. Amber's legs felt like some giant alien held them riveted to one spot. She didn't want to think who lay in the casket.

The reverend intoned Sarah's name as he touched the black box. Amber's knees gave way. Perry kept her from crumpling to the ground. Tears flowed down her face.

"My God, this is Sarah's funeral," Amber muttered. "But it can't be!"

Perry hugged her tight and whispered, "I'm so sorry."

The reverend mumbled more kind words to the mourners passing by the casket; many placed flowers on top, before they wandered off to their cars. Amber remained motionless, staring helplessly. Perry gripped her waist as the attendants, using a hand crank, lowered the casket into the ground.

Someone cleared his throat near where Perry and Amber stood.

Amber, who'd been staring at her feet, peered up through her blurry eyes at a stocky man in a black suit, his dark eyes tear-filled. He said, "I'm pleased you made it.

You don't look anything like your picture that Sarah has by our bed. You are Amber Rockwell?"

Amber wiped her runny nose. "Are you Mr. Lancaster?"

"Please call me Cash." He dabbed a handkerchief to the corners of his eyes, and ran a hand through black wavy hair. His sideburns were a mottled gray. "We attempted to locate you."

His gaze drifted towards the grave, then back to Amber. He gently enclosed her hand in his. "I'm very sorry, Sarah's dead."

Amber depended on Sarah her whole life. Without her presence... it was impossible to accept anything would seem real with her gone.

"No," she whispered. "I just spoke with her on Friday. Didn't she..." Amber talked slightly louder. "Didn't she tell you I phoned? That we'd be here today?"

"I didn't get a chance to talk with her on Friday. That's when she died."

"Oh, God, no!" Amber twisted away from Lancaster's grasp and fell against Perry, sobbing. Her boss patted her back until her racking cries became a low moan and her body calmed.

"Amber, this is such a shock," Lancaster said, "Please, ride back to the house in the limo with me. We'll have a few moments alone to talk. Your friend can follow us in his car."

Amber sniffed and swiped her tears away. Searching beyond the man to the dark hole in the ground, she said, "I don't understand. What happened?"

"She was very depressed." Lancaster shook his head. "I don't know why. I was next door attending a party at the Martins. When she didn't come over, I went home. Found her on our bed."

As he hesitated, a tear rolled down his cheek. Lancaster

stared at the grave. "I thought she'd fallen asleep. I bent down to kiss her. Oh..." The tear dripped off his chin. "When my lips met her cold skin, I couldn't believe it. Her face was so pale."

He looked back to Amber. "She was already dead. Nothing I could do for her."

Anguish laced his voice. Amber studied him. The politician's grin Sarah had so vividly described had been wiped off his face. He brushed tears aside. Amber shifted away from Perry and rested her hand gently on Lancaster's arm. "I'm sorry."

The reverend walked over. "Mr. Lancaster, if there's anything further I can do for you, please call."

"Thank you, Reverend. You did fine."

"I'm confused. You're not a Catholic priest," Amber stated. "Sarah and her family, they're Catholic."

"No, young lady, I'm not a priest, but I assure you Sarah is in God's hands now."

"Thank you, Reverend," Lancaster said. "This is Amber Rockwell and..."

"I'm Perry Cole. We work together."

"Ah, you're her boss," Lancaster said. "I've heard about you." He addressed the reverend, explaining, "They just arrived. Amber didn't know about Sarah."

The reverend clasped Amber's hands. His were warm, clammy; hers were ice cold. "I'm so sorry for your loss. Come see me if you need to. However, I regret that now I must attend another funeral. If you'll excuse me." He nodded at Perry, patted Amber's hand, and strode away. His black suit jacket flapped in the breeze.

Amber ran to the grave, slumping to the ground. The Astroturf prickled her knees and hands. She leaned over and gazed down through the machinery that had lowered Sarah's coffin into its final resting place. She smelled freshly dug earth and spotted the black casket. She flashed back to high school. *This should have been me.*

Her parents had been on a drinking binge that day. She walked into the room and her father slurred "You're so fat, Amber, why don't you lose some weight." She fought back tears. Her mother screamed, "Don't call her fat!"

That started the routine argument. The voices grew louder, the name-calling heightened. She couldn't live like this any longer.

Amber ran from the room, gathered as many pills from the medicine cabinet as she could, and hurried out back to Sarah's and her tree house.

Tears flowed down her face as she swallowed the pills. The empty bottles littered around her. She grabbed a notepad and wrote to Sarah explaining why she couldn't live any longer.

She lay down, put the note on her chest, and closed her eyes.

"Rocky! Rocky! Are you here! Wait 'til you see our pictures," Sarah yelled as she rushed into the tree house.

Sarah screamed.

She shook Amber until her eyes fluttered open. Tears streamed down Sarah's face. "What have you done?"

Sarah opened the cupboard where she'd stashed all kinds of medical supplies. After cutting herself once in the tree house, she stocked it with everything so she would always be prepared for any future emergencies.

She forced Rocky to drink the ipecac so she would throw up. After Rocky puked her guts up, Sarah took her to her own house and paced with her all night to keep her awake.

Sarah and Amber told no one what had happened. Back at the tree house, Sarah cleaned up the mess, and said, "Rocky, we'll make a sacred pact. We will *never* commit suicide. Besides being a sin, we *won't* do that to each other. When things get bad, no matter what, we'll find each other and talk it out."

She showed Rocky the picture they'd had taken of each other together. She'd made a copy for each of them. Sarah pricked their thumbs with a pin and on the back of each picture, they pressed down leaving bloody thumbprints. Sarah wrote "I swear" and below, they signed their names to seal the solemn pact.

Amber carried hers in her wallet. She'd just looked at it on the plane. Sarah kept hers in a silver frame by her bed. If it hadn't have been for Sarah, Amber would have been in this grave her junior year in high school.

Oh, God, Sarah, how did this happen? Amber's tears dripped down onto the casket.

The men walked up behind her.

Perry asked Lancaster, "How did Sarah die?"

Amber jumped up. "For God's sake, how *did* she die?"

"Oh, dear, I'd like to think it was an accident." Lancaster reached out and clutched her arm. "However, the official version, I'm afraid, is suicide."

"Suicide?" Amber blinked several times and stepped away from Lancaster's touch. "No way. Sarah would never do such a thing!"

"You haven't been around her lately. She'd changed."

"We kept in touch. I talked to her on Friday. She sounded down, depressed, but she made no mention of..." Amber stopped, struggling to think clearly. "No, no that is not possible. I don't believe it."

After Amber lost her parents, she'd not been able to figure out what happened. Now her best friend was gone and she knew she'd never have committed suicide. Not with *their* pact. *My God, I can't go through another death without finding the truth.*

Sarah's death brought back horrible memories from a year ago. She received the call at work in New York: her mother murdered and her father disappeared. Blood at the scene indicated both parents were involved. Was her father dead, too? Even though she had searched to find out what happened, that tragedy never achieved closure. This time she would find an explanation for Sarah's death. *I will find out what happened to you. This time I'll uncover all the circumstances.*

"Mr. Cole," Lancaster said, "it's a good thing you're traveling with Amber. I'm only now beginning to accept Sarah's death, partially recovering from the shock. Amber will be just starting."

"True," Perry said, moving closer to Amber. "This trip started out so wonderfully. She was ecstatic about seeing Sarah."

"We tried desperately to reach you. Mr. and Mrs. Hudson asked constantly, 'Where's Rocky? Where's Rocky'? The person at your store said you'd be here today, but didn't know what time. I'm so relieved you made it when you did."

"Why didn't you leave a message on our cell phones?" Perry asked.

Amber was relieved Perry asked the questions. Tears flowed like lava, searing her heart. She couldn't find her voice.

"Told your manager not to," Lancaster said. "It would have been awful to hear that way."

"We didn't call Tom back," Perry said. "When we finally got reception, Amber saw a call from Tom, but assumed it was business related. She wanted to wait and see Sarah first. By the way, where are Mr. and Mrs. Hudson?"

Amber wondered the same thing.

"You just missed them. I'm afraid they didn't approve of having the reverend. Said it should have been a priest. But the reverend is a friend of mine. Sarah and I attended his church. The Hudsons' limousine drove away when you arrived." Lancaster glanced down at his wrist, peering at his watch. "I'm sorry, but I'd better get to the house. Everyone will be waiting for me."

"Of course," Perry said. "The caterer is the one who informed us about the funeral. I still can't believe it's Sarah."

Amber gripped Perry's arm, glaring at Lancaster. "Neither can I."

"I'm very sorry. I'm sure you have many questions. Perhaps we can discuss this later," Lancaster said. "I need to leave now."

Amber couldn't stop crying. She hated it whenever she lost control. Someone else must have invaded her body. This whole scene reminded her of one of those bad horror movies that Sarah and she used to watch. Any minute the coffin would rise up. Sarah would climb out and yell, 'Gotcha!'

Amber did need to talk. But she didn't know Lancaster. She wanted to hear this from Sarah's parents. She yanked a strand of hair that found its way into her mouth away from her lips. *Dang, that blasted habit.* "You're right. We should go."

"Please join me in the limousine. We can talk on the way."

"No, thanks," Amber said. "We'll follow you."

Limousines weren't abundant in Carsonville, so Amber didn't worry that Perry would get lost. He had no trouble following the sleek, black car.

Amber sat silently for several blocks.

"Are you okay?" Perry asked.

"No. I want to figure out what's going on." Her voice cracked. "Sarah can't be dead."

"I felt that way when I buried Mark. With AIDS and then his heart condition, I at least could prepare for his death." Perry reached over and grasped Amber's hand. "I know how this has shocked you, but you have to find a way to calm down."

"Sarah would never kill herself."

"I'm positive you feel that way, but admit it—you haven't seen her for awhile. You said she told you about her depression."

"But she sounded excited about our visit. She mentioned something about helping her escape Cash."

"Amber, *escape* was not the word you used earlier when you told me about your conversation."

"All I know is I have to talk with Sarah's parents."

CHAPTER 4

Amber sat in the Mustang parked behind Lancaster's limousine. A tall man dressed in tails came out from the driver's side. At the back of the car, he stepped onto a lawn so manicured his footprints bounced back. After the chauffeur opened the rear door, Lancaster emerged onto the brick walkway that led up to the stately two-story Victorian.

Perry came around and Amber exited the rental car. A whiff of the citrus scent from the Mexican orange hedge that surrounded the house drifted past. For a minute, the smell took her back to when she lived in Carsonville. Her own family home had the same hedge. She loved coming home to the smell. That fragrance should be a perfume— probably was.

However, this massive house was double, or even triple, the size of the one she'd lived in. Stained glass glowed in the windows, but they gave her an eerie feeling, as if someone watched her every move.

Her unease meandered in with the fog as it wended its way around the Victorian's green towers and turrets, creeping along the widow's walk. She felt anxious, doomed. Something terrible was going to happen. Something terrible *had* happened.

Lancaster walked over. "Welcome to my home. I wish this was under different circumstances. Amber, this is James." Lancaster motioned to the chauffeur. "He's my driver and my butler. If there's anything you need, just ask him. James, this is Amber Rockwell and her boss Perry Cole."

"Mr. Cole." The butler inclined his head, but did not smile.

As he turned to Amber, thick eyebrows shaded his dark eyes like an awning. His look was so sinister it reminded her of old Boris Karloff horror movies.

"Ms. Rockwell," James said. "It is such a blessing you arrived today. Mr. Lancaster was so agitated when he could not contact you."

"I was. James, would you please see to the guests inside the house. I'll walk Amber and Perry in."

"Very good, Mr. Lancaster. Ms. Rockwell, Mr. Cole, if you will excuse me, I will see that all is well inside. A pleasure meeting you."

"Thank you, James," Amber said to the retreating butler.

"Come in," Lancaster said. "People insisted on coming to honor Sarah out of respect for me. I had to have a wake or some sort of a gathering after the funeral. They've arrived from all over the country. I'd like you to meet some of them."

Lancaster escorted Amber up the walkway. Perry stayed one step behind. Purple pansies, orange marigolds and other flowers bloomed in the cultivated beds. The colors soothed Amber's anxiety a little until she noticed the blood-red roses. How she hated that color since her parents died.

As the three of them climbed the steps, the murmur of voices and music drifted out from the ornately-carved mahogany front doors that stood ajar.

On the porch, Amber moved away from Lancaster and clasped Perry's hand. She gave it a squeeze. He lifted his chin and she nodded, knowing she had to be strong.

"Are you coming?" Lancaster asked.

"Go on," Amber said. "I need a minute." She took a gulp of foggy air and straightened her spine.

Lancaster hesitated, but then continued on into the house.

"Can you believe this place?" Amber scanned the façade.

"Impressive. I can hardly wait to see inside. All the antiques Sarah talked about." Perry slipped his arm through Amber's. "Shall we go in?"

"Guess we better. Let's find Sarah's parents." By the time they entered the house, Lancaster had been swallowed up in the throng.

"May I take your coats?" James asked in a deep resonant voice.

"Thank you, James."

"If you need anything, please ask." The butler took their coats, and then maneuvered his way through the assembled guests. He disappeared before Amber could ask if he knew where Dan and Linda Hudson were.

Standing on the marble foyer, Perry and Amber stared. "Sarah wrote and told me lots of details," Amber said. "But not enough to prepare me for this."

"Get a load of those paintings along the stairwell," Perry said. "Too bad they're not the originals." He pointed. "That particular Monet is in the Louvre in Paris. I've seen that original Renoir in The Metropolitan Museum of Art in New York City."

A noisy crowd arrived, pushing the two of them farther

into the house. People in the drawing room held champagne glasses, eating caviar and canapés. A curved-back couch overflowed with beautiful women with slender legs, long flowing hair, and perfect makeup. Men, dressed in dark suits with somber ties, stood behind the women. Some of the men stole glances down the women's ample fronts.

An Elton John song, Sarah's favorite singer, blared through unseen speakers. A Tiffany lamp, with crystals swaying to the music's beat, sat on a table near the settee. The light shined through the prisms, bouncing red, blue, and yellow around the room.

Amber overheard bits of conversations highlighting food, music, arts, and modeling. Like a wave, the voices rose and fell. She missed the beginning of a story by two women nearby. "... and Sarah threw a fit." She caught disconnected snatches until one woman's voice rose: "... broke one of his best pieces. Can you believe that maid's behavior around her boss..."

Her chance at fitting the puzzle pieces together shattered when Perry's voice pierced the din. "Shall we split up or search together to find Mr. and Mrs. Hudson?"

Amber wished she could have heard more of the women's conversation, but one of them squinted at her and steered the other off into the crowd. Although she considered that she might learn more without Perry's presence, she said, "Don't you dare leave me. I'll never find you again."

While she pondered which direction to proceed, a waiter offered them wine from a silver tray.

"Thank you." Amber took a glass. As she looked around, she swirled the Merlot within the fine crystal. "Have you ever seen anything like this?"

Perry studied the glass. "Why, yes—"

"No, not the glass," Amber interrupted. "This party. This bash." She gaped at the antics. "Perry, he's throwing a real party. Not a wake or celebration of life, but a party! They just lowered Sarah into the ground. How could he?"

When a deep voice from behind said, "Everyone handles grief in his or her own way, Ms. Rockwell," Amber flinched. The butler then said, "I believe it is the custom to have family and friends close, to comfort one during a time of grief."

James circled around, peering down his nose at her. A twinge of fear surged through her as she saw his eyes darken to inky, inscrutable pools. Amber backed away before they could suck her in. His squared shoulders reminded her of a football guard, protecting the all-important quarterback. He grew in stature right before her. "He loved your friend a great deal. She should not have killed herself," he stated matter-of-factly, and marched off.

Amber stared open-mouthed after him. "That man appears and disappears like a sorcerer. I still didn't get to ask him where Sarah's parents are."

Perry set the two half-filled glasses on a nearby table. "Come on. Let's find them."

They searched the main floor, hoping the next room would lead to the Hudsons. Instead, loud people crammed each space. Snatches of conversations were again overheard: "... I don't understand...," "... too young, too beautiful...," "... but her depression lately...," "... so different from when I first met her...," "... that maid is impossible...," "... wish something could have been done...," and "... we should have paid more attention to her latest actions...," "... a big clue...,"

Amber wondered about Sarah's actions. What behaviors were different?

No one seemed to know where Sarah's parents were.

Amber felt most of them didn't even know the Hudsons. After a thorough search downstairs, including the kitchen, Amber asked, "Where are they? I haven't seen Lancaster either."

Perry stroked his chin as they stood near the staircase. "Perhaps we should call their hotel room?"

"Which motel or hotel?"

"Why don't we try the next level?" Perry pointed up the stairs lined in red velvet where more people stood on each step, looking like models posed for a magazine. Some held champagne glasses, others bottles of Perrier.

"Why not? Can't find them downstairs, so they must be up. I have no intention of leaving this house until I figure out what's going on. After we talk with the Hudsons, we'll leave and check into a hotel."

Climbing the steps, they jostled their way through the crowd. At the landing, Amber noticed a sculpture of a Michelangelo angel—another reproduction. She knew from Sarah's description of the house that the master bedroom was to the left.

The bedroom door stood open. Amber stepped inside the room and stopped suddenly. Perry bumped into her. Lancaster and another man were poised in front of a dressing table with their backs to the door, staring down at something in Lancaster's hand. The tall, blond man, dressed in a black suit similar to Lancaster's, had his head bent studying whatever commanded their attention.

"She was distracted," Lancaster said, "but I did not attach any significance to it. She even mumbled to herself." His cheeks appeared sunken, face pale. "I never dreamed she was that depressed."

"Suicides are often perplexing," the man said. "I met her for the first time a couple of weeks ago. Even so, I wouldn't have thought someone so vivacious would kill herself."

"Sarah would not do that," Amber blurted out.

Both men spun around. Lancaster almost dropped the silver-framed picture. Amber recognized his blonde-haired companion. *Oh, my God, why did he just lie about when he'd met Sarah?*

Lancaster shoved the picture into the man's hands and rushed forward. "Oh, Amber, this must be so difficult for you."

"But she told me—"

"Excuse me, Ms.—"

"I'm sorry, Steve," Lancaster said. "This is, you know, *the Amber*—Amber Rockwell, Sarah's best friend. This is Police Detective Steve Burns." He hesitated, then said, "Oh, and Steve, this is Amber's boss Perry."

"Perry Cole, Detective." They nodded at each other. The detective hadn't moved. Perry said, "Amber learned about Sarah an hour ago. She hasn't come to grips with her death."

Amber couldn't believe Steve Burns had become a detective. When he dated Sarah in high school, he couldn't find a black rabbit in a snowstorm. Now, detecting was his job.

His lips parted slightly. Burns furrowed his brow, examining her face as if studying it for imperfections. Then he gazed down at the picture Lancaster had given him and shook his head. He placed the framed photo atop the nearby dressing table. "I understand. The assistant coroner and I handled this investigation."

Why didn't Steve acknowledge her? Amber wondered. He looked as shocked as she felt. She wasn't sure what held her back from asking him why. Instead, she said, "Then, as usual, you handled it all wrong. Sarah would never do something like this. Where are Dan and Linda?"

Lancaster glanced from one to the other. "Do you two—"

"I don't think they're here," Detective Burns said. "Are they, Mr. Lancaster?"

"What?" Lancaster asked, running his hand through his hair. "Oh. No. Mr. and Mrs. Hudson refused to come here because of the suicide."

"Quit saying that." Amber walked to the table and picked up the silver-framed picture the men had been scrutinizing. Sarah still had their blood-pact picture. Sarah appeared the same, but... Amber grimaced. Since this picture had been taken, she'd lost a lot of weight, let her hair grow, and now wore contacts.

She sighed, still studying the photo. "We were best friends. I may live in New York, but we kept in close contact. I would have known if Sarah were about to do what you said."

Suffocating silence filled the room.

Burns cleared his throat. "I'm sorry for your loss. I understand what it's like. Miss Hudson was dear to us all."

Amber tore her gaze away from the photo. She glared into Burns' blue eyes. "She was, Detective." The word "detective" stuck in her throat. She couldn't fit the "high school Steve Burns" with this man.

"You're in shock." Burns placed one hand on her shoulder. "But I assure you, I'm an experienced police investigator. All the evidence pointed to suicide. Even the Hudsons were concerned about her depression."

Clearing his throat again, Burns held up a hand, warding off any comments. "The coroner investigator on this case, a Dr. Mayhill, checked and rechecked. So did I. As much as

I hoped for another diagnosis, Dr. Mayhill ruled it a suicide.

"You don't agree with any of this now, but come to the station tomorrow. We'll discuss the particulars. Ms. Hudson left you a note. I didn't know you'd be here, so I don't have a copy with me. Besides, now is not the proper time."

Amber, too stunned to respond, just blinked. Sarah wrote her a note.

"Mr. Lancaster, I'd better go." Burns shook hands with Lancaster and Perry. Digging in his wallet, he removed a business card and thrust it into Amber's hand. "Please call me. I'll answer all your questions. Again, I'm very sorry for your loss." The detective marched toward the door.

Amber stared at the card. "Steve, wait. What *did* the note say?" She ran after him and grabbed his arm. "Please, tell me now."

He lifted her hand off his arm. "She wrote, 'I'm sorry,' but as I said, we'll discuss it tomorrow when you've worked through the shock. Get some rest."

Unable to utter a sound, she watched him hurry off. He was right about one thing: The shock had beaten her like a punching bag. *Why didn't he acknowledge me? And what did he mean, get some rest, as if I could.*

From behind her, Lancaster asked, "Steve?"

"What?" Amber turned around. "Isn't that what you called him?"

"Well, I did," Lancaster said.

"That man is so infuriating." Amber rubbed the back of her neck. "Why wouldn't he say more about Sarah's note?"

"He's a little abrupt," Lancaster said, "but he did a thorough investigation. This is hard on all of us. For now, can't we push this nasty business aside?"

Lancaster guided her gently through the doorway into

the hall where they strolled past the fake angel. Perry followed.

"Do you have any idea what the note said exactly?" Amber waited for an answer.

"Just what Steve, er, the detective told you. 'I'm sorry.' Please, I can't talk about this anymore. Let's talk tomorrow, but for now, I don't want to even think about it." He took a deep breath. "It's too painful. Please—do as Detective Burns suggested and discuss it with him tomorrow."

A little farther down the hall, Lancaster opened a door. "This will be your room, Amber. Perry is across the hall, two doors down."

Amber's lower jaw dropped. She couldn't help but think how Sarah used to tell her if she didn't close her mouth, she'd catch flies.

Her suitcase lay open on the bed. A woman, about her own age, dressed in a low-cut, black and white uniform, hustled about the room, unpacking for her. "How?" Amber managed to ask.

Lancaster clasped her hand in his and gazed into her eyes. "I took the liberty of having your suitcases brought up. I assumed you planned to stay here. Even though Sarah is gone, she would have wanted you to." He squeezed her hand. "Perry, I believe James is unpacking your things as well."

Amber hated it when men did things without asking. Women were not objects. Sarah said Lancaster controlled everything. Amber resented his actions all the more. But, she held back the anger threatening to boil over, and inhaled deeply. She exhaled, withdrew her hand from Lancaster's, and entered the room. The men followed. Her jaw tightened, but she forced a smile. "Thank you, Mr. Lancaster."

"Please, call me Cash."

"Cash," Amber said, although the word sent a cold shiver through her. "I'm sure Sarah *would* have wanted us to stay here. However, if you'll excuse me, I'm very tired, and I would like to rest."

"Oh, of course." Lancaster backed out. "I'll see you—"

"In the morning. I can't handle any more."

"I'm sorry. Get some rest and I'll see you tomorrow morning." Lancaster smiled.

Oh, my God, Amber thought. *There's that grin Sarah told me about.*

Lancaster's smile resembled a politician who had just won an election. It was brief and blank. This smile either meant nothing, or covered something up. He headed down the hall.

Amber thought about slamming the door, but remembered the maid, who still hustled about in the room, so she shut the door slowly. She whirled around.

Perry reached out and squeezed her hand. "You okay?"

Amber eyed the maid. Unpacking completed, she now lifted the suitcase up onto the top closet shelf. "Oh, Perry, this whole thing is just too much."

Pastel flowered wallpaper hung from ceiling to floor. Scatter rugs covered most of the polished hardwood flooring. Amber ran her hand along the intricately carved footboard of the bed. It had a matching headboard. The Japanese double-grained oak antique furniture reminded her of her own bedroom from her teenage years. The set included a highboy dresser and another smaller dresser with an attached mirror. It was so familiar.

Curtains, pulled back and secured with a pink silk rope, framed the windows, revealing gray fog beyond. It threatened to billow in, enveloping the town, as usual.

Next to the bed she smelled fresh-cut roses from the garden that had been arranged in a Waterford crystal vase.

She murmured, "Great room."

Perry stood just behind her. When Amber tapped his shin with the toe of her shoe and tilted her head toward the maid, Perry stammered in response, "It… it is. Just like the entire house. I could spend hours inspecting all the collectibles here." He sauntered over to the dresser and examined a large piece of rose quartz.

The maid turned down the bed, and with a flourish, fluffed the pillow. "Will there be anything else?"

"No, thank you," Amber said.

The maid closed the door behind her with a gentle click.

"What are you up to?" Perry raised an eyebrow.

Amber tiptoed to the door, pressing her ear against it. Loud music still blasted through the house. She pointed to the bed. They sat. She whispered, "Something terrible happened in high school, and I know for a fact Sarah would never kill herself. I'm going to get to the bottom of this. What better place to start than here in this house? Get close to Lancaster."

"What happened?"

Amber shook her head, not ready to tell her horrible secret. Her lip trembled.

"All right, don't tell me," Perry said, "but you should rest up. You'll think clearer in the morning."

"No, Perry, something is not right here. Does Lancaster act like a grieving lover?"

"Well…"

Amber pressed her fingertips lightly against Perry's lips. "We all grieve differently. But all this," she motioned with a sweep of her hand, encompassing not only the bedroom, but also the bash happening downstairs. "It's unbelievable.

"And, that detective's acting odd. I know him. Sarah dated Steve Burns in high school. The three of us were close. That is until Sarah refused to marry him and came to New York with me after graduation.

"He really knows you?" Perry stared at her.

Amber, feeling nervous, walked to the dresser. Another vase filled with roses sat on top. "Why didn't he acknowledge me?"

Perry rubbed his chin. "I don't know. You have changed a bit since then. However, it is odd."

"I have to resolve all of this." Amber trailed her finger down the stem of a rose until it caught on a thorn. She sucked the tiny dot of blood from her finger. "I need to discern just how Sarah died. I'm not sure how I'll manage getting close to Lancaster, but I'll find a way. Sarah told me only beautiful things interested him, including women. That leaves me out. But, somehow I'm going to endear myself to that man and learn what happened to her."

CHAPTER 5

As I walk down the stairs, the music blasts a snappy beat. I smile, thinking about my new acquisition to the collection. The new plan is working well. Glad I can think fast. I put Amber right where I want her. Mr. Cole will not be a factor, nor Sarah's letter. Why had she written that stupid letter? Well, it doesn't matter. I will take care of it just as I did the other letter.

Mingling amongst the mourners, I think of poor Sarah. She would have enjoyed this party. At first, I believe she's the right one—so beautiful, and she cares for people. Not full of herself like other models. But, damn it, she changes—becomes vain. Give women money, some authority, and all of a sudden they think so much of themselves, as if they're better than everyone else. Too bad—but it is my job to show them.

I must keep a close eye on Amber. Help guide her in the right direction. I know she *is* the one. She can fulfill my dreams and plans. If she changes like the others... Well, no, I refuse to think about that possibility.

First, I have to retrieve that letter Sarah wrote before Amber sees it. Good thing I hear Sarah mention it over the phone. A slight problem, but nothing I cannot handle. I have practiced.

CHAPTER 6

Amber stepped into the claw-footed tub that served as a shower. Antiques and period replica plumbing gave her the impression she'd gone back to a safer time. She drew closed the white lace curtain hanging from the gold-colored frame shutting out the dull morning light. The curtain surrounded the tub. This all reminded her of her own bathroom when she'd grown up here in Carsonville. She twisted the shiny brass handles. The water heated. She flipped the lever and the showerhead sprayed warm droplets over her body.

After lathering up, she rolled her shoulders, easing her nervous tension from last night. She basked in the warmth of the water cascading down, rinsing her off.

As she reached for the faucet handles, she froze. She strained to listen.

The hairs on the back of her neck rose. She pictured a knife plunging down, ripping through the lace into her torso. With her trembling hand, she yanked the curtain back.

No one.

Get a grip. Amber banished images from the movie *Psycho.* She'd have to keep a tighter control on her over-active imagination. This house revved it up. All kinds of sinister scenarios ran through her mind. She shivered. *This house makes me want to put on my clothes and run away as if a mountain lion is chasing me. Or, maybe the people are getting to me? Is this how Sarah felt?*

Wrapped in a towel, Amber stared into the oak-framed mirror hanging above the marble sink. It still seemed as if someone watched, even now, but only her face reflected in the mirror. Sunken eyes, dark circles, pale cheeks. Then Sarah's voice echoed in her mind. "No matter what you look like, you can change it with make-up." Amber smiled. Then her throat tightened. She fought back tears. As kids, Carsonville was their playground. Sarah and she used to ride bikes all over the city, even along this street. *Where did that thought come from?*

How did this happen to you, Sarah?

Amber donned her bathrobe and went down the hall. Back inside her room, the bed was made. The staff was too efficient. She wanted to crawl back under the covers and mope all day, but, no—too much to do. Dressed in a navy blue pantsuit with low-heeled matching shoes, she surveyed the room one last time, and closed the door behind her.

Perry's door remained shut. She didn't want to bother him. He needed his sleep. Amber descended the stairs slowly, gliding her hand along the polished banister, studying the paintings. *Sarah hated museums. Maybe Lancaster believed she'd never know when he bragged he had originals. Or had he found out Sarah knew the paintings were copies? Could that be why Sarah was dead?*

The butler greeted her at the bottom of the staircase. He wore the same crisp uniform as the night before. He stood erect, chin high in the air, his eyebrows knitted. "Ms.

Rockwell. I trust you had a restful night. Breakfast is served in the dining room. If you will follow me, please."

Amber thought as he strode away, *He walks as if he's been starched. I bet if he bent any part of his body it would break, or at least make a horrible creaking noise.*

"Your friend, Mr. Cole, is partaking of his breakfast. I am afraid it is too early for Mr. Lancaster. He has not yet arisen."

Amber glanced at her gold Timex. "It's eight A.M." In New York, she would have been up for hours by now. It surprised her that Perry awoke early, but that Lancaster still slept. She remembered Sarah said he rose early. *I bet the party last night kept him up into the wee hours.*

"That is correct. Eight A.M. is quite early, Ms. Rockwell." The butler opened the dining room door.

"Good-morning." Perry forked food into his mouth. Speaking between bites, he said, "Breakfast is wonderful. Anything you could want."

Scrambled eggs, pancakes, bacon, sausage, and Danish pastries were laid out on individual warming trays on a white lace tablecloth that covered the long, mahogany dining table, set for four.

Perry swallowed a bite. "Help yourself to whatever you're hungry for. It's delicious."

"If you need anything further," the butler said, "just call, or press the buzzer on the wall, and I will come. In case you have forgotten, my name is James."

Amber whirled around to eye the tall man behind her. "James? Isn't that a stereotypical name for a butler?"

For the first time, the man smiled. "It is, Ms. Rockwell. James Jefferson, the Third. It is rather traditional. However, all the men in my family were butlers. I believe it is an honorable profession." He bowed robot-style and began pulling the dining room doors closed as he backed from the room.

"James," she called before he disappeared. "Do *you* know how Sarah died?"

"Indeed I do, Ms. Rockwell. She killed herself. I am sorry." Before she could say another word, he finished closing the doors.

On the sidebar sat a large carafe of steaming coffee and another of hot water with a cut crystal bowl next to it, overflowing with a variety of tea packets. Amber selected mint and let the tea steep in the DeHavilland china cup. The pattern was the one her mother used to use, now packed away in a box in storage.

Amber pulled out a chair and sat across from Perry. "Everyone seems to know Sarah took her own life. But how? No one wants to tell me."

Wrinkles creased Perry's forehead. "Aren't you going to eat?"

"No. But I'm glad your appetite is back. Are you about done? I have to find Dan and Linda Hudson. They'll tell me how Sarah died."

Perry dabbed at his mouth with the linen napkin. "I'm surprised they haven't phoned."

"I get the feeling they don't like Lancaster, not just this house."

"Try not to jump to conclusions," Perry said. "How would they know we're here? After all, we missed them at the funeral yesterday."

"True." Amber sipped her tea, staring across the table. Perry shoveled in another mouthful. "How can you eat like that?"

"I'm hungry. Besides, I hate to see all this food go to waste."

"Food's the farthest thing from my mind."

Perry set down his fork. "I know how difficult this is. After what I've been through…" He hesitated. "You'll eat again, eventually."

"I'm sorry. Mark was a terrible loss for you. I guess you, of all people, understand what I'm going through."

"When Mark died," Perry said, "I thought my world had ended. But my friends helped me survive. You were one of them." His gaze bored into Amber's eyes. "I'm here for you. I'll help you get through Sarah's death."

Amber blinked back tears. "I know. But, I need *answers*."

Her mother's murder still haunted her. Not knowing what happened to her father made her envision him on street corners even though he wasn't there. *I must have closure this time.*

"Okay." Perry rose and threw his napkin on the table. "Let's go get some answers."

He pushed his chair back, and hurried over to her. He cupped Amber's chin, lifting her face upward. He smiled. "We will get to the bottom of this! You ready?"

After grasping his hand, she said, "Let's go."

At the end of the driveway, Perry slowed the Mustang and faced Amber. "Where to?"

Seconds ticked by. The only sound—the car engine's rumble. "Let's try the Carsonville Inn first. That's a popular place."

Following Amber's directions, Perry drove down F Street. He parked at the intersection of Seventh. Amber loved the large Tudor Revival-style inn. Her father told her it was built in 1922. Inside the grand lobby, overstuffed elegant furniture suggested stability and comfort. Something Amber sorely needed, especially now.

She strolled to the registration desk and introduced herself. She asked for Dan Hudson's room. The clerk tapped on his computer keys beneath the counter then rang a room. "Mr. Hudson, there's a Miss Amber Rockwell and friend hoping to see you." The clerk listened. "Yes, sir, I'll send them right up." He placed the phone on the hook. "Mr. and Mrs. Hudson are in room three-twelve. The elevator is there." He pointed. "Or you can take the stairs. Go right on up."

"Thank you."

Perry and Amber approached the room. Taking a deep breath she raised her arm to knock, but before her knuckles touched the door, Dan Hudson yanked it open. Amber rushed into his arms. "Oh, Dan, I'm so sorry I missed you yesterday."

"You made it? Where've you been? We've been frantic trying to contact you. Your cell phone isn't working and we refused to leave a message—no way to hear about Sarah."

"Unfortunately," Amber said, "we turned the phones off. There was no reception when we switched them back on."

Dan held her at arm's length. "They say Sarah was so depressed she committed suicide. We can't believe it."

"I won't believe it either." Amber shook her head. "Not possible."

Perry cleared his throat.

"Oh, Dan, you remember Perry Cole, don't you?" Amber asked.

Dan released his grip on Amber's shoulders and extended his hand. "Nice to see you again, Perry. You joined us at that great restaurant when we visited Amber in New York."

After taking a breath, Dan continued, "The man I talked to at your store said you'd be here Tuesday. But, he didn't know where you were. How'd you find out?"

"First," Perry said, "let me say how sorry I am about

your daughter." Without waiting for a reply, Perry continued, "We drove up to Lancaster's house and learned about a funeral from the caterer. By the way, how's Mrs. Hudson?"

The bathroom door opened. Dan's wife stepped out. Amber gasped. She had uncombed hair and dark circles under red puffy eyes. Linda usually took great care to look her best.

Amber hurried over and wrapped her arms around the disheveled woman. "Oh, Linda."

Tears flowed down Linda's gaunt face. Amber couldn't hold her own tears back any longer. She guided Sarah's distraught mother to the bed. They both sank onto the bedspread.

Through gasping breaths and loud sniffs, Linda said, "Rocky, Sarah loved you so much. You... oh, Amber."

Amber swiped at the tears streaming from her own eyes. She eyed Dan and then Linda. "I phoned Sarah Friday from the airport. I *spoke* to her. She knew we'd be here on Tuesday to see her. She sounded *happy*, even *excited*."

"You spoke to her?" Dan asked.

"I did. She was anxious to see me," Amber said. "Knew I was coming."

Linda stared wide-eyed. "Now I'll never believe she took her own life. If Sarah was depressed and knew you were coming, she'd have waited for you. I know it."

Dan motioned to a chair. "Perry, please sit down." Dan sat on the bed on the other side of his wife. "I don't understand any of this."

Linda smoothed back Amber's hair. "I'm so glad you're here. Oh, Rocky..."

It saddened Amber to see Linda so upset. She used Amber's nickname when she was mad, or hurt.

"It was horrible," Linda said, "when Steve phoned us in

Florida and told us about Sarah. Can you believe he's a police detective? He always thought he was such a super jock, we figured he'd go into sports."

She placed her hand over her heart. "I was relieved when Sarah flew with you back to New York instead of marrying him. He was very angry with her about that decision."

Linda wiped away tears. "I don't trust Mr. Lancaster, either." She glanced at her husband. "Sarah would not have done this to herself... or us."

"I feel the same way," Amber said. "Steve acted strange, as if he didn't even know me. Or, he didn't want Lancaster to know that he knew me. He hasn't changed much from high school, ignoring me then, too. I don't know Lancaster, other than what Sarah told me."

Amber clasped Linda's hand. "This is hard, but can you tell me how Sarah died?"

Dan cupped his wife's hand. "They say a combination of Valium and champagne killed her. She was so depressed. Steve was shocked to see her for the first time in years, lying dead that way. The poor boy's had a lot to deal with.

"Did you know he lost his sister two years ago to a murderer?" Dan took out a handkerchief and blew his nose. "He's been so helpful to us."

Amber remembered that Steve and Dan were close. Sarah's father had been the only one disappointed when Sarah had not married Steve. *I'll have to watch what I say in front of Dan,* Amber thought. "Champagne and Valium? She might have taken them accidentally?"

Dan shook his head. "Steve said because of the note, the bottle of pills and champagne, they didn't seem to think so."

"He wouldn't tell me anything."

"Amber, you were a bit hysterical last night," Perry said. "After the caterer told us about the funeral, we rushed to the grave site. A few cars and a limousine pulled away as we arrived. We must have just missed you. Lancaster told us about Sarah."

"Oh, how awful. You poor dear. We couldn't take another minute of that farce of a funeral." Linda grabbed a Kleenex and wiped tears streaming down her face. "Lancaster planned the whole thing, including renting us a limo. That should have been a priest, not some reverend."

Amber nodded in agreement.

"The reverend is a friend of his," Linda said. Her mouth turned down, appearing disgusted.

Amber stood and paced. She stopped, facing the Hudsons. "There's no way Sarah would do this. I'm going to get to the bottom of it."

Dan furrowed his brow. "Now, Rocky..."

Amber smiled. He seldom used her nickname, and it made her feel special. "No, I'm right. I might not have seen Sarah for almost a year, but we've been in constant touch, and we're still as close as we were in high school. I would have known if something had upset her enough to make her do such a terrible thing."

"Sarah told you on the phone she wrote you a letter," Perry said. "Possibly it will have an explanation. Or, it might have been an accident."

"We tried to convince the police it happened that way," Dan said. "An accident makes more sense to us, except because of that note, Dr. Mayhill wouldn't listen."

"Note?" Amber questioned.

"The note to you. Isn't that what you were just talking about?"

"No, Sarah told me on the phone she mailed me a letter. Steve told me about a note last night. I haven't seen it yet. Have you?"

Dan nodded. "Steve showed it to us. Sarah addressed it

to you. They found it propped up against the picture of the two of you that she kept in the bedroom. No details, she just apologized.

"As Steve explained, because of the evidence, the coroner wouldn't budge from the suicide findings. Sarah's friends said she'd been acting weird, depressed, mumbling to herself. The note clinched it for the coroner."

Linda whispered, "My little girl was a good Catholic. She wouldn't do that, no matter how depressed."

"We know, but what can we do about it?" Dan patted his wife's hand.

"She could have been apologizing for anything," Amber said. "I'll go to the coroner, and then I'll talk to Steve."

"We've been that route," Dan said. "They won't listen to you, Rocky."

"Then maybe it wasn't a suicide. Or an accident."

Linda turned whiter, clasping her hand over her mouth. Amber gazed from one to the other. "It's something that should be explored."

"Wait a minute, Amber," Perry said. "I know you don't believe Sarah killed herself, but with advanced technology... I'm positive the coroner did a thorough job."

"Well, I don't know about the coroner," Amber said, sitting on the end of the bed, "but I think you could fool that so-called detective any time of the day."

"Amber, I've never seen you act this way." Perry scratched his chin. "I don't know how he behaved back then, but I bet he's changed. You have. The evidence pointed the coroner and him in that direction. He must have had his reasons for not acting as if he knew you." Perry's speech trailed off. The group sat for a beat in gloomy silence before Perry continued. "I admit that it's odd, but let's go talk to him and find out."

He looked at Dan. "Besides, the coroner signs the death

certificate. We'll talk with both of them. I'll be with Amber every step of the way. We aren't scheduled to go back for more than a week. Tom can handle the store in New York."

Dan hugged Linda to him. "Good. We need to know the truth, no matter what. We can stay."

"Did Sarah seem odd to you?" Amber remembered that Sarah and she could talk to both of Sarah's parents about anything. If Sarah had problems, she would talk with them.

"No more than usual," Linda said. "She did complain about this new habit of talking to herself. Don't we all do that? I do know she was depressed, but we all get depressed. Sometimes she hid her true feelings from us to protect us. You know how she acted."

"Remind me to call and ask Tom to check for that letter when he goes by your place to water your plants," Perry said. "I bet it will explain things. Tom could fax it to you or mail the letter overnight delivery."

"Good thinking," Amber said. She noted on her cell phone to remind her to have Perry call Tom. Then she asked, "Linda, did Sarah ever confide in you about someone wanting to hurt her? Did you pick up on something she said?"

"We've spoken on the phone a couple of times recently. She didn't mention any angry person. Who could get mad with Sarah? Steve's the only person who's ever been really upset with her, back when she refused to marry him. That was a long time ago. I'm sorry."

"Don't be. And, don't worry," Amber said. "We'll get to the truth. However, you can't waste your time here. Who knows when we'll find any information out?"

"But we can't leave this to you," Dan said.

Amber inspected Sarah's father. A walking zombie. Pale.

Thin. The bald patches in his hair jarred her. "But, you must. You have your chemo treatments."

"He has to keep his appointments," Linda said. "I can't lose him, too."

"Take Linda home," Amber said. "We'll keep in close contact."

"Well, if it was suicide—"

"No, Dan. I *know* our daughter."

Amber stood and placed both hands on her hips. "And I *know* my best friend." *Especially with our sacred pact.* Something about Lancaster bugged her. "Were you aware she wanted to leave Cash?"

"No," Dan said. "She never discussed her love life with us. That's one area we stayed away from. We didn't approve of her not being married and living with a man."

"And she never let on that anyone acted jealous over her, or that she had trouble with someone?"

Dan and Linda gazed at each other. Amber waited for an answer.

"No, Rocky," Linda said. "She mentioned something about an overbearing, over-sexed maid, but... Do you really think someone killed her?"

"Her death might have been an accident, or something else, but I'll never believe suicide." Amber pictured that awful day in high school and the disgusted look on Sarah's face. "I'll not rest 'til I get to the truth. Did she say the maid's name?"

"No," Dan and Linda said in unison.

"Mr. and Mrs. Hudson, you go home," Perry said. "We'll figure out precisely what happened and inform you the minute we discover the truth, no matter what it might be."

Tears welled up in Dan's eyes. "Thank you. Our little girl wouldn't do what they said she did."

Amber's heart constricted. Everyone in this room understood what it was like to lose someone close. She went to the Hudsons and hugged them tight. She whispered, "We'll find out, don't you worry."

CHAPTER 7

Even in July, the coastal California fog sucked into Carsonville, shrouding it in mist, dampening spirits. Amber felt quite miserable. *Good thing I remembered a jacket.* She slipped it on. After entwining her arm with Perry's, they descended the steps into the bowels of the dark county building.

The coroner's offices resided in the basement, alongside the morgue. The hallway was cold as if it stood out on a pier buffeted by the ice cold ocean winds. "I hate this fog." Amber shivered. They continued on down the hall accompanied by the sound of her heels clicking on the white-tiled floor.

They reached the door marked, 'Coroner.' Amber hesitated then pushed it open. A blast of chilly air hit her face, sending more tremors through her body. The strong odor of formaldehyde gagged her.

A woman in a stained, white lab coat sat behind a gray metal desk. She looked up. "May I help you?"

"I hope so." Amber walked toward her and smiled. "We'd like to speak with the coroner. Is he in?"

The stout woman rose and placed both hands on her desk, displaying clean-scrubbed fingernails. "I'm the assistant coroner. How may I help you?"

Before Amber could speak, Perry asked, "Ma'am, your name is...?"

The woman studied Perry's features. The assistant coroner's face softened and she smiled. She thrust out her hand. "I'm Loretta Mayhill. Dr. Mayhill, one of the coroner investigators." She pumped Perry's arm up and down.

"I'm Perry Cole." He winced as she continued shaking. She must have noticed his pained expression, because she suddenly released her grip. She eyed Amber.

"Dr. Mayhill, it's a pleasure. I'm Amber Rockwell." She extended her hand.

The assistant coroner shook Amber's hand briefly then sat down behind the government desk. Papers and files littered the top. A Styrofoam cup with visible teeth marks sat on one corner. A file lay open alongside, exposing a picture of a nude female body.

"Have a seat." Dr. Mayhill closed the file. She motioned toward two metal folding chairs. "We don't get many visitors down here. How can I help you?"

"Dr. Mayhill," Amber said, "we're here to discuss Sarah Hudson's death."

"They tell us Miss Hudson committed suicide." Perry examined the chair carefully before sitting. "She was Mr. Cassius Lancaster's girlfriend."

"I know. I handled that case. Are you a relative?"

"No," Amber said. "But I'm her best friend, and her parents want more information."

"I see," Dr. Mayhill said. "Miss Hudson seemed to have everything going for her. Such a shame she ended her life. Is modeling that tough, Miss Rockwell, that you would end your career so young?"

"I'm not a model," Amber muttered. "Sarah enjoyed modeling, but she'd been away from it for a few years."

Amber couldn't believe this woman thought she modeled. But that wasn't why she was here. "Mr. and Mrs. Hudson asked me to discover what really happened to their daughter." She inhaled deeply. "How did Sarah die?"

Dr. Mayhill leaned forward in her chair and rested her head on one fist. "I told them what happened. Have you talked with Detective Steve Burns?"

"He couldn't find his way out of a paper bag," Amber murmured. "I want your opinion first."

Dr. Mayhill sat back in her chair and laughed out loud. She brought herself under control and said, "I'm sorry for the outburst. You don't like Detective Burns much, do you?"

"I don't know the *man*." Amber couldn't tell this woman that she only knew him as a teenager. *I don't know what secret Steve is keeping or why he pretended he didn't know me, but I'll soon find out.*

The assistant coroner frowned. "But you've already formed an opinion of our famous detective. He does his best to make a woman feel inferior. Comes across as some male chauvinist wanting to take care of you because you couldn't possibly take care of yourself."

Amber smiled. When she got past the creepy job and stained lab coat, she believed Mayhill could be trusted. "Sarah was my best friend. It's hard to believe she killed herself."

Dr. Mayhill said, "I know first-hand how hard it is to lose a best friend."

"Then, you understand. The Hudsons gave me their written permission." Amber removed an envelope from her purse and handed it to the doctor.

The coroner assistant waved the envelope aside. "Oh, our records are public. Let me get the file."

She pushed her chair back, the scraping sound echoing around the room. At the steel file cabinet, she unlocked the drawer and searched through dog-eared files. She stopped about halfway through. "Here it is."

"May we see it?"

"Not the entire file, Miss Rockwell. There are pictures in here you shouldn't see. But I'll summarize my findings for you. Later, if you want a copy of the report, it'll cost you $25.00."

Amber dug in her purse and handed over the money. "I'd like a copy."

"Fine." Dr. Mayhill stuffed the money in her center drawer and wrote out a receipt. Then she handed it to Amber. Dr. Mayhill opened Sarah's file and thumbed through several pages. After removing a two-page report, she closed the folder and made a copy. The doctor handed it to Perry. "You might not understand the medical terminology and other anatomical and physiological references."

"I've gotten pretty good at reading medical reports," Perry said. "I spent the last year in and out of a hospital with a friend of mine who had AIDS."

"I'm sorry."

"Thank you," Perry said. "He died two months ago."

"Unfortunately, there's a lot of that in this country. I lost a friend to AIDS last month. Again, I'm sorry for your loss." Dr. Mayhill clasped her hands together. "Basically, I found an overdose of Valium and alcohol in the blood stream. Miss Hudson died as a result."

The doctor held up one hand. "Before you ask, let me finish. I know what you're thinking, but believe me, Miss Hudson swallowed those meds of her own free will. I checked for any signs of force. Nothing marked her body signifying a sign of a struggle. Nor was there any evidence at the scene that someone slipped the drugs in her drink. We checked with her friends about her state of mind. Her attitude for the last month, combined with the note, *and* the presence of drugs in her system, led me to rule it a suicide.

"I'll let Detective Burns give you further details. But, we fully concur. And, believe me, we lock horns nine times out of ten. It's a shame that Miss Hudson committed the act most family and friends cannot accept. There is no evidence suggesting otherwise."

Dr. Mayhill returned the original report to the manila folder. She stood and walked over to the file drawers, jammed it inside and shoved the drawer closed.

After locking the cabinet, she faced Amber. "Suicides are hard on the ones left behind. Even if the two of you were close, it wouldn't stop her from killing herself. If she were determined, nothing you could have done would have stopped her."

"But what if you knew Sarah and I had talked on Friday. That she knew I'd be here on Tuesday. Would that change your thinking?"

The assistant coroner hesitated for a moment. "She might have been excited, but, I think her depression... She did leave you the note apologizing, after all, even though it's not much comfort to you."

Amber took the report from Perry. "I haven't received the note. Her parents told me it was addressed to me. Do you have it?"

"No." Dr. Mayhill shook her head. "Figures. Talk with Detective Burns. I'll be glad to talk with you again after you've discussed it with him. If you discover any new evidence to the contrary, I'll take another look." She strolled over to a side door. "Now, if you'll excuse me, I have to get back to work."

With the doctor gone, the room grew icy. Amber couldn't ever remember being so cold.

CHAPTER 8

Amber stopped so quickly, Perry stumbled into her. She stared through the open doorway into the detective room, which had five desks. One woman talked on a phone, scribbling on a notepad. A red-headed officer typed on a keyboard, watching a computer screen. Steve Burns sat at a black metal desk in front of him, drinking a cup of coffee.

Perry whispered into her ear. "What?"

Amber kept staring. The detective glanced up. Before he uttered a word, Amber flashed back to high school: the football field, Steve the super-jock, lifting Sarah—her heart-shaped face bright, her smile wide—into his arms. Amber, jealous of his relationship with her best friend, took an immediate dislike to him.

She realized that she still carried a bit of that jealousy.

Burns motioned for them to come over. "Mr. Cole, Miss Rockwell, please come sit down." He stood and brought over another folding chair, setting it next to the other one across from his desk. Then he settled into his swivel seat.

Perry nudged the small of Amber's back. Two other

officers, standing by a coffee maker, watched her as she walked straight to Burns.

She stared into his bright-blue eyes that peered at her from beneath dense white-blond eyebrows set amidst a tanned complexion. His hair still thick and tawny blond. The detective rested his chin on the tips of his steepled fingers. "What can I do for you?"

"Give me Sarah's note," Amber said.

"Miss Rockwell, please sit."

Amber hesitated, and then lowered herself into the nearest chair. Burns' desk top appeared too clean, as if no other business awaited his attention. All of it would be focused on Perry and her. He had been arrogant in high school. Arrogance and public service, what a combination.

Even back in high school, he'd been fastidiously neat and tidy. Amber, the opposite, stacked her desk with junk mail and every scrap of paper she used. Burns displayed a picture of a blond woman who shared his features. It figured he married someone who looked just like him.

Perry cleared his throat.

Amber said, "I see you still wear black. Same as in high school." He had on a freshly pressed black suit similar to the one he wore at last night's party. Amber called it a party—no other word described it.

Burns continued smiling, but said nothing. His Brut aftershave permeated the air. He still wore that same stinky cologne.

His silent smirk drove her crazy, and she knew he knew it. Well, she could play that game, too. "For a detective, you have a lousy memory," Amber said, crossing her arms. She lifted one eyebrow. "You act as if you don't remember me. I suppose you don't remember your late girlfriend, either?" She uncrossed her arms, glaring. Before he could utter a response, she asked, "What's your version on how Sarah died?"

Burns didn't blink. "I've never forgotten Sarah. I told you last night, she took her own life."

Amber held up the copy of the report. She waved it in front of the detective. "We just came from Dr. Mayhill. These words mean nothing to me. Sarah loved champagne. Maybe she took the pills by accident. Dr. Mayhill, Sarah's parents, and even you mentioned something about a note addressed to me. Where is it? I want to know why you could ever think Sarah would have killed..." Amber hesitated, and then continued, "taken her own life."

"We spoke with Sarah's friends here, Mr. Lancaster, and all his staff," Burns said. "Dr. Mayhill concurred. Sarah killed herself. You were not available to interview. Plus, you haven't seen her for some time."

Amber leaned back against the cold metal chair. She felt icy, and the detective's words hurt. He still could push her buttons and make her feel inferior. This time, she wouldn't give in. "But we were in constant contact. I spoke to her on Friday. She mentioned being depressed, but sounded excited about my visit."

She softened her voice. "If only I'd come out sooner. Steve, please tell me about Sarah's death."

He didn't answer right away. His face showed a glimmer of sadness right after he adjusted the picture on his desk.

"Listen, Detective," Perry said. "You're possibly not accustomed to explaining your findings to friends of the victims, but believe me when I tell you if you don't do so this time, you'll get no peace." He paused, and looking at Amber, said. "She might not have been persistent in high school, but now you can't get her to quit searching for something until she knows about it down to every last detail."

"Okay. Let me get the file."

Burns teeth gnashed so tight Amber feared he might break a tooth. She recognized the expression on his face—she'd seen it whenever Sarah turned him down. Was he going to explode?

He spun around to the man at the desk behind him. "Hey, Red, do me a favor and grab the Hudson file out of the 'closed' drawer for me."

"Why not? I don't have any work to do except be at your beck and call." The officer stood and sauntered off, looking as if the chip on his shoulder weighed him down.

"Thanks," Burns called after him. Amber wondered if he was counting to ten. After he blew out his breath, he said, "It'll be a few minutes. Care for some coffee, tea, water?"

"No thank you." Amber focused her attention on the wall next to Burns' desk. Some sort of diploma or certificate hung in an oak frame. Through the window, she glimpsed the fog swirling outside. She shivered, feeling hollow and lonely, just like the day. Moisture collected on the windowpane. Droplets formed, running down in rivulets. A typical gray Carsonville summer day.

"It's been a long time," Burns said. "Tough to find Sarah dead after all these years, and harder yet to call Dan and Linda. Have you seen them? I had a note to call Dan, but when I phoned their hotel, they'd checked out."

"I convinced them to fly back home to Florida." Amber remembered Sarah telling her how hard Linda was taking Dan's cancer. After each treatment, he suffered the ravages of the cure. Amber prayed the treatments would work. "I promised them I'd get to the bottom of this and let them know what I discover."

"There's nothing to find."

Before Amber could reply, the officer returned. He

threw the file onto the desk and marched back to his seat without a word.

"Thanks, Red." Burns opened the file and skimmed his finger back and forth down the page. "Miss Rockwell, where would you like me to start?"

"For starters," Amber said, "why are you calling me 'Miss Rockwell?' Don't you remember me?"

Burns grinned. "It's been awhile. You don't look anything like you did in high school. I barely recognized you, or Sarah for that matter."

"Oh, come on." Amber wanted to wipe that smirk off his face. "Me, I've lost a ton of weight and wear contacts, but Sarah? She hadn't changed much since high school. For God's sake, you dated for over a year. We worried you might even get married. And you didn't *know* her?"

"She had changed. Besides, I only ran into her a few days before her suicide. I'd become close friends with Lancaster, but hadn't met his girlfriend yet."

"And her name didn't sound familiar?"

Perry said, "That's hard to believe."

"It never came up. Mr. Lancaster is campaign manager for Henry Longreen, who's running for Congress. The candidate interested me, not Lancaster's love life. Surprised me to see Sarah again. A few days later, shocked me that she'd killed herself. As far as you're concerned,—"

"Lancaster doesn't know about you and Sarah, does he?"

"Sarah didn't mention it," Burns said. "So, I figured I'd keep my mouth shut for her sake. He might know, he might not, but I haven't said anything. And, I don't plan to."

Amber mulled that over. It made sense. But why wouldn't Sarah want Lancaster to know about Steve?

"Okay. Start from the beginning? Tell me about Sarah's death. And, where is that note?"

Amber thought back to her Friday telephone conversation with Sarah. "Guess who I ran into?" she'd asked over the phone. Was it Burns?

The detective reached into his drawer and handed over a piece of paper.

Amber snatched it from his hand. The note read: 'Dear Amber, I'm so sorry. Love, Sarah.' Through blurry eyes, Amber reread the note. "Okay, Sarah left me this note, acting depressed, unlike herself. There's no evidence of foul play—I understand all that. But she intended to... She had plans for the future. Something... I can't put it into words yet... feels all wrong about deciding she committed suicide."

"Believe me, I do understand."

"How could you?" Amber asked.

"A young person's life ending too soon is all wrong," Burns said. "Sarah's death will never feel right."

His gaze flickered to the photograph of the woman on his desk. He no longer sneered. Even his eyes seemed less bright. Grief?

Amber studied the photo again. She recognized the face: his younger sister, two years behind him in high school. What was her name? Denise? Debbie? Though Burns' face resumed a neutral expression, Amber caught a glint of yearning in his eyes. Dan Hudson told them Steve's sister was murdered. Amber understood the grief caused by the unexpected loss of a family member. She kicked herself mentally for her earlier unkind thoughts about Burns. She should reconsider why she was raising such a ruckus about Sarah's death since everything pointed to suicide.

"I need to know more," Amber said. "I can't leave it like... this."

Perry leaned over and patted Amber's shoulder. "She really can't."

Burns averted his gaze from the picture. He tapped the file. "I wasn't the first on the scene. Mr. Lancaster found Sarah. She was supposed to have met him at the Martins, Lancaster's next door neighbors. They were having a cocktail party. When she failed to arrive, he got worried and went home to look for her. She lay on the bed. After he discovered she was dead, he dialed nine-one-one. Officer Williams arrived. Finding Sarah deceased, Williams immediately reported it to the Homicide Detectives."

Burns held up his hand, and before Amber could interrupt, he continued, "Let me explain. That's standard OP. When there's an unexplained death, operating procedure specifies that we're always called in. I was next on the rotation. I understand this is hard for you. If at any time you'd like me to stop, please tell me."

"This is hard, but I'm not as frail as you may think. Sarah's dead. You say she killed herself—so far, you've not convinced me."

"Let him finish," Perry said.

"Anyway," Burns continued, "when I came onto the scene, Lancaster stood in the hall, looking like hell, even crying. Unless he's a good actor, he was upset. A champagne goblet lay at her fingertips beside her. Pills, her own prescription for Valium, littered the nightstand. A count of the pills compared with the number on the newly filled prescription indicated that most of the pills were gone. The note you're holding sat propped up against the silver-framed picture of Sarah and you.

"You look a lot different in that picture." He drummed his fingers on the file. "Anyway, after reading the hand-written note, I phoned the coroner's office. You've met Dr. Mayhill. I assume you know what she uncovered?"

Amber remained silent.

Perry said, "Just what's in the report. She said talk with you first."

"I'm surprised the good doctor didn't tell you everything. She and I don't see eye to eye."

Burns gave the arrogant little smile that Amber detested in high school. Then he said, "Dr. Mayhill arrived, and even though we had the suicide note, we took the same precautions as if it were a homicide. Again, this is standard OP. Dusted for fingerprints, bagged Sarah's hands to preserve her fingernails in case there had been a struggle, and snapped numerous photographs."

Amber's eyes filled with unshed tears. *Oh, Sarah, why?* She reread the note. There in Sarah's bold, beautiful handwriting, "Dear Amber..." She stopped and knitted her eyebrows together.

"Where's the original?" she asked, glancing up at Burns

"That's evidence. You have an exact copy. Keep it."

"This doesn't mean she killed herself." Amber waved the note. "This could refer to anything."

"But we found it at the scene, propped up against the picture of the two of you by her bed."

"You said that before." Amber jerked her head up after reading the note again. She handed it to Perry. "Sarah didn't write this."

"That's not her handwriting?" Burns walked around the desk and peered over Perry's shoulder. "Dan and Linda identified it."

"Well, it looks like it, but she wouldn't have written that."

"Miss Rockwell—"

Amber glared at Burns as he sat on the corner of his desk, one foot dangling above the other on the floor. "Quit calling me that! We've known each other a long time. Are you trying to annoy me?"

"I'm sorry, Rocky," Burns said, using her nickname. "It's easier to be formal in order to maintain some distance."

Amber could kick herself for always thinking the worst about this man. "Fine. Sarah calls me, called me Rocky. You, yourself, just used it. Sarah gave me that nickname in grade school."

"So?"

"So," Amber said, exhaling loudly. "This note is addressed to 'Dear Amber,' not 'Rocky.'"

"She was too embarrassed to use your nickname this time."

"No!"

Burns rose. From the full height of his six-foot frame, he examined her. He still had his football physique. Broad shoulders, barely any neck, but still handsome in his black suit. Sarah always fell for good-looking, arrogant men, who shared the conviction that a woman had no brains.

The detective retrieved the note from Perry and stared at it. "Look, Miss... Amber, Rocky, I'm sorry, it is her handwriting."

"No way."

"All her friends here," Burns said, "noticed a change in Sarah. Depressed. Even you said she admitted that on the telephone Friday." He sat back down in his chair and placed the note in front of him. "She mumbled to herself all the time, yelling at Cash's staff one minute, apologizing the next. She told one of them that she wasn't herself.

"She was alone in the house when she died. It's tough, but she committed suicide." Burns brushed an imaginary piece of lint from his sleeve.

Amber wanted to scream. In high school, she couldn't get anything through this man's thick skull. Why did she expect to be able to get through to him now? What if she told him about their pact? No, she wasn't about to tell

Burns now. She wanted to put a strand of hair in her mouth and chew, but left it alone. "Sarah adored life. I know for a fact she'd never take her own life."

"How?" Burns studied his nails.

Amber bit her lip. How could she convince him without telling her story? No one knew but Sarah, not even Perry. "I just know."

Burns raised one eyebrow. "Dr. Mayhill tested both the bottle and glass. Pure champagne. Pills were not forced down Sarah's throat. No one else's fingerprints were on the pill bottle. No other evidence pointed to anything irregular. We ruled out murder—there's no motive. Now, maybe, and I'm reaching here, it was an accident."

Bile rose in Amber's throat. She forced it back down. Her face flushed. Burns' tone of voice reminded her of a patient schoolteacher trying to explain a simple problem to a child. He'd acted the same way in high school. She would not be dismissed so easily.

Grabbing the note, she waved it in his face. Amber gritted her teeth. These men couldn't hear. They never listened.

She jumped up out of her chair and balled the note in her fist. "That proves nothing!"

Burns rolled his eyes. Silence ensued.

Amber paced back and forth. How could this man possibly be a detective? If she were a man, he would listen to her. Perspiration formed half-moons under her arms. Her bra felt damp and constricting. Sticky, she inhaled and expelled loudly. She plopped down in the chair.

Burns continued in the calm voice that irritated her, "So, there's no evidence of foul play. Now, I may concede, she took that combination as an accident. But if she did, why the note?"

"I don't know." Amber snapped her fingers. "Wait a minute. Sarah said something over the phone."

She tapped her forehead trying to remember. "You got me so upset, how could I have forgotten?"

"Forgotten what?"

"You're wrong about a motive." Amber pictured Lancaster's 'party' for Sarah and the fact Sarah had planned on leaving Lancaster. *Could he have killed her? Or someone else?* She couldn't say this to Burns. He and Lancaster behaved like golfing buddies. "You wouldn't believe me anyway.

"Thank you for your help and understanding." Amber rose and spun around. Over her shoulder, she said, "I *know* you don't want further evidence, but I *will* find it." She marched to the door and under her breath, she mumbled, "But how?"

"Why do men have to believe they're the only ones with intelligence?" Amber crossed her arms and leaned against the car.

Perry chuckled as he opened her door. "Not all men. I don't feel that way."

Amber's face softened as she patted her good friend's arm. "No, and I appreciate that." She climbed in, smoothed out the note, and put it in her purse. "Let's go."

Perry sat behind the wheel and inserted the key in the ignition. "Where to?"

"Back to Lancaster's. There are a few questions I'd like to ask the SOB."

"Now, Amber, you can't just barge in on the man and accuse him of foul play."

"Did I say anything like that?"

"No." Perry scowled at her without starting the car. "Possibly Sarah was more depressed than you could ever imagine."

Amber gazed out the windshield and into the summer fog. The earlier wisps had increased and now shrouded some of the buildings. A perfect set for a horror movie. Amber braced for the ax murderer to appear. "That could be true."

Silence grew heavy between them. Then Perry said softly, "Those last weeks with Mark..."

Amber shifted to face him.

"Every day, he asked me to help him die." Perry's voice became faint. "Every hour. Every minute."

She covered his hand. "I'm sorry."

"So am I." He gave her a wistful smile.

"But Sarah wasn't in that sort of pain."

"There are all different types of pain. True?"

She had to agree. "True."

"And you'll keep that in mind?"

"I'll try."

"If someone murdered Sarah, your poking around might alarm the killer. You could be at risk." Perry ran his hand over his head. "This is selfish, I know, but... I don't want any more losses. I can't handle any more pain."

Her chest tightened. She didn't want any more losses either, and she could be risking Perry's life, too. *How responsible we are for others.* "I give you my word: You will not lose me. I promise."

The lines in his face eased. She wondered if this was a promise she could...

Perry started the car and pulled away from the curb.

"But," Amber said, "I have to pursue this. You could be in danger, too. Why don't you go home? I can do this without you. Although, I still need to get close to Lancaster, and I'm not sure how." She grabbed a strand of her hair and chewed. "Any ideas?"

Perry steered the car around a corner. "I believe Sarah

killed herself." Before Amber could retort, he continued, "But, you'll never rest until you're positive. And, I'm not leaving you."

He glanced her way, and then maneuvered the car through the small amount of Carsonville traffic. "You want to get close to Lancaster. You should offer him our services."

"What do you mean?"

"He's a collector. We're in the antique business. You're familiar with most of his collectibles, even though you haven't seen them all. Sarah kept you informed of each piece he obtained, plus some of the ones he already had."

Amber spat out her hair. "So?"

"Use that information. Help him with his collections?"

"You think he'd be interested?"

"You kidding? He's interested in you. He'll jump at an opportunity to keep you close."

"That's a horrible thing to say. I mean, if he loved Sarah, he better not be interested in me." Amber wanted to wretch. The idea made her stomach roil and she belched. "Why should he be?"

"I get the feeling the man won't mourn long. He'll move on with his life. And if he loved Sarah, he'd want you around because you're the next best thing."

Amber's stomach grumbled again. "I know my work. Perhaps that would attract him. Sarah did say he adores amber and we have some in the shop. Maybe they're quite different from the ones he has? Perhaps we could help him to acquire some new pieces?"

Perry muttered, "Of course, Amber, for his collection."

CHAPTER 9

Before Amber rang the bell, the massive mahogany doors opened.

"Good afternoon, Ms. Rockwell. Please do not feel that you must ring the bell to enter." James waved them inside. "That goes for you as well, Mr. Cole."

"Thank you, James," Amber said. "It's very kind of Mr. Lancaster to make us feel welcome. And you, of course." She stepped over the threshold onto the marble foyer and again unease assaulted her. "Is he in?"

"I am afraid Mr. Lancaster is away at the moment, but please make yourselves at home. If there is anything I may help you with, please let me know."

Amber hesitated.

Perry said, "Amber, don't you have a question?"

"I do. James, could I have a word with you?"

One bushy eyebrow rose to his hairline. "If this is about Ms. Hudson—"

"Nothing like that." With a nod of her head, Amber motioned for Perry to go on upstairs.

"Well," Perry said, walking to the stairs. "I'm going up to my room."

James escorted Amber into the parlor. "May I get you any refreshment, Ms. Rockwell?"

"No, I'm fine, but I could use your help."

"Help? I am afraid I do not understand."

Amber sat on the settee. Just yesterday, it held beautiful women who thought it disgusting that Sarah took her own life. Amber would prove those women wrong for dissing her friend.

Two gold candelabra set atop the fireplace mantel. A large portrait of Sarah, with the frame draped in black hung above it. Amber didn't remember the black from yesterday. She stared at her friend's picture. *How did he pull this off?*

"Ms. Rockwell?"

James stood ram-rod straight, waiting for her to speak.

"How long have you worked for Mr. Lancaster?"

The butler half-smiled and his eyes twinkled. "A very long time, Ms. Rockwell. I find him a most wonderful man."

"I'm sure he is." Amber could see the admiration the butler had for his employer. "You've known Mr. Lancaster since he was a boy?"

James walked farther into the room. "In a manner of speaking." He rearranged some lilies in a crystal vase on the table next to the settee. "What may I help you with?"

"I'd like to repay Mr. Lancaster for his kindness."

The butler eyed her. "Oh, I assure you, that is not necessary."

"But, it's what I want to do. Do you think he would be interested in allowing me to help him acquire some new pieces for his collections?" Amber imagined the wheels working in James' head.

With a slight smile, the butler said, "I am certain he would be most pleased with the suggestion."

"Does he have someone who normally helps him? I don't want to put anyone out of work."

"Cash, er... Mr. Lancaster does most of his own selections. He is quite knowledgeable in his acquisitions."

"Is it too soon after Sarah's death to talk with him about this?"

"On the contrary, Ms. Rockwell, I believe it would be perfect timing. It will take his mind away from this horrible misfortune."

"Thank you, James. You've been very helpful."

"Wherever Mr. Lancaster is concerned, I try to be."

Resting her hand on the banister, Amber glided down the stairs for dinner. She remembered Sarah said they always dressed semi-formal for the meal, so Amber took considerable time to achieve the right appearance. She settled on a black dress, and arranged her auburn hair in a chignon at the nape.

She wondered where they were going when James led her to the parlor, not the dining room. Both Lancaster and Perry held drinks in their hands. When she entered, Perry smiled and gave her a low whistle.

Lancaster grasped her hand and kissed it. He gazed into her eyes. "I'm sorry I missed you today. You look stunning. Would you like a drink before we leave?"

"Leave? I thought we were dining here."

"No, I'm taking you to Sarah's favorite seafood restaurant." He steered Amber to the couch. "It has a magnificent view of the harbor. The fish is fresh and the shrimp scampi is delicious."

"Sounds like an interesting place to eat," Perry said.

The maid, who had unpacked Amber's things the night

before, sauntered toward them. She wore a black Bolero jacket, a short black skirt, and a low cut white blouse that showed plenty of cleavage.

She carried a silver tray laden with sliced Gouda, cheddar, and smoked salmon on crackers. A basket of baked sourdough baguettes sat on the coffee table. The aroma made Amber's mouth water. Next to the bread sat three plates, hand-painted with roses; three green linen napkins, shaped into fans; and three gold forks with a rose pattern.

"Would you care for an hors d'oeuvre?" the maid asked, stopping in front of Lancaster. She bent low to place the tray on the coffee table. Her bright red-painted lips formed into a broad smile. With her dark brown eyes meeting Lancaster's gaze, she murmured, "I hope everything is to your liking."

"It is, thank you, Marie." Lancaster laid his hand upon hers, but then moved it abruptly away as his gaze met Amber's.

Amber bit on the salmon-covered cracker. Crumbs fell to her lap. She watched the woman with Lancaster. Was this the maid everyone talked about? *I better keep a close eye on her.* Amber brushed the crumbs from her dress. "Mr. Lancaster, we don't have to eat at a restaurant if you'd prefer to stay home."

"Call me Cash. Mr. Lancaster is my father." He took Amber by the elbow and glanced at Marie, who frowned. "Perhaps we should go."

The maid marched out of the room, her spine rigid. Amber wondered about the hors d'oeuvres. Why didn't he want to stay and eat them? Was it something to do with Marie? Amber allowed Lancaster to escort her out the front door to the waiting limousine.

~~~~

From the back of the limo, Amber observed James maneuver the car through the narrow streets near the wharf. She let Perry and Lancaster talk during the drive while she examined her host and the driver. Lancaster seemed so at ease chatting with Perry. Every now and again he brushed his leg up against hers. When that happened, she felt like a snake had just crawled across her. Was Lancaster capable of killing? Or James? She had no doubt that the butler/chauffeur would do anything for Lancaster.

The limousine eased to a stop in front of the restaurant. James came around and opened the back door. They climbed out.

A tight knot of patrons stood outside a rustic wooden building. Some sat on a rock planter filled with seashells and flowers. The place appeared packed. As the breeze swirled around, she caught the smell of cooked fish and shrimp mingling with the aromas of garlic and baked bread. Her stomach growled.

"Smells wonderful," Perry said.

A man rushed out the red door and shook Lancaster's hand. "Oh, Mr. Lancaster, welcome. Come on in. Your table is ready." He hurried them past the people waiting outside.

Their table had a panoramic view of the harbor which was filled with motor and sail boats. The man lowered his voice. "Mr. Lancaster, I'm so sorry about Miss Hudson. Such a beautiful, friendly woman. So young."

"Yes, Victor, thank you."

Amber wondered how Lancaster could sound so nonchalant.

When Victor placed a linen napkin on Amber's lap, she

flinched. She wasn't used to this happening here, but it reminded her of a favorite New York restaurant.

On the white linen tablecloth, a candle flickered. Points of light danced across the table, illuminating a cut crystal vase supporting two deep red roses.

"Joanne will be your waitress this evening," Victor said. "She'll be right with you, Mr. Lancaster."

"You come here often?"

"Yes, Perry. Sarah loved the place."

"This used to be a place named Lazio's." Amber remembered when Sarah and she came here. "Looks like the restaurant's still packed with people."

"Locals and tourists." For some reason, Lancaster's grin made Amber shudder.

A few minutes later a blond waitress appeared. Amber ordered the fresh lingcod, Perry asked for the shrimp scampi, while Lancaster wanted the freshly caught salmon. He also special-ordered a bottle of white Napa chardonnay.

Amber toyed with the bread sticks, unsure of what to say to Lancaster. She tried not to think of him as Sarah's killer, but who else could have done it?

Everyone in the restaurant knew Lancaster. They stopped by to give their condolences. He sat rigid in his chair with that politician grin, the "famous grin," glued onto his face.

Amber hoped people here missed Sarah a little, and that they weren't merely curious about the new woman sitting with Lancaster. She mentally kicked herself for that last thought. She'd been giving herself a real beating—so unlike her, to think such thoughts of others.

"I apologize for all these interruptions," Lancaster said. "Sarah and I came here quite often. People adored her. I hope this is not too painful for you."

"It's comforting to know so many people cared about her."

"It makes me proud. She was kind and really beautiful, at least in the beginning."

Amber furrowed her eyebrows. "What do you mean 'in the beginning'?"

"She'd changed from when I first met her." Lancaster's shoulders sagged. His smile disappeared. "She'd become full of herself... oh, I don't know... I guess very vain."

"Are we talking about Amber's friend?" Perry said. "Not the person I knew."

Amber shook her head. "No way." *The vain person here is you.*

"I trust you had a somewhat pleasant day today."

"I did." Amber marveled at the abrupt change of subject. "Perry and I visited with Sarah's parents. We said our good-byes."

"They've flown back?" Lancaster asked. "I hoped we could have gotten together. If only I'd taken better care of their daughter." He lowered his lashes. "I had no idea Sarah was that unhappy."

Lancaster's dark brown-eyed gaze bored into Amber's. "Believe me, if I had, I would have tried to help her. I would have contacted you myself. Perhaps Sarah wrote to you. We could ask James if he'd mailed anything. He usually mailed all her letters for her."

"As a matter of fact," Amber said, "Sarah told me Friday that she'd sent me a letter."

"Well then, hopefully it will help you with closure."

"That reminds me," Perry said. "I forgot to tell Tom. I'll have him run by your house on the way to the store and pick up your mail."

Amber nodded. "That sounds good."

"I'm certain you have misgivings," Lancaster said.

"Believe me, I found it hard to accept Sarah's suicide." He took a bite of his salad, chewing slowly. After placing his fork at the edge of his plate, he reached across the table and covered Amber's hand with his.

Amber wanted to yank it away, but his words and expression stopped her.

"Believe me, I loved Sarah. I thought she loved me, too. I don't understand why she did this." He squeezed Amber's hand. "I would have preferred it to have been an accident, but the police wouldn't listen to me. Not with the note they discovered."

Amber slid her hand away from his and picked up her wine glass. "Although it wasn't much of a note."

"But it was more than she left me."

"I suspect one leaves a note to the one they love most," Perry said. He patted Amber's shoulder.

She shifted in her seat and pictured throwing her wine in Lancaster's face. Now she mentally kicked herself, again. To Lancaster, she said, "I'm sorry I've been difficult. I guess I hadn't thought about what you'd be feeling. I'm sure you did everything you could for Sarah. You shouldn't feel guilty." Could she be wrong about Lancaster killing Sarah?

Perry came to the rescue of an awkward silence, asking Lancaster questions about the town and some of the man's paintings and antique furniture.

Amber eyed Lancaster from beneath her long lashes as he spoke with her boss. She understood why Sarah had fallen for him. He was dynamic, confident. A touch arrogant, just Sarah's type.

"Amber, are you listening?" Perry waved his hand in front of her face.

"What? Oh, sorry, guess I was reminiscing? What did you say?"

Before he could speak, the waitress brought their dinner. Lancaster said, "That salmon smells delicious."

After the server departed, Perry said, "I was telling Mr. Lancaster about your recent buying trip, the pieces of amber you'd seen, and the one you bought that had a scorpion inside. He's quite interested."

"Really?" Amber took a bite of her ling cod. Memories of eating here with Sarah flooded her mind. "Why does amber fascinate you so?"

"Amber is beautiful." Lancaster studied her face intently. "I love the feel of it, the fact that it's not like other gems or minerals. Each piece is unique."

"That's true. It's a mineraloid, not a mineral." Amber spun her finger over the lip of her wine glass. "It occurs within the earth and is produced through the agency of living organisms."

"I knew it wasn't a stone," Lancaster said.

"No, it's amorphous. It doesn't have a crystalline structure. Call it petrified tree sap."

"Funny to think of it as tree sap," Lancaster said.

"Unless it's a plastic imitation."

"Like Chinese amber?" Lancaster asked.

"Or a commercial plastic of the Bakelite variety."

"Can you tell the difference between real amber and an imitation?"

Perry smirked and ate his shrimp.

Amber sipped her wine. *Are you testing me to see if I know my stuff?* "I do know the difference. With the correct tools, it's easily tested."

"How?" Lancaster asked.

"By touching it with a hot needle. If the amber is genuine, white, pine-smelling smoke will come from it. If it's not real, then a black mark appears on the piece."

"Wouldn't that ruin it?"

"It has to be done in an inconspicuous place." Amber took a bite of her fish and swallowed. "You know Sarah wrote to me about many of your collection pieces. She enjoyed the watercolors, the tulip-shaped Tiffany lamp, and the amber in your bedroom. Perry and I could find you a few more authentic collectibles. As a gift, for your hospitality, helping me to adjust..." She hesitated, and then continued, "Adjust to the reality of Sarah's death."

"It is not necessary to buy me a gift. Sarah would have wanted you to stay."

"Thank you, but Perry and I would like to do something. We could tour the house and take an inventory. See what new pieces would augment your collection. Then we could search for a collectible that would suit your taste."

"I'm afraid I'm tied up in meetings all day tomorrow."

"No problem. Perry and I can manage without you. We can make a list and discuss it over dinner."

"Will you be able to work?" Lancaster asked. "After Sarah's death... sometimes..."

"I can manage," Amber said, "like you're doing. I, too, need to keep my mind busy." Her involvement would keep her closer to Sarah's life.

She decided to learn more about Lancaster. "Are your parents still living?"

"They're back east, retired, and live in a trailer park, collecting gnomes for their small yard."

The waitress cleared away the remains of their meal and asked, "Would you care for any dessert?"

Perry and Amber shook their heads.

Lancaster smiled. "No, thank you, Joanne, I think we're fine, but I would like some coffee. Perry? Amber?"

After they ordered two coffees and a tea for Amber, Perry asked, "What state were you raised in?"

"Back east." Lancaster asked, "So, did Sarah truly enjoy my collections?"

There's that change of subject again. Amber wondered if he was touchy about his parents? "She thought the Monet was exquisite."

"I'm glad." Lancaster raised his coffee cup.

Amber sipped the herbal tea that the waitress set before her. "Why do you collect beautiful things?"

"I enjoy beauty," Lancaster said.

"Including women?" Amber asked, watching him intently.

"I love to have beautiful women around me."

"I suppose you've had a string of them."

Perry choked on his coffee. Amber waited for Lancaster's response.

"Well, I wouldn't say a 'string' is the correct word." Lancaster put his coffee cup down. "I've been fortunate to have been acquainted with a few."

"Have you ever been married?"

"No."

Amber wondered what had happened to any of his 'significant others', if anything? She wanted to ask him if it was just the looks, or if their personality counted, but she held back.

"How long have you worked for Perry?"

"Didn't Sarah tell you?" Amber questioned.

"I see you can avoid answers as well as I." Lancaster drank some more coffee. "Perhaps we should stay on safer ground and discuss antiques."

Amber fidgeted with her teacup. "It's no mystery. I figured you already knew. Five years."

"How'd you get interested in antiques and art?"

"Growing up in Carsonville, a Victorian town that takes great pride in its history, buildings, and antiques—kind of difficult to avoid. My parents owned a Queen-Anne. We had a grandfather clock, some Tiffany lamps, and a crystal collection. I had a creative mother. She loved art and I guess I inherited that from her. What about you?"

Lancaster looked out the window. Amber followed his gaze. A fishing boat passed, heading out of the harbor. The lights sparkled off the water.

"It's no secret. James interested me in the 'arts.' You know he's more than my butler. I wasn't always as comfortable financially as I am now. James instructed me in so many things and guided me concerning investments."

"A butler?"

"Butlers are knowledgeable in a variety of areas. They do not just run the household, but also know the ways of the world. Of course, only if they're good at their profession. James is worth every penny I pay him, and then some. I couldn't function as well without him."

Before Amber could ask another question, Perry asked, "How long has James been with you?"

"Since I was a young man."

"You're not that old now." Amber finished her tea. "Did he work for your parents?"

Lancaster laughed. "Heavens, no."

The waitress picked up the leather folder containing Lancaster's credit card and the bill. "I'll be right back, Mr. Lancaster. Was everything satisfactory?"

"Excellent as usual, Joanne, thank you."

Beaming, she scurried off. Amber stifled a yawn.

"Am I boring you?"

"Not at all," Amber said. "Must be the time change. Of course, it could be the wine and the emotional strain."

"How inconsiderate of me. I should have thought… We'll go straight home. I have some business to attend to anyway."

"At this hour?"

"Campaign work has no off hours, Amber."

"That's right. Steve said you were some sort of a campaign manager."

"I see you're on a first name basis with our detective."

"Oh, well..." Amber cleared her throat. Her cheeks burned. She wouldn't be the one to let Lancaster know about Burns and Sarah's past.

Perry coughed. "Detective Burns has been quite helpful."

Amber looked up at the ceiling.

"Good," Lancaster said. "I hope he's cleared everything up for you." His "famous grin" returned as they exited the restaurant. He said his good-byes to the patrons who had acknowledged them. Lancaster shook hands and expressed compliments to Victor.

Seated in the limo, Lancaster said, "I guess James could show you around the house tomorrow. He knows about everything I own."

Amber hadn't learned much, but it was a start. "Good. Then it's all settled. Perry and I will catalogue all of your collections. Then we can find you a new piece of furniture, or a lamp, or a piece of amber..."

Lancaster reached over and patted her hand. "I'm certain it will be authentic and as beautiful as you."

CHAPTER 10

The next morning Amber dressed and hurried downstairs. She found Perry eating his breakfast. "Are you through yet?"

"Aren't you going to eat?"

"No, Perry. I managed to keep dinner down. My stomach can't handle much this morning. Let's get to work."

"You sound eager. I didn't know cataloguing excited you so or I'd have you do it more often."

"Really funny."

"You think snooping through the house will turn up any clues?"

"Shush." Amber glanced around. "James could be lurking behind the door."

"What? Like in those horror movies you're so afraid of? A bit cliché, don't you think?" Perry swallowed a last sip of his coffee. "Let's go find that starched man and get started."

The butler was in the parlor.

Amber slowed her pace and strolled over to him.

"James, you don't have to show us around." She smiled and surveyed the room. "Perry and I can list the items if you have other duties."

"Oh, it is no trouble at all, Ms. Rockwell. My other obligations are completed. Mr. Lancaster asked me to assist you."

What other business has he asked you to assist him with?

"This must be rather boring for you," Perry said.

"Quite the contrary. I encourage Mr. Lancaster's collecting. My previous employer purchased art, furniture, and other valuables. The right antiques are a wise investment." The butler picked up a vase, holding it with care. "We purchased this vase," he pronounced the word 'vaz,' "back east. It is a piece of Paul Revere Pottery. It is beautiful. Do you not agree?"

Perry held the vase James handed him and examined the base closely. "It's an original."

Amber couldn't believe it. Some of Lancaster's paintings weren't originals. She took the vase. Impressed on the bottom: 'Boston,' a picture of a galloping horse with a rider, and 'Paul Revere Pottery.'

"'The Saturday Evening Girls' produced the vase," James said.

Amber eyed the butler. "You know about 'The Saturday Evening Girls'?"

"A librarian, Edith Guerrier, who wanted to better the intellectual and social needs of girls and women, began the club. These young women started making pottery for family income. The Paul Revere Pottery was founded in 1907 with the help of two other women: Edith Brown, an artist, and an upper class patron, Helen Osborn Storrow."

"I'm impressed, James."

"Thank you, Ms. Rockwell." The butler nodded.

Amber wrote down the item on the list. Since James had

to tag along, she'd try and get more information about Lancaster from him. She needed to know everything she could about the butler's relationship with him.

"The vase is beautiful," Amber said to James. "You know a lot about antiques."

"I assisted my former employer in acquiring some of his pieces. When Mr. Lancaster employed me, I passed along my knowledge of antiques to him."

"So you interested Cash in collecting beautiful things? Or had he already developed it?" Amber thought, *Lancaster had admitted that last night*. But she wanted to get the butler's opinions and his reactions. Maybe James hadn't approved of Sarah and wanted her out of the way.

"Mr. Lancaster inherited a number of these items. However, I taught him to appreciate other beautiful things, Ms. Rockwell and some he already showed great interest in." He stared down at her, making her skin feel prickly. Heat rushed to her cheeks. She felt like a butterfly caught under a microscope.

Several beautiful women wrapped around Lancaster popped into her mind. She shuddered, erasing the image. Sarah should've been the only woman in Cash's life. "There seems to be no... all the furniture is so different. Everything else, too."

She saw Perry roll his eyes. All this jumble of furniture seemed like several people collected all of it, or someone with a split personality. She scanned her list and then gazed around the room filled with different Victorian era pieces. Some were dark, reminding her of those dreaded horror movies again. Or was it because Sarah had been murdered in the house? This fact she was sure of.

"No." James stood behind a Lambert Hitchcock chair. He clutched the oar rungs that were decorated with many-colored designs in stencil. "Mr. Lancaster picks things he enjoys. Some of it came with his inheritance. It does not necessarily fit the décor, but he will not part with much."

"I can see that." Amber wondered how he usually parted with his women, she just knew about Sarah. "What inheritance? Aren't Lancaster's parents still alive?"

"They are." James' fingers whitened as he gripped the rungs tighter.

When James didn't elaborate, Amber asked, "If he didn't inherit from his parents, who did he inherit from?"

"I suggest you speak with Mr. Lancaster. Did you list this 'Daffodil' Tiffany lamp?"

"Marked it down. I like the daffodil flowers against the blue ground. It appears he likes Tiffany glass."

"He does, Ms. Rockwell. Besides his amber, the Tiffany throughout the house is another of his prized possessions." Amber noticed his fingers relax a little.

She made a separate list for the hand-made Tiffany favrile glass. She marveled at the swirling patterns, strange iridescent colors, marbled designs, curious free-form shapes, and clear brilliant patterns in texture of object. She appreciated Louis Comfort Tiffany's creations so much, she'd even splurged, purchasing a vase and a lamp for her apartment in New York.

Lancaster's Tiffany collection consisted of lamps, various styled vases, and a few paperweights. Amber studied each piece, imagining the worker creating it.

Pieces of amber were scattered throughout the downstairs rooms. She wondered what she would see upstairs. Her room contained a large rock of rose quartz. Was it the only one? She hadn't noticed any other rose quartz, yet.

Rose quartz was known as the love stone. It helped the user feel a strong sense of self-worth, therefore being worth love. It's the stone of universal love. Was that why Cash had it as part of his collection?

"Mr. Lancaster has some exquisite collectibles," Amber said. "It'll be difficult to top any of these."

"I have no doubt that he will appreciate any object you find for him. I feel certain the item will be beautiful, coming from a lady like you."

Amber's face grew warm. She hated being devious, but she told herself this was the way to discover who murdered Sarah. She chewed on a strand of hair,

Perry raised an eyebrow and shook his head.

She spat the hair out.

"You are quite refreshing compared to other women," James said. "Not like your friend."

"You didn't like Sarah very much, did you?"

"On the contrary, Ms. Rockwell, I adored her. In the beginning."

"What changed your mind?"

"I should not speak ill of the deceased."

"But?" Amber encouraged him to continue.

"Well, she did believe she was quite gorgeous."

"She was, but are you sure we're talking about Sarah?"

"I am, Ms. Rockwell."

"That's not the Sarah I knew."

"Precisely."

Amber turned her head so James wouldn't see the tear that leaked from the corner of her eye. She wiped it away and brought another strand of her hair into her mouth to chew on. Why did everyone keep reminding her that she didn't know Sarah? Why hadn't she come out earlier? Could she have prevented her death? Doubts festered.

Then Amber thought, *No, I did know her better than that. Besides, after my stupid high school episode, and that pact... Sarah would never have broken it.*

Perry whispered in her ear, "Try not to chew on your hair."

She pulled the wet strand from her mouth and tucked it behind her ear. She faced James.

"I apologize, Ms. Rockwell," the butler said. "I have upset you. Perhaps I could get you some tea?"

"No, thanks. Let's continue. Why don't we inventory the study next?"

"Well..." James hesitated.

"Is there a problem?"

"Oh, no. However, Mr. Lancaster's study is private. I do not believe he would approve of us being there without him present."

"That's okay," Perry said. "We can do the study when Mr. Lancaster's around."

"Very good, Mr. Cole. Follow me to the next room." James headed down the hall and entered a small sitting room.

Amber grabbed Perry's arm and they lagged behind. "Why'd you say that?" she whispered, glaring at him.

"You can't go through drawers and things while James stands by."

"No, but there must be something in there that Lancaster doesn't wish anyone to see. And, that's what *I* want to get a look at."

"Get a grip," Perry whispered.

Amber peeked into the room. James looked out a window. She stepped away from the doorway.

"If Lancaster committed a crime," Perry said, "he's not going to leave proof lying around. Be reasonable. He's entitled to a little privacy."

"Not if he's guilty of murder, he doesn't deserve it."

"Since when have we started believing Sarah was murdered?"

Amber said in a low voice, "Since I learned about that so-called suicide note addressed to 'Amber.' Sarah didn't write that." Amber gritted her teeth and squeezed the pen in her hand. "No way. She was murdered."

Amber crossed the threshold into the room where James still stood over by the far wall near a curtained window. Tasseled cords fastened with curtain bands held back the brown velvet drapes. Amber had never seen anything like those bands. The stamped gilt metalwork was studded with glass flowers.

Perry didn't have a chance to respond to her whispered outburst about the note as James said, "This sitting room will not take much time. Then we may have lunch and after proceed upstairs."

In the middle of the room, Amber made a slow circle, eyeing the contents. On the wall behind James hung a George Baxter print of a small landscape. She nodded her head toward the wall.

Perry walked over to the print and lifted it down. He examined the mount. "It's an original." He read the words, "Printed in Oil Colours by Geo. Baxter Patentee." He hung it back.

On the end table by the settee, Amber reached her hand into a bowl of glass marbles. She picked up one of the playthings from the 19th Century, rolling the smooth, round finish between her fingers. "Imagine creating these marbles. A glass blower cut a solid glass rod in lengths. When molten, they were introduced into another mold lined with colored rods or twists of glass. After they cooled, the glass blower withdrew the 'clear' glass. The colors fused into a mass, and then the blower rotated them in a small furnace. The rough edges and the rotary motion created round marbles."

"Very interesting, Ms. Rockwell. You do know your work."

"I played with my father's marble collection when I was young." Amber replaced the marble and closed her eyes, remembering briefly. "He told me all about them." Thinking about her father's disappearance made her all the more determined to discover the truth about Sarah.

She filled her notepad and flipped the page to list another piece of amber. A few of the amber items had ancient creatures trapped within. This room contained the first rose quartz she'd seen downstairs. It was shaped like a pyramid.

Amber put a question mark by the antiques Perry and she could not identify—things that would require research at a later date.

"James," Amber said, getting his attention, "Mr. Lancaster told me last night that he'd been raised back east."

"That is correct, Ms. Rockwell."

"Can't remember what town."

James inclined his head. "Did you get this Bottle-Jack hanging over the fireplace?"

"Yes." Amber wrote it down on the list. "They used those in Victorian kitchens with a motor, hanging the meat on the hook to cook."

"The motor slowly rotated whatever hung from it in front of the fire," Perry said. "Aren't you glad you don't have to cook that way?"

Amber ignored him. Perry knew she couldn't cook at all. "James, did you know Mr. Lancaster's parents?"

"I have worked... met them. Admirable people. I am certain you would like them."

"How often do they come for a visit?"

"Cash does not see his parents."

"Ever?"

"Not for a long time. They prefer not to travel. Did you list this lily pad-shaped Tiffany lamp base?"

"Of course," Amber said. "Mr. Lancaster doesn't have much of an eastern accent."

"He has worked diligently on his speech, Ms. Rockwell."

Amber thought about the different East Coast accents. Sensing James's reluctance to talk about his boss, she decided to make a guess. "He's from the Boston area, isn't he?"

"He is. May we proceed with the cataloguing? Lunch time approaches. I must oversee the preparation."

She felt like yelling, "Hooray!" Finally she'd gotten something right. "If you need to leave, James, please do. We're about finished in this room."

"Fine. I will see that lunch is ready in half an hour." James hurried off.

"So now you know Lancaster's from Boston." Perry scratched his head. "Why's that so important?"

"It's a start. Why is everyone so tight-lipped around here?"

"Possibly they like their privacy?"

"Maybe a little too much." Amber brought the notebook to her chest. "I'm not through with James. And, I need to get into that study, with or without Lancaster."

"I wonder if you'll ever meet a man who will let you do everything your way, all the time."

When Perry looked down at the list, Amber stuck her tongue out at him, but deep down she knew he spoke the truth. "Is that everything from this room?"

"We listed everything in here. Let's go get ready for lunch. I'm starved."

"Perry, I'm glad to see your appetite's back." Amber walked out of the room.

After freshening up, Amber knocked on Perry's door, and then they headed downstairs. As they descended the steps, she said, "Let's finish cataloguing down here before we begin on the second floor."

"I still don't know what we're looking for."

"I don't either." Amber bit her lip. "I just hope when I see it, I'll know."

CHAPTER 11

During lunch, James brought in a tray of desserts. Amber ignored the chocolate-coated pastries. After three days in Carsonville, she felt ten pounds fatter. James had set the table with the silverware precisely one inch from the edge of the table. Amber noticed that after he put the tray down, he squared it up. The pastries were in perfect alignment.

She scrutinized his actions, realizing he performed all of his duties in this obsessive-compulsive manner. "With the exception of the study, I believe we've inventoried all the downstairs. So, after we've peeked at the study, we're ready to move to the second floor."

While examining her notebook, she hoped what she said next would influence James into helping her. He was all about precision and order.

"Organization is my key." Amber smiled. "I'd really like to complete the downstairs inventory first. Is there a way to contact Mr. Lancaster? Ask if it'd be all right to itemize the study without him?" She held her breath.

"I suppose I could telephone him."

She exhaled slowly. "That would be great, James. It would make it all much more orderly."

"Very well. Please, while you finish your lunch, I will telephone Mr. Lancaster and discuss the matter with him." He raised his finger, like an admonishing father chastising his children. "Mind you, though, if he says no, I cannot allow it."

"Thanks. I know you'll stress the importance."

"I have a few other duties to perform, so after lunch, I suggest you take an hour's rest. We may meet up after."

James marched out of the room.

Perry said, "So precise, it's like living inside a clock."

An hour later, Amber rapped on Perry's door. "Ready?"

James stood at the bottom of the stairs, waiting. Perry and Amber followed him to the study. As he unlocked the private domain, he said, "Mr. Lancaster didn't see any reason why you and I couldn't inventory this room together."

Amber's gaze locked on the center of the room, where an oversized roll-topped desk sat by a matching high-backed rolling chair. Three pictures, facing both back and front, were arranged above the desk's closed cover that masked the secrets Amber ached to discover. Those photos were of different women: one was Sarah, the other two Amber didn't recognize. Books, both antique and modern, lined two walls from floor to ceiling, interspersed by pictures and paintings mounted between shelves.

"Are these all family pictures?" Amber neared the desk. "This picture is of Sarah. Who are these two women?"

"Dear friends," James said.

Well, that's evasive. But Amber let it go for now.

A Venetian Tiffany desk lamp with bright blues surrounded by green trees adorned a side table. Two overstuffed dark brown leather chairs with a matching couch created the room, giving off a masculine feel. Amber closed her eyes and envisioned the study with cigar-smoking men reverently swirling brandy snifters. She could almost smell the lingering smoke.

In one corner stood a four-drawer oak file cabinet with several pieces of amber on top, each distinctly different in size, shape, and color. One had a leaf trapped inside. A rose quartz, unlike any that Amber had ever seen, sat on a shelf on the third wall. It was shaped like an elephant; different from the rose quartzes in the sitting room and her room.

Amber couldn't pull her gaze away from the file cabinet. If she could just get a look inside. That wouldn't happen. Time, and James' patience, were working against her. Lancaster had to be cleverer than to leave anything incriminating in those files.

Mentally, she inventoried what she knew so far: One, Lancaster didn't appear outwardly broken up over Sarah's death, but that in itself meant nothing. Two, he had a great collection of beautiful antiques; some had been inherited, some acquired. Three, he loved beautiful things, including beautiful women. What man didn't? The only new bit of knowledge? Number four, his inheritance. That information brought with it a new set of questions.

However, she did uncover that James was a father figure to Lancaster, more than his butler or chauffeur. Amber wondered which relationship outweighed the other. Maybe she could learn where James had come from. How long had they known each other?

Was she going about this all-wrong? She needed to come up with a plan to get James to open up. He might be easier than Lancaster to get information from. Amber was too self-conscious around Lancaster. She didn't feel beautiful around him and knew he only responded to beauty. Even though the butler scared her, she could be herself.

Beautiful. She hated that word. Why did women have to gaze into a mirror and be uncomfortable with themselves? Why couldn't she just look in the mirror and say, "I'm beautiful," no matter what she looked like?

"Ms. Rockwell, did you hear me?"

"What? Sorry, James. This study is so..." She waved her hand, encompassing the room, trying to think of an appropriate word.

James nodded. "This is Mr. Lancaster's favorite room."

"I can see why." She smiled at James. "Thank you for arranging this. You've been so helpful, and your knowledge is invaluable."

Amber didn't think it was possible, but James stood taller. She wished she had the room to herself. Perry stood next to her. To get rid of him, she asked, "Have you gotten hold of Tom at the shop?"

"No, not yet."

"Why don't you go ahead? Oh, and please don't forget to ask him to pick up my mail." Amber faced James. "The two of us can handle this room."

"Mr. Cole, if you need to discuss business matters, I am quite certain Ms. Rockwell and I can manage."

"You're positive?"

Smiling, Amber motioned toward the door. "We can inventory this room without you."

"I would like to speak with Tom." Perry walked to the door. "I'll run upstairs to my room and use my cell phone."

"Okay." Amber followed him and slowly closed the door behind her boss.

That's when she noticed the heart-shaped rose quartz necklace encased in glass hanging by the door. She wondered why the pendant would be on the wall and not in some woman's jewelry box.

"Where would you like to start?" James asked.

Amber faced the room and leaned back against the hard wood. She tried her best to be subtle. "Why don't you settle yourself into that chair behind the desk? There's history here. I can feel it. Tell me about each piece."

James droned on and on about each collectible, how they acquired it and where it came from. Amber wrote down the item, and then as James talked, she browsed through the leather-bound books behind him. She scanned through a few. While leafing through a large, red-leather bound volume, a torn piece of paper slid out. James, absorbed with the telling of his story, didn't see the paper slip to the floor. Amber snatched it up.

She stared at the yellow-lined scrap of paper. Someone had written the name "Amber" and "Sarah" over and over. The last lines resembled Sarah's handwriting. Amber stuffed it into her notepad and scribbled the title of the book into her notes. Then she replaced the book on the shelf. Trying to keep her voice calm and James talking, she asked, "All these books weren't procured by Mr. Lancaster, were they?"

James set down the vase he had been discussing and swiveled in the chair to gaze at the books. "No. My former employer purchased most of the volumes as well as other pieces in this room."

"Does Mr. Lancaster read much?"

"Sometimes." His gaze told of his appreciation for the tomes. "Mr. Lancaster allows anyone access to these wonderful books. I have enjoyed reading some, and even some of the other staff has. And, of course, his friends, including, I think, Detective Burns."

Burns, Amber thought. *Didn't know he read.* Was he that

close to Lancaster? "Hmm, a lending library." She watched James's face soften, something she didn't believe possible. "How does he keep track of the books?"

"He keeps a logbook. You have to sign out and sign back in."

"That's orderly. May I borrow one?"

"Oh, dear, I am afraid the logbook is locked up in this desk. If you would like to borrow a book, I am certain you may ask Mr. Lancaster this evening."

"I'll do that." Amber wondered why Lancaster kept the desk locked. It seemed odd that James didn't have a key. She mulled it over. If he had it, why didn't he want her to know? What was so valuable that even James might not have access to the desk?

"How did Mr. Lancaster end up with all of these items from your former boss?" Amber held her breath, hoping James had been lulled into a talkative, remembering-when state.

"I suppose it is not a secret. Mr. Lancaster was engaged to my previous employer's daughter. Mr. Fullerton was so excited and happy that his daughter had found the perfect match. He admired and befriended Cash."

James spoke with a faraway expression and bemused smile on his face. He hadn't noticed he'd slipped by referring to his employer as "Cash."

"Before the wedding, Mr. Fullerton's daughter, Harriet, passed away. That's her necklace hanging by the door. Anyway, after she died, the Fullerton's still invited Cash over for dinner and treated him like family. He filled the void that remained after the loss for their only child. When Mr. and Mrs. Fullerton died, they gave everything to Cash. They even mentioned me in their will. Suggested he keep me on as his butler."

"You don't mean you were bound to him in their will?"

"No, nothing so archaic. However," James said, "I could not very well leave everything in his hands alone. He needed guidance. He asked for my help. I could not refuse.

"The loss of the Fullerton family devastated him, so we left the East Coast and came to California. Eventually, we settled here in Carsonville. Cash cherished this romantic setting with so many Victorian homes. This area has everything for him."

Amber smiled. She added information number five to her ever-growing mental list. Lancaster said he'd never been married, but no mention of being engaged. How did his fiancée die? What happened to her parents? What did this have to do with Sarah? Amber had more questions than answers. She didn't know where to start.

With her mind drifting, she almost missed James saying, "Mr. Lancaster loves beautiful women. I can see he is attracted to you."

Amber coughed and gripped her notebook. "I... I doubt that," she stammered. "I'm... I'm sure it's because I was so close to Sarah, and the fact that I'm helping him to acquire a new item for his collection."

James lifted an eyebrow. "You are so refreshing after some of the others." He arose from the desk chair. "Now then, I think we have covered everything in this room. We have finished the downstairs. Tomorrow, Mr. Lancaster will be available for the upstairs. May I suggest you prepare for tonight's dinner? A few friends are coming over, and dress is formal. If you should need any help, let me know.

"I believe you and Mr. Lancaster will get along just fine." He picked up a piece of amber and examined it. "Amber is his favorite and most prized possession out of all of his collections." He set down the large Baltic amber with an ant trapped inside and walked to the door.

Once again, Amber felt the hairs on the back of her neck stand up. She shivered when James opened the door wide, waiting for her to pass.

She heard the final click of the lock behind her.

CHAPTER 12

While Amber showered, she peeked out from the curtain, feeling like someone watched her. No matter how hot the water, she felt cold. After toweling off, she donned her robe and rushed to her room.

She held up the black cocktail dress, and then gazed at her favorite one. The vintage bottle green sheath with tiny gold buttons might be a better choice. She hoped Lancaster would open up more if she didn't wear mourning black.

Amber hung the black dress in the closet and slipped into the green one. Since Sarah never mentioned Cash's past, Amber intended to discern as much as she could at tonight's dinner.

Perry waited for her in the hall. He wore a black suit, yellow shirt, and a burgundy tie. "James said formal attire is appropriate for this evening's gathering of friends. Hope they're not all in tuxes."

"Come on." Amber clasped his hand. "It can't be that formal. Besides, James said it was just a few friends."

They descended the stairs to discover Marie standing at the bottom, talking with Lancaster. The maid's low-cut uniform bulged with cleavage. She'd painted her lips a bright red, the same shade as her long fingernails. Her hand rested on Lancaster's arm.

Marie smirked after she spotted Amber. She withdrew her hand and flounced off down the hall. *My God,* Amber thought, *she's too hot for the housekeeping position.* Who has hair like that? Did Lancaster give her those antique silver hair-clips? They were similar to ones Sarah owned.

Lancaster offered Amber his arm. "You look lovely."

"You're not so bad yourself." Amber swallowed. She flicked an imaginary speck of lint from his tuxedo's lapel. She glanced at Perry with an expression that conveyed, "What can I do?" She wanted to bash Lancaster's head in, but instead, she entwined her arm through his. She hated the way he seemed to have forgotten about Sarah.

Cocktails were served in the drawing room. Amber was wrong about the level of formality. Tall, beautiful women glided by in designer dresses, their necks and arms glittering with jewels. Handsome men wore expensive suits or tuxedos. All sipped champagne or Perrier from crystal flutes. *He sure puts on expensive parties.*

Amber clenched her jaw. Her right eye twitched. She couldn't believe the number of people in the room—at least thirty. Where were this man's feelings for Sarah?

James materialized at her side. "Champagne, Ms. Rockwell?"

Amber stared at him in amazement. She was underdressed. Of all times to have a bad hair day. She reached up and patted the unruly mass she hastily piled atop her head. "A few friends?" she whispered to the butler.

He winked. Lancaster grabbed a glass of champagne from the tray and handed it to her. "Help yourself, Perry."

Lancaster cupped Amber's elbow and guided her farther into the room. "There are people I'd like you to meet."

Introductions passed in a blur. Who were all these people? How could Lancaster be having yet another party so soon after Sarah's death?

"Don't you agree?" a tall man asked her.

Lancaster squeezed her arm. "Are you all right? Henry, I'm afraid Amber is still reeling from the shock of Sarah's death."

"I imagine you both are. I do appreciate your continued support of my campaign, but I would have understood if you had bowed out of this dinner. If you'll excuse me." Henry nodded his head slightly and ambled off.

The rest of the group muttered, "We're so sorry," and, one by one, they too wandered away to mingle with others, sipping their drinks.

Alone with Lancaster, Amber said, "I thought tonight Perry, you, and I would be discussing your collections? But this..." She pointed to all the people.

"Does it bother you?"

"Did you have to throw a bash?" Amber couldn't hide the contempt in her voice.

"There are important people here." Lancaster's gaze skimmed the crowd. "See that man over there?" He motioned toward the man he'd called Henry.

A few gray hairs streaked his golden locks. He had a long nose, jutting chin, and blue eyes that lied by saying you were the only one in the room he was paying attention to.

"Henry Longreen will be our next Congressman," Lancaster said.

Amber didn't think the man looked like a politician. "I still don't understand why you want to party when the dirt's barely been shoveled over Sarah's grave."

Lancaster flinched. "Time didn't stop when Sarah died.

We both wanted Henry elected. Sarah planned this gala fundraiser several weeks ago. I take my job seriously and I have to carry on with the campaign work. As you said, it keeps my mind occupied. I'm not spending all my time thinking of her, as you are."

They stood in front of a large gilded mirror. For a moment before turning to Amber, Lancaster appraised himself. "You do look nice this evening, however somewhat austere. Sarah would have understood if you let loose and dressed up a bit."

Before Amber could reply, Perry came and draped his arm around her shoulders. "Have you eaten any of these little shrimp things? They slide down easy."

As she opened her mouth to say "No," Perry popped the seafood in. Not having a choice, Amber chewed, and then grinned at Perry. The scent of garlic assaulted her as he held up another shrimp. Leave it to him to defuse her before she ruined everything. "That's delicious."

"I'll tell the chef," Lancaster said with that arrogant tone of voice Amber didn't appreciate. "Now come along." He tugged on her arm. "I want everyone to meet you. Stay focused."

Amber wanted to snap at him for being rude, but he continued, "I know Sarah would have wanted you to get to know some of her friends."

She blinked, realizing he spoke the truth. Sarah would have wanted her to know some of these people.

"You come, too," Lancaster told Perry. "Some of my guests are interested in antiques. Perhaps you can drum up some West Coast business."

"Speaking of business, Amber," Perry said, adjusting his tie, "I reached Tom. He'll swing by your place sometime in the next couple of days to check your mail."

"Thanks, Perry."

"I told him he could forward it here. I hope that's all right, Mr. Lancaster."

"Of course." Cash said to the butler. "Be on the lookout, James." The butler nodded. "Now I suggest we mingle."

Amber visited with Henry, met his assistant, and a couple who were interested in antiques. Her mind whirled. Before sitting down to dinner, she strolled past the dining room on the way to the bathroom. Marie bustled about the table, removing a dish, silverware, and glasses.

Earlier, Amber noticed a blond woman standing next to Henry Longreen, talking. The woman matched his height. Amber hadn't met her yet. She'd been standing near them when Perry talked about Tom, but wandered away before being introduced. Amber hadn't seen her since then. Was the place setting for her? If so, who was she? Where had she gone?

After James announced dinner, Lancaster escorted Amber to her chair. She wanted to ask him about the removed setting from the other end of the table. Before she could, Detective Steve Burns rushed through the dining room doors.

"So sorry I'm late."

James seated him across from Amber on Lancaster's right.

The detective leaned toward Lancaster and in a low voice everyone could hear, said, "I had some unexpected business." He handed Lancaster a check. "For Henry's campaign."

"A thousand dollars." Lancaster lifted his eyebrows. "You've a right to be late. Thank you, Steve." He stuffed the check in his coat pocket.

Burns glared at Amber. "I'm surprised you're still here."

Shocked to see Steve Burns, and hearing of the amount

he'd just handed over, Amber forgot about the blond woman. "Perry and I are inventorying Mr. Lancaster's collections. I want to acquire a nice piece for him to add to it."

"Staying here at the house?" Burns' voice sounded to Amber like he was shocked.

"We are." She grinned. Having her around would irk the good detective.

Marie swished in and set down the salad plates. Another young woman placed plates farther down the table. When Marie served Lancaster, she made sure she bent low so her breasts touched his shoulder. "Hope everything is satisfactory, sir."

He smiled. "I'm certain it will be."

Between Burns and the maid, Amber couldn't concentrate. She heard snippets of conversation about food, dinner, and California politics, but Sarah's name never came up.

James rested against the wall behind his boss, ever vigilant. If a wineglass appeared half empty, he glided forward and poured more. He guarded the table like a Royal Grenadier in front of London's Buckingham Palace.

After dinner, the guests withdrew to the parlor for liqueurs. Amber felt as if she were driving in a tunnel against traffic. Too many people were unconcerned about Sarah.

She thought she caught a glimpse of the blond woman, but when she looked again—no sign of her.

Amber stood next to Perry. Lancaster introduced them to a couple and said, "And this is her boss, Perry Cole." He lifted his hand and dropped it limply. Amber couldn't believe he gave the cliché movement portraying a gay man.

"Perry, of course, owns an antique store back in New

York," Lancaster said. "Perhaps he could help you purchase that perfect Tiffany lamp you're looking for."

Amber blinked. Why would Lancaster infer Perry was gay? She waited for Perry's comment. The couple and he gaped at each other. But then Perry grinned and said, "I would enjoy that. I just love shopping." He waved his hand and dropped it like Lancaster had motioned. "I'd be glad to help you find a lamp you'd like."

Amber recognized this version of Perry's personality. He was having a great time. He loved attention and wasn't ashamed of being gay. Why had Lancaster brought up Perry's sexual preference? Maybe to let people know that she was not involved with her boss. But why would that matter? She needed air to clear her mind. Amber strolled out onto the patio.

"Why are you still here?" Detective Burns whispered as he slipped up beside her.

"You're not doing your job, so someone has to."

"You fool." His hiss reminded her of a snake. "Even in high school you didn't believe in me."

"No, and you never took me seriously either." Amber stared into unblinking blue eyes. *Why do I keep baiting this man?* "Did you know that Lancaster was engaged before?"

"So?"

"Have you ever checked his past?"

"Why?" Burns laughed that annoying chuckle that meant he didn't believe her.

"I take it he still doesn't know about our being in high school together?" Burns' face flushed. "Ah, I see I'm right."

Before he had a chance to respond, a woman stepped out onto the patio. She wore an elegant flowing gown in some shade of red, a neck entwined in diamonds, and perfectly coiffured dark hair. "There you are Detective, darling. How do you manage to sneak off so successfully? You disappeared tonight the same way you did at my party last Friday." She wagged a finger at him. "Naughty, naughty."

The woman eyed Amber. Smiling, she extended her hand. "How do you do? I'm Barbara Martin. Cash's next-door neighbor. So you're Amber. A model like Sarah?"

"No," Burns said, "Sarah's best friend."

Barbara put her hand over her heart. "Oh, my. I'm so sorry for you, darling."

Amber, reeling from what the woman said about Burns being next door when Sarah died, couldn't respond.

"Have I interrupted you?" Barbara asked. "I'm terribly sorry."

"No... no." Amber found her voice. "Excuse me. I get caught up in my memories of Sarah. I was leaving anyway." She hurried into the din of other people's conversation, letting men and women surround her, engulfing her in a safe cocoon. Amber's stomach roiled with acid. She should have spoken more with Barbara Martin, but needed to consider the ramifications.

Where was Perry? Amber searched room by room. She wanted to tell him what she just learned. He talked with Lancaster, a heavy-set man in a tuxedo with a yellow cummerbund and a woman with a page-boy hairdo that made her appear old. Perry wore that expression on his face that told her he was about to make a sale. She'd talk to him later.

Amber wandered around, and every time she spotted Burns, she darted to another room. She went into one and ran into him. He pulled her over by a chair in the corner where they were alone.

Visions of the torn paper flashed in her mind. Before he

could say anything to her, she asked, "Detective Burns, how many books have you borrowed from Lancaster?"

"What?" The detective wrinkled his forehead. "I returned two a couple weeks ago."

"One you'd recommend?"

Burns raised an eyebrow, studying her. "That was a while back. I was too busy to read them." He looked around the room. Amber followed his gaze. Barbara Martin waved to him. "Excuse me." He hurried off.

Standing alone, Amber observed Marie flitting about serving cognac. The maid's gaze stayed glued on her boss. Whenever she could manage, she brushed up against him. In his usual stance, James stood by the door at the ready. Amber kept a close eye on Lancaster and the staff. She believed one of them was a killer.

CHAPTER 13

The gala over, Amber sat on the bed in Perry's room, one leg tucked underneath her. They talked in low tones. "Did you find out any more information about Lancaster?"

Perry, under the covers, leaned his head against the headboard, eyes closed. "Yes, these people respect Cash. No one even remotely believes Sarah's death was anything but a suicide."

Amber chewed on a strand of hair. "I couldn't believe Cash invited Detective Burns to this party."

"Why not? They seem to get along quite well. Two of a kind."

"Or the detective's a wanna-be tycoon?"

"Without opening my own eyes, I know yours are blazing green. And quit chewing on your hair."

Amber spat out the wet strand. Her cheeks burned. "That man infuriates me."

Perry opened one eye, raising his eyebrow. "Which one? Lancaster or Burns?"

"Really funny."

113

Perry closed his eye and yawned. He looked tired, or bored, or both. "What did the poor detective do this time?"

"Burns doesn't believe anything I say. I suggested he check Lancaster's Boston past, and that he'd been engaged." Amber placed her hands on her hips. "The man just laughed."

Her boss chuckled. "Why should he investigate Cash? You've still come up with nothing suspicious." He yawned again.

"Am I keeping you awake?"

"Sort of."

"Well, I'm sorry. Then I suppose you wouldn't be interested in a few suspicious things I discovered."

With halfway opened eyes, Perry peered through their slits. "Like what?"

"Like, your good detective was next door at the Martins' party when Sarah died. How come he never mentioned that?"

Perry's eyes widened. He sat up straight and opened his mouth to speak. He sputtered and managed to say, "What?"

Amber smirked. "Next door. Furthermore, I found something in the study." With a grin that was a mixture of triumph and spite, she handed the torn paper to him.

Perry examined it. "Appears someone wrote yours and Sarah's name over and over."

"Notice how in the beginning the handwriting occurs one way, but in the end, it's different." Amber reached over and tapped the last couple of lines. "Those develop into Sarah's handwriting, but not the first attempts."

Perry gaped at her. "Did you tell Detective Burns?"

"No. He had access to the study and he told me he borrowed some books. That paper fell out of a red, leather-bound book entitled *The Last Honest Man*. How do I know who wrote these names? I asked Burns which ones, but he told me he returned them, and couldn't remember their titles."

"Can you remember names of books you read last week?"

"If they were fancy books I signed out of a rich man's library, maybe. This is important."

"You don't suspect the detective, do you?" Perry studied the writing again.

"He was angry with Sarah when she refused to marry him."

"Amber, that was a long time ago."

"Maybe not for him. What am I supposed to think? He was next door at the Martins. He disappeared during the party. We need to figure out if he was gone long enough to come over here and kill Sarah."

"I can't believe he did that." Perry covered his mouth, unsuccessfully hiding another yawn. "Hey, it's been a long day. Can we discuss this later? I drank a bit much, not to mention, I'm bushed."

Even though Perry was eating well lately, his drawn, pale complexion worried her. The T-shirt he wore was too baggy. "Sure," Amber said. "Sorry I kept you up."

He placed his hand on her arm. "I think you're onto something, hon, and it frightens me. But, I can't think with a muddled brain."

She kissed him on the forehead and snatched the slip of paper from his hand. "Don't worry. I'll be careful. We'll talk in the morning. Get some rest."

Amber reached for the handle of her bedroom door. She stopped, thinking everyone was probably as exhausted as Perry. It was after two in the morning so they'd be sound asleep.

Moonlight filtered through the fog and streamed

through the windows, lighting her way as she tiptoed about the house. *Don't let me trip over my feet as I did with Sarah one night when we were trying to sneak out to a high school party.*

She went down the stairs toward the study determined to find the logbook. She glared at the different handwriting samples still clutched in her hand. If she could discover who had checked out *The Last Honest Man*, then she'd have a solid suspect. Right now, she suspected everyone: Lancaster, James, even Burns. Were there more? That maid acted as suspiciously as everyone else. It seemed like they all danced on Sarah's grave.

One way or another, Amber needed to see the logbook. The only reason someone would have the handwriting appear as Sarah's—to write that suicide note. She'd never received closure on her parents' death, but she was determined to have it with Sarah.

She grasped the study's cold metal doorknob in her hand and twisted it.

Locked.

Amber held her breath, struggling to listen. The Victorian house groaned as if protesting for what she was about to do. She removed a bobby pin from her snarled mass of hair. A thin strand fell, tickling her neck. She knelt in front of the door, pushed the bobby pin into the keyhole, and swiveled it around.

Five minutes later, the door remained locked. She wiped away the sweat trickling down her brow. They did this so easily in the movies. Straightening up, she stretched her back and stopped in mid-stretch. Footsteps resounded on the stairs. Unsure of what to do, she dashed toward the kitchen. Strolling back, she retraced her steps.

Lancaster halted in mid-stride, staring. He had on gray silk pajamas with a black silk dressing gown. "What are you doing up?"

Amber yawned. "I couldn't sleep. Thought I'd raid the kitchen. Hope that's okay."

"Of course. What did you find?"

"Decided I really didn't need to eat."

"That's one way to keep your figure." He eyed her from her toes to the top of her head.

Amber still wore her evening clothes. She hated it when she blushed, the heat burning her cheeks. Now they must be bright red. She crushed the paper tight in her fist. "Well, guess I better get off to bed."

Lancaster reached out an arm preventing her from passing. "Are you certain you didn't want anything?"

She hesitated for a minute. "As a matter of fact, when James and I inventoried your study, I found a book I'd like to read."

"Why didn't he give it to you?"

"He said the logbook was locked in your desk. I'd have to ask you."

"That's true," Lancaster said. "But everyone knows where I keep the key."

"Oh, where?"

He laughed. "I'll be right back." Lancaster hurried into the kitchen. Amber thought about following him, but decided not to. He returned, holding a set of keys and inserted a long, old-fashioned one in to open the door. At the desk, he unlocked it with a small key and pulled out a red binder. "Which book did you want?"

Amber pretended to browse for a certain book. She removed one, and then grabbed another, which was the one she really required. "Would it be all right if I borrowed two?"

"Of course. Those choices are excellent."

"Have you read them?" Amber asked.

"I just finished *The Last Honest Man* last week. I think you'll enjoy it."

Lancaster marked both of the titles that she chose into the records. She made out the date he wrote, but his body blocked the rest of the binder, so she couldn't read any entries.

"James told me about your system. May I see?"

Lancaster closed the book. "How about tomorrow? I need sleep." He shut and locked the roll-top and walked to the door. "Ready?"

Amber gave the desk a last once-over. She'd seen nothing of importance, except for the logbook. "I am." She sighed. "Thank you."

In her room, she flattened out the handwriting clip. She held the books upside down and shuffled the pages. No other pieces of paper fell out. Had someone borrowed the book after Lancaster read it? She had to be sure. How was she going to get a look at that binder?

She fell asleep with the book open on her chest.

CHAPTER 14

Retrieving that ridiculous letter is a last annoyance. At least I can take care of it before Perry's assistant goes by Amber's place. Thank goodness for airplanes. With Amber's address in New York and my connections and talents—easy to get that letter so she will never know.

People are like pawns on a chessboard, easily influenced, readily sacrificed. It's almost lonely, standing with my back to this wall, knowing not one guest at this party is capable of strategy; timing; elegance. Henry will be a shoe-in. He'll be another pawn, but he'll do, if he obeys instructions.

This fund-raiser is a huge success. It pleases me to see everyone adores Amber. She reminds me of a dolphin swimming among sharks: wary, gentle, and yet ready to strike or flee if the need arises. It's great the way she holds herself erect, making everyone feel at ease, even though to my discerning eye she seems uncomfortable.

Her loyalty and persistence will be an asset. My choice to include her in the collections and other possessions is a wise one.

She suspects foul play, which means I have to be

especially careful and keep an eye on her. I am not too worried—my ingenuity will pay off. I laugh out loud and look around quickly. No one even notices.

Amber will snoop a little to satisfy some inner need, but she'll find nothing other than what the coroner concluded. I make sure of that.

Amber brings to mind, Sarah. I can*not* stop thinking about her. I have to get rid of Sarah's images. I do not want to focus on the other women, just Amber. Sarah's face refuses to disappear. The dreaded letter could have been damaging. She was depressed, I heard her tell Amber. No matter, I will make certain the new letter tells about her depression in more detail.

Sarah took her own life. She could not pass a mirror without admiring herself.

Vanity. Makes me shudder. It made Sarah ugly and unacceptable—just as it did the others.

No time to think about that now. Must concentrate on Amber. From what I see and hear, once she gets an idea it doesn't shake loose. Can I convince her Sarah committed suicide? Perhaps with the help of the new letter. Writing it will take some thought, but I've manipulated situations far trickier than this one.

Setting up the car wreck—lots of devious planning. But the plane crash—ingenious. Yes, I handle all kinds of situations.

And, I know what I'm doing. Things will work out. This time, my choice is right. Amber fits in nicely, as long as she never realizes just how beautiful she is. I hate to have to get rid of her, too.

CHAPTER 15

The morning was foggy as usual. Amber drove Perry downtown and parked in a spot on Third Street.

"Hard to believe I talked with Sarah last Friday and it's Friday already."

She and Perry stood on the sidewalk. He surveyed the street. "So, where are these great antique shops you've talked about?"

Amber swiped at a tear and entwined her arm with Perry's. She led him down to Second Street. They strolled along the brick-lined walkways. "Don't you love the multi-colored paint with blues, browns, oranges and reds? Those Victorian homes have been refurbished into offices." Aging storefronts were reconstructed with big picture windows. "Second Street's known as Old Towne. Lots of cafes and antique stores."

"This area looks fun," Perry said. "But since we haven't gone into any shops, what are we doing here?"

"Finding an old friend of Sarah's and mine named Max Kazinsky. You're helping me. Sarah and I came here and brought his horse, Wally, apples and carrots. He drove for the carriage company back then and showed tourists around."

Amber paused in front of a brick-paved park with black wrought-iron benches. Water overflowed out of the top of the brick fountain like lava bubbling up from a volcano. Several couples stood under the covered gazebo, gazing down a narrow street to a view of Humboldt Bay. A slight breeze blew. Amber caught a whiff of salty air mixed with smells of fresh fish. Sailboats, fishing boats, and tugs patrolled the water. Some bobbed at the docks.

She pulled her gaze away from the harbor. "I know you think we should go see Detective Burns, but I have to talk with Max first. Sarah adored him. She confided in him and he might know something important."

"Possibly. But, I think we ought to ask the detective to check out Cash's past."

"What if Burns had something to do with Sarah's death? He had the opportunity."

"Just because he was next door?" Perry rested a fist on his hip. "What's his motive?"

"I don't know." Amber chewed on a strand of hair. "Jealousy? Maybe he wanted to frame Lancaster."

"Take the hair out of your mouth. You need to break that habit."

Amber removed the strand of hair and tucked it behind her ear.

Perry asked, "Why make it look like a suicide?"

"How should I know? The more I delve into this, the more questions I have."

"Precisely why we should involve Detective Burns. He could answer some of those questions."

"I hate unanswered questions."

Perry reached over and patted Amber's shoulder. "This is not going to be like your parents."

Amber didn't want to think about how her mother had been murdered. What had happened to her dad?

An old-fashioned leather-seated carriage pulled by a gray-dappled horse came up the street by the park. The gelding wore blinders. The rig parked nearby next to a curb. The Old Town Carriage Company's driver wore a top hat and tails. After he climbed down, he faced the horse and fed the animal a carrot.

"Mr. Kazinsky, it's me, Amber Rockwell." She ran over and gave the old man a kiss on the cheek.

"Rocky, I can't believe it's you." Max used her childhood nickname.

She patted the old horse. "Wally hasn't changed much, gray hairs underneath his chin. He still has that white stripe on his leg."

"You came back for Sarah's funeral?" Max asked. "Such a shame. I remember the two of you were like two ponies pulling a cart—always together and so close."

He motioned his head toward Perry. "Who's this?"

"I'm sorry, Max. This is my friend and boss, Perry Cole."

Perry stuck out his hand for a shake, but Max ignored it and simply nodded. He glanced around as if someone might overhear and leaned closer. "Climb aboard." He motioned toward the carriage. "We need to talk."

They stepped up into the buggy. The ride meandered through Old Towne and along the waterfront. Max narrated the historic sites and elegant Victorians. Three minutes into the tour, he brought up Sarah.

"She was unhappy living with Mr. Lancaster, thinking about leaving him," Max said without turning around.

"How did you know that?"

He looked over his shoulder and smiled. "She still came here to visit me. I'd give her a ride, just as we're doing.

We'd talk. She'd bring apples for Wally the way the two of you used to do."

Amber remembered the horses slobber as he nibbled an apple from her hand and how Sarah laughed from the tickling chin whiskers. "So she hadn't changed."

Max faced Wally and jiggled the reins. "Sarah, change? Never! She still laughed at Wally when he took food from her hand, and she still put on parties for the Senior Center. The day she died, she'd been to see me. You know she'd run into Steve Burns again?"

"I found that out." Amber couldn't rush the old man. He'd tell her all about Sarah in his own way. If she questioned Max, he might clam up.

Perry sat next to her, viewing the sights.

The carriage rolled to a stop in front of the famous Victorian Eureka Mansion. Max swiveled in his seat and gazed down at her. "Rocky, you've heard this before, but I'll tell your friend the story. Back in 1885, the mill slowed down. To keep his mill workers busy, our local lumber king had this 'castle' built." Max pointed to the Eureka Mansion.

Amber watched Perry as he admired the gray and green towers and turrets that rose high into the sky. Surrounded by a spacious, manicured lawn, the mansion guarded the bay like a sentinel, keeping a vigil not only over the water, but Old Towne as well.

Perry pointed to the large estate. "Boy would I love to see inside of that place."

"You can," Max said. "It's a private men's club now, and Mr. Lancaster is a member."

"Mr. Kazinsky, do you believe Sarah killed herself?" Amber waited for his answer feeling her heart rate increase. If he did, then maybe she'd been wrong.

He locked gazes with her. "Of course not. Sarah was going to leave that Lancaster fellow. Steve has been enamored with wealth all his life. Do you think he would let anything get in his way?"

"I don't understand. What's Steve have to do with it?"

"He had just gotten in good with the man. If she left, who would be blamed for it?" Max lifted an eyebrow.

Before Amber could reply, the horse swished his tail and blew out through his nostrils.

Max continued, "Once Lancaster learned about their past, he'd have to blame Steve 'cause his ego wouldn't have it any other way." Max leaned over and said in a hushed undertone, "I've never thought much of Steve. Too full of himself if you ask me."

"But you were so nice to him." Amber pictured Steve and Sarah riding in the carriage, laughing at Max's jokes.

"I did that for Sarah. At least she came to her senses. That Mr. Lancaster wasn't any good for her either. She showed me pictures of some of his paintings. I think one of them was stolen."

"Why do you think that?" Amber asked.

"I read this article on stolen paintings that had pictures. It resembled one of the paintings in the article."

"Perhaps it was a copy?" Perry shifted in his seat.

Max snorted. "I mentioned it to Sarah. What if she confronted Lancaster or told Steve?"

"We just inventoried all Lancaster's collectibles," Perry said. "We didn't find any stolen items."

"Good. Why'd Sarah always have to pick the same kind of man?" Max sniffed. He took out a white handkerchief, wiped his nose, and stuffed the cloth back in his pocket.

Suddenly, he changed his behavior. He straightened, and while making gestures, in a louder voice, said, "If you want some good food, go down M Street, turn right on Third. Restaurant Three O One has a good selection."

Again, in a lower voice, he stated, "We shouldn't be seen talking too long."

"Why?" Amber looked up and down the streets, not seeing anything sinister.

"Police have ears everywhere. I don't trust Steve."

"All right," Amber said. "Thank you, Mr. Kazinsky. May we talk again?"

"I'd be disappointed if you didn't come back. Bring old Wally here an apple or carrot next time, the way you did in the good ole days. You're old enough to call me Max. Nice to see you again."

Perry and Amber climbed down from the carriage. She asked, "Are many of our old school friends around town?"

"Most of your gang are gone, except for Steve. Sarah had to make new friends, mostly Mr. Lancaster's." Max tipped his hat then clicked his tongue. The old gelding plodded off, horseshoes clopping along on the cement street.

"See, I knew Sarah wouldn't kill herself."

"Wait a minute, Amber. Just because that old man told us a story—"

"Story? He and Sarah were close. She loved horses, always came around to talk with Max. At least he confirms I shouldn't confide any information I detect to Burns."

"Your Max Kazinsky didn't make much sense. Sounds like he has it in for the detective. We can't do this on our own. Besides, why would Cash blame the detective if Sarah left?"

"Because Sarah and Burns were lovers. Lancaster would have to blame somebody. Maybe he'd think she'd wanted to get back together with Burns. Max made plenty of sense to me. And, there's no reason why we can't figure this out on our own."

"Maybe we should confront the detective?"

"Oh, Perry, I thought you wanted me to be careful. If he's the killer, we'd be tipping our hand."

"I wish you'd quit saying 'killer.'" Perry glanced around, as if searching for someone. "There's no proof. Possibly it was a horrible accident. If Detective Burns isn't involved, we could try to convince him to help us."

"We don't need his help. You could go back to Boston and investigate Lancaster's past."

"No!" Perry's voice rose. "If you're right, and I'm not positive you are—"

"How can you say that? What about the handwriting?"

"I admit that's suspicious, but it doesn't prove your point. But, if there is a killer, you could be in serious danger. I'm not leaving you. That's final."

Knowing her boss, Amber assumed Perry wouldn't budge on this. "Okay, if we have to talk with Burns, let's ask about Lancaster's past and nothing else. Don't mention the paper I discovered in the book."

"I promise, I won't."

CHAPTER 16

Men loitered around the coffee pot in the detective's room as the sergeant told Amber to come on in. The reek of stale coffee assaulted her. Her stomach grumbled when she caught a whiff of maple donuts. Those pastries were the reason she'd gotten so fat as a teenager. She hadn't eaten a donut in a long time. Sarah and she ate one every day in high school. Of course, Sarah never gained weight, but it took Amber over three years to get the donut fat off and keep it off.

When would everything stop reminding her of Sarah? Amber ignored her rumbling tummy and focused on Detective Burns. He sat behind his desk, sipping from a Styrofoam cup and reading a file. He looked up as they approached.

Before she opened her mouth, Perry said, "Good-morning, Detective. We have a favor to ask you."

Burns smirked. "I guess it depends on what it is."

"You believe I couldn't possibly know what I'm talking about," Amber said. "And, I have no proof, yet. But, I'm working on that end. Would you at least humor me? Help me out? Think of all the satisfaction you'll have when you prove me wrong."

From the twitch in Burns' jaw, she touched a nerve. Back in high school, he tried to be the better in Sarah's eyes. Burns and she always competed for Sarah's affection. "Please check out Lancaster's past, if you haven't done so."

"Even if I did that or have done that, the law prohibits me from telling you."

Amber stood in front of the desk, biting her lip. "Okay. But if Sarah was murdered, then he's the first person who would be a suspect. Right?"

Burns inclined his head slightly.

"Will you prove to me that I'm wrong about him? I learned he was engaged back in Boston to a Harriet Fullerton who died. Afterward, he stayed close with her parents. After they died, he inherited everything. How did they all die? Why did Lancaster inherit the money?"

Burns placed both hands on his desk and pressed down until his fingers turned white. "And if there's nothing criminal about all this, then what?"

Amber shrugged.

"Detective," Perry interjected, standing next to Amber, "what would it hurt to check it out? We have to admit that if Cash loved Sarah, he has a funny way of showing it." He held up a hand. "Wait. Let me finish. Grief is different for everyone, but I haven't seen any form of it in that house. I have seen what appears to be immense relief from Lancaster, the butler, and others close to Sarah."

"I'll admit," Burns said, "Cash and Sarah were having problems. He might have wanted her to leave as much as she wanted to go."

"How do you know Sarah was leaving?" Amber crossed her arms over her chest and waited for his answer.

"She told me. Asked me to help her figure out a way to do it without hurting him."

Amber dropped her arms to her sides, mouth gaping. "And you didn't suspect anything when she died?" She couldn't believe Burns would be that indifferent.

"Of course I did. The evidence didn't point toward him."

"Ever hear of 'Domestic Violence'?"

Burns gazed heavenward. "Cash could have any woman. Why would he hurt Sarah?"

"Then how come she's dead?" Amber leaned forward, placing her hands on the desk, glaring.

"She killed herself. I don't understand why." Burns shrugged. "But I don't think her death has anything to do with Cash's past. So, she wanted to leave him. Happens all the time. The man was engaged before. Big deal. People get engaged before they marry. Besides, you said this Fullerton woman died before her parents, so I'd have to rule out that he was after her money."

"Unless he knew he'd already been written into the parents' will."

Detective Burns rolled his eyes so hard he tilted sideways and almost fell off of his chair. Amber hated his drama performances in high school.

Before she could speak, he said, "Let's say the parents had great affection for Lancaster, especially if Harriet was an only child. They let him take her place. Since they had no one else, they would naturally pass on everything to him."

"She *was* an only child." Amber straightened, balling her hands into fists. "But how did you know?"

"Because I'm not stupid." Burns glared up at her. "If Lancaster inherited, there might not have been other siblings. There's no crime in loving someone and giving them their inheritance. Can't you believe that someone loved Cash?"

"Sarah loved him. Now she's dead." Amber looked down at the picture on Burns' desk. He followed her gaze.

The detective rose from his chair and leaned over. "You and I never got along in high school, so why should things change now? Look, Rocky," he emphasized her nickname, "You thought I was a screw-up back then, but I know what I'm doing.

"Besides, Dr. Mayhill ruled Sarah's death a suicide. This case is closed."

He straightened with a shrug of apology. "Sorry. Nothing more I can do, unless you uncover solid evidence that will make me re-open the case."

Amber blew a strand of hair away from her face. *I will not let him get to me like he used to.* What had Sarah ever seen in Steve Burns? "Okay, but deep down in that little pebble you call a heart, do you truly believe Sarah killed herself?"

She glared back to the photo on the desk. "If you don't, I'd think you'd do *everything* in your power to catch her murderer."

Amber reached down and picked up the picture of Burns' sister. Before he could answer, she asked, "What happened to Debbie?"

The detective's face grew red.

"Well?"

"She was murdered."

"How?" Amber glared at him.

He squirmed.

"And?" Amber coaxed.

"Her husband killed her," Burns said. "No one had a clue that he'd been stalking and harassing her for over a year. I worked with him. I had no idea." He wiped a fallen strand of hair from his forehead.

Amber felt sorry for him. The pain in his voice matched her feelings. She turned the photograph toward him. "What if this case is like Debbie's?" She set the picture back on the desk gently.

Without waiting for a response Amber pushed past the tall redheaded detective who had just entered the office and called over her shoulder, "Come on, Perry. We can do this ourselves. This was a bad idea."

CHAPTER 17

After Perry and Amber left the detectives' office, Steve removed his laptop computer from his briefcase and hooked it up. He entered a password. A file headed Cassius Robert Lancaster appeared on the screen. Steve pushed the print button and waited.

He remembered high school as if it was yesterday. Sarah and Amber were almost inseparable, but senior year he managed to pry them apart. Amber had been shy and quiet. Sarah—outgoing and lots of fun. He smiled thinking about the prank when they toilet-papered the football field. Sarah climbed on his shoulders to string paper over the goal posts, laughing the entire time. He could still picture her cheerleading outfit with a short skirt and those lace red panties when he looked up. From the beginning, he knew Sarah was made for him, that they would marry.

That was a blow, when after graduation, she and Amber fled to New York. If only he hadn't gotten so mad when she declined to marry him. It scared her when he put his fist through the wall. He never forgot the wide-eyed look she gave him before she ran out. She refused to take his calls. When he went to see her, Mr. Hudson said she headed for New York with Rocky.

He missed Sarah. Surprisingly, he even missed Amber. She may not have said much, but when she spoke, he liked the sound of her voice. What she said made sense and was right.

The printer finished running. Several sheets lay in the tray. He could have told Amber he checked into Cash's past, but she brought out his stubborn streak. She pushed, and he shoved back. He had to prove something around her. Besides, he followed the rules.

He eyed the papers. Some of Cash's past was familiar to him. Cash, a murderer—Steve doubted it. If Cash was a killer, it would change a lot of things. What would Longreen's chances of winning the election be if his campaign manager and long-time friend turned out to be a murderer…

Why was he letting Amber get to him again? Steve never doubted his work until she came along. Cash—involved— No! Sarah committed suicide. He'd make sure that stuck.

Steve stuffed the papers in his desk drawer and put away his laptop. Then, he grabbed his coat. After he exited the office, he walked a few blocks away. The scent of salty sea wafted by on a slight breeze. He scanned the brick façade offices. A storekeeper swept the sidewalk three doors down. He'd put that business owner away for tax fraud. Hard to believe he was out and back to business. Cars sped past on the one-way street. The sun shone, but he could see fog drifting in.

The guy sweeping hadn't noticed him. Steve ducked into a newly renovated building. Inside, the receptionist took his name. He sat on a soft, leather couch. Two floral, high-backed winged chairs were at either end. The coffee table in front of him held a stack of magazines, and Steve flipped through a *People*. A few minutes later, the receptionist said, "He'll see you now. Go on in."

Steve opened the carved door and stepped onto the plush carpet. The smell of new leather greeted him. Cash rose from the desk chair and extended his hand. "Glad to see you, Steve. Please, sit down. Just bought a new couch and chairs."

Steve sank into a chair. "Very comfortable. She came by to see me again."

"She, meaning Amber?"

Steve nodded.

"I don't doubt it." Cash perched on the corner of the desk, crossing his arms. "She's having a hard time with Sarah's death. Even I still find it hard to believe."

"You can't blame yourself. Sarah changed, became—"

"But I should have sensed something," Cash said. "Someone in the house or close to her should have seen it coming."

"Suicide often comes as a surprise. You have to let her go. Longreen needs you."

"I believe Amber wishes I was the person who died."

"Don't let her get to you. She's still in shock."

"But what if Sarah didn't commit suicide?"

"Not you, too?"

"I know." Cash walked to his chair and sat. As he leaned forward, it squeaked. "But Amber's so persistent. I think she suspects me."

"If Sarah was murdered, you'd be the logical one. She's curious about your past, but there's nothing there for her to find. Right?"

Cash eyed Steve. "Is that a question?"

Steve remained silent, hoping for an explanation.

Cash settled back. "There's nothing in my past to make her believe I'm a murderer. What about you?"

"Me?"

"You and Amber seem... you know each other. She doesn't like you much."

"Must be my winning personality."

"Ha! Don't insult my intelligence. Wealthy men don't take friendships for granted. I check out people. Unearth their backgrounds. Carsonville isn't a big city. Hard to keep secrets in this town, especially when the people attended school together."

Heat rose under Steve's collar. His cheeks burned. "You know—"

"Of course. I'm not certain why you and Sarah kept quiet about your history, but I appreciate you keeping me informed about Amber. We don't want people getting riled up around here for nothing. How close an eye *are* you keeping on her?"

"I'm doing my job. Besides, I'm the police. She comes to me. Are *you* watching her?"

Cash put on his politician grin. "Why should I? Is she a threat?"

"What can she find? Dr. Mayhill ruled it a suicide. No evidence to the contrary."

"Believe it or not," Cash said, rubbing his temples, "I miss Sarah."

"I thought you said she was becoming a pain—always admiring herself whenever she passed a mirror,—"

"I complained, but what man doesn't with the woman he loves? I still miss her. Amber's upset over her and feels guilty."

"She'll snoop around for a few days," Steve said. "When she discovers nothing, she'll realize I knew what I was talking about. With Perry's help, she'll conclude we were right."

"Fortunately," Cash said, "there's no other conclusion she could come to."

"Are you positive?" Steve asked.

CHAPTER 18

After lunch, Amber followed Lancaster as he guided Perry through all the upstairs rooms. She examined everything, searching for any information that suggested Sarah had been murdered. Without it, Steve would not even consider re-opening the case. All she had—her gut instinct, and that wasn't enough. So far, she discovered nothing incriminating, except that paper from the book, *The Last Honest Man*. Could she be wrong?

They approached the last room—Lancaster and Sarah's bedroom. Amber's heart raced. With each step, her breathing grew more labored. She crossed the threshold and imagined Sarah lying in bed, reaching out a hand toward her, saying, "Help me."

"Are you all right?" Lancaster asked.

Sarah's image vanished. Amber saw the canopied bed. A crystal vase, with fresh, yellow roses, sat on the dresser. The scent of the flowers filled the room. She stepped onto the Persian carpet. "I'm fine."

"Okay, then." Lancaster glanced at his watch. "You'll

have to excuse me, but I have some campaign work. I feel certain you can manage this room without me."

Amber, too stunned to talk, watched him leave. She studied the master bedroom. "He left us alone at the crime scene? Makes me wonder why?"

Perry stood by the dresser. He reached past the crystal vase to pick up a piece of amber with a beetle trapped inside. "Has a crime been committed? We haven't found any evidence."

"You don't think a torn piece of paper with someone practicing handwriting that ends up resembling Sarah's is significant?"

Perry placed the amber back on top of the dresser. "You should have given that to Detective Burns."

"No way. Not until I'm sure he had nothing to do with Sarah's murder." She walked to the armoire. "Another thought. Did you notice one of the rooms appeared as if it might have a guest?"

"I did. Two of them," Perry said. "Yours and mine."

"Really funny. No, one of the other bedrooms felt lived-in."

"Your 'Spidy Senses' kicking in?"

"Ha. Ha. I can't put my finger on it—"

"Oh, oh." Perry hummed the Spider Man's theme song. "Are your super heroes or sci-fi aliens appearing?"

"Thanks, Perry, you're no help. Leave my heroes and aliens out of this." Could he be right? Did she look too hard, letting her imagination take over? Granted, she prayed the disappearance of her father didn't mean he'd killed her mother, but that had nothing to do with imagination. Or was it wishing? She grabbed a strand of her hair and chewed on it.

She noticed the bottom of the armoire and spat out her hair. Leaning over, she ran her hand across a dent. "Looks like someone threw a shoe at the mahogany here. I see a stiletto heel imprint. Wonder why?" She straightened and flung the door open. "What the..." Amber hurried to a low dresser with a tilting mirror, and pulled its drawers open one by one.

"What are you doing?"

"Sarah's clothes are all gone!"

"Did you really expect him to keep them around?" Perry asked.

"Well, I thought maybe he would have let me go through them."

"He didn't know you were coming. Besides, James probably disposed of them. It would have made it much easier on Cash."

"But..."

Perry slipped his arms around Amber. "I understand. You wanted a piece of clothing or perfume that belonged to her. But, trust me, it's for the best. I knew Mark would die. But, I still had to get rid of everything he owned as soon as I could. Having his things around—way too painful. I thought about keeping a sweater or two. But Tom, and you, I also believe, convinced me not to.

"This is hard for you," Perry said, "but believe me, Cash's actions aren't out of the ordinary. He may not behave as you are, but he's acting somewhat as I did." He waved his hand. "Can we get on with our work here or at least pretend we're listing inventory?"

Amber squirmed out of Perry's arms and glanced at her notebook. "Oh, all right. I'm making too much of this. It's difficult. This reminds me of my parents all over again. You remember when the police told me Mom was murdered. I felt as if I'd been kicked in the gut. But when they said Dad disappeared, they suspected him... well, it didn't ring true. My dad's not a murderer. Just because they found his blood at the scene. For God's sake, he could be dead. That investigation is at a dead end. I want... No, I *have* to have answers this time."

Perry smoothed back Amber's hair. "I understand. But, sometimes we don't find the answers. I'm not saying we give up. But be prepared to discover that Sarah took her own life. You may never understand why. I've wondered why some of us die from AIDS and others don't. Why do good, young people die? Sometimes, answers just aren't there."

Amber thought about her own suicide attempt back in high school. Perry didn't know anything about that, nor about Sarah's and her "Suicide Pact." She was too embarrassed to tell him. But, if she did, would he understand why she believed Sarah would never kill herself? "Oh, Perry," Amber said, "I'll try to keep a perspective, but I need those answers."

"Come on. Let's get back to work."

After examining a painting, Amber marked it on her list. She catalogued the furniture, including the Persian rug, another painting, and the amber with the beetle. Writing in the notepad and thinking about the pieces calmed her jangled nerves.

Fifteen minutes later, Amber stood in the middle of the room. She did a slow three hundred and sixty degree turn. "That's odd. There isn't any rose quartz or Tiffany glass here. My room and downstairs have both and the other upstairs rooms contain Tiffany. Wonder why this one doesn't?"

"Possibly they don't fit the décor."

Amber motioned with her hand, encompassing the room. "If you can figure out the *décor* in here or this house, you're a better person than I am. I'll check the bathroom. Be right back."

The bathroom had a pine smell, but contained no pieces of rose quartz. Did that mean anything? Her footsteps echoed on the Italian tile. She opened the medicine cabinet. She ran her hand over the wood frame where Sarah must have touched it so many times. Amber searched through the medicine to the back. Hidden behind several bottles that belonged to Cash on the top shelf, she grabbed a prescription bottle and couldn't believe what it was.

Valium for Sarah.

She slipped the vial into her pocket and closed the mirrored door. Perry's square-jawed face reflected in the mirror behind hers. She flinched.

He leaned toward her and whispered, "What did you put in your pocket?"

Her smile twitched at the edges. "My hand." How did Perry sneak up on her? Amber tried to step around him. Looking down, she saw Perry' black Converse All-Stars move to block her exit.

He cocked his head, narrowing a stare that went straight to her heart.

Her gut told her not to tell him about the Valium—not just yet, anyway. Why would Sarah call in for a prescription when she already had some in the back of her medicine cabinet?

Amber didn't say this to Perry. She felt very alone.

Later that evening, Amber sat at the dining-room table. Mrs. Martin was next to her and Mr. Martin across the table. Cash, on her right, took the head of the table spot. Perry was at the other end with Burns across from Mrs. Martin. The detective arrived late again. Talk centered on Henry Longreen's chances for Congress.

While Amber picked at her food, she listened for information about Sarah. But, again, no one mentioned her friend's name. Amber hoped she'd learn something she hadn't known before.

Nothing unusual came from the conversation, and after dinner, Amber wandered off into the parlor while the others were still discussing politics. Suddenly, Burns stood next to her. They were alone.

"I hear you've finished listing Cash's collectibles. Now what?"

Amber shrugged. "I'll type up the inventory so he'll have a catalogue. Then, Perry and I will find a special Tiffany object, or another collectible for Lancaster. He's been generous in letting us stay in this house. After all, he doesn't even know us."

"That's true. Did you uncover anything sinister lurking in his closet?"

Amber wanted to tell him she had. "No, nothing *sinister.*"

"Then you're satisfied?" Burns asked.

The other guests sauntered into the room. "Not yet," she whispered. "What have you discovered?"

Burns didn't have a chance to answer. Lancaster strolled over. "What are you two chatting about? Old times?"

Amber glanced at Burns, surprised he told Lancaster they knew each other in high school. When Burns looked blank, she said, "No, we were discussing your collections and what I might purchase for you."

"I see." Lancaster raised one shoulder toward his ear. "As I told you before, you don't need to buy me anything. It's been a pleasure having you." He placed an arm around her shoulder and glared at Burns. "I just wished it could have been under different circumstances."

Still talking to Burns, he said, "I also wish Amber wouldn't suspect me of foul play."

She pulled away from Lancaster and blinked. *My, God, he knows I suspect him. Thought I'd been subtle.*

Lancaster gazed into her eyes. "I've upset you. It's quite evident you believe I did something terrible to Sarah. But, I didn't drive her to suicide. I'm really upset she killed herself."

He reached out and clasped Amber's hand. Her first reaction was to pull away. His touch made her feel dirty. But he appeared so sad. She left her hand in his. "Sarah was so beautiful. The way she always admired herself in front of any mirror she passed was becoming tiresome, but that's not enough to kill somebody over, is it?"

"No, of course not," Detective Burns said. "No one's accusing you of anything."

Lancaster ran his thumb over Amber's hand. "No?"

Perry wandered over to Amber's side. He put his arm around her shoulders and drew her close. Her hand slid away from Lancaster's. "It's too bad Sarah's gone from our lives," Perry said. "Nothing will bring her back."

"True." Amber wiped away a tear, wishing she wouldn't cry every time Sarah's name came up. "But she can remain in our hearts. Is there anything wrong with trying to understand what happened to her?"

"No," Lancaster said. "I'm certain we'd all like to understand."

After the guests disbursed, Amber said her goodnights and trudged up to her room. She sat on the bed, staring at the paper with the altered handwriting. Who wrote this? She didn't recognize the original handwriting. She'd seen a brief glimpse of Lancaster's and had not seen James'. She hadn't seen Burns' handwriting since her senior yearbook.

Her attention glommed onto the bottle of pills. Tomorrow she'd contact the doctor. See what he had to say. Would he tell her anything? If not, she would have Sarah's father call him.

"Oh, Sarah, what happened to you?" Amber whispered.

She moved the steaming cup of herb tea James left on the nightstand, and set down the bottle and torn paper. The silver-framed picture Lancaster gave her while staying here drew her attention. She reached out and lovingly picked it up. Lancaster didn't want to let the photo go permanently because it was the only picture he had of Sarah and Amber together. He said he wasn't ready to keep it near him yet, but perhaps Amber would like it. He didn't know she had a duplicate, the one in her wallet.

She removed the one out of the frame and the other from her wallet and flipped them over. She stared at the backs where their blood-thumb prints and signatures reminded her of their pact. Could this have been a tragic accident? No, Sarah wasn't that careless.

After fluffing up her pillows, Amber leaned back to read her book, and sipped some tea. Her eyes kept drifting closed. She realized she'd read the same page over again.

Why did she feel so tired?

CHAPTER 19

No need to get rid of her. My luck is turning. She *is* perfect.

Not like Sarah at all. That woman infuriated me after she became vain. She couldn't pass a mirror without admiring herself. Gave me the creeps.

But Amber is refreshing. She has no idea she's beautiful. She glides by the hall mirror and doesn't even glance at herself.

I slip unnoticed into her room. On the dresser is the list she's working on: rose quartz, Tiffany objects, amber, the Monet paintings, other artists, and the roll-top desk and other furniture and collectibles. She even marks whether they are originals or reproductions.

That Tiffany scarab she notes is an imitation. She really knows her antiques. Even I didn't know that. Thought it was real. What a great asset she is.

She annoys me with this tireless quest to discover what happened to Sarah. I made Sarah's death appear like a suicide. Everyone is convinced until Amber shows up. But, when she finally receives the letter that will change. This time Sarah's letter begins: "Dear Amber," but I use 'Rocky' elsewhere. I hate that nickname, but I pretend it is a great name. After all, Sarah gave it to her. I like that she uses "Amber" now. It suits her better.

Makes me happy she lost the weight and uses contacts, too. Keeping an eye on her is fun. She's not only pleasing to look at, but I respect her natural intellect. She is organized, and when she doesn't have the information, she is not afraid to admit it, or learn more about something.

She fits like a warm scarf.

I gaze upon her sleeping form and I smile.

Suddenly, she flails her arms and knocks things off the nightstand. I hurry from the room.

Out in the hallway, I stop. Everyone is sound asleep. Besides, they're so used to me coming and going, I slip around the house unnoticed.

I peek back into Amber's room, but she's still asleep. Must have been a nightmare. She tosses again.

No one knows I even enter her room.

This one is much more interesting than Rose, or Tiffany. She even outshines Sarah. Amber and I will have so much fun together: going shopping, dining out, discussing antiques. I can hardly wait.

The new prized possession.

CHAPTER 20

Amber bolted upright from the bed. Her adrenaline rushed. She gasped for air—a dream about zombies chasing her. She shoved hair away from her eyes and took a deep breath. Then she slowly exhaled. Daylight slipped around the edges of her drawn drapes. Her door remained closed as she'd left it the night before.

The silence in her room, aside from the noise thumping in her ears from her pounding heart, stretched on.

She untangled herself from the sheet. Her skin felt clammy. Swiveling around, she set her feet on the carpet and switched off the nightstand lamp.

The teacup James brought in last night lay on its side on the saucer, the tea spilled out. In Amber's haste to right the cup, it fell to the carpeted floor. *Thank God it didn't break.* She picked it up. Her gaze widened. The silver-framed picture now lay face down on the floor and her purse sat between the bed and the nightstand. But the Valium and the incriminating paper were gone.

She rose so abruptly she nearly fell. Amber wiped the sweat from her forehead, feeling dizzy and a bit nauseated.

A picture of someone standing over her flashed through her mind and vanished. "Calm down. Think," she told herself.

One book lay on the dresser. What about the one she'd been reading? She couldn't remember when she fell asleep. Where was the red, leather-bound book? She started for the dresser but halted in the middle of the room. "Concentrate," she ordered herself.

Nothing came to mind.

She stared toward the bed and nightstand. While chewing on a wild strand of hair, she imagined everything where it was before falling asleep. So, where was the book?

Back by the bed, she dropped to her knees and lifted the dust ruffle.

The red book lay on the floor. The heat rushed to her cheeks. "Get a grip," Amber told herself.

She grabbed *The Last Honest Man*, and felt around for the piece of paper.

Gone.

Amber flipped through every page, but no piece of paper spilled out.

The bedroom door burst open, revving Amber's heart rate higher. Marie swept in, balancing a silver urn and a bone china cup and saucer on a tray. "Good morning. Mr. Lancaster asked me to serve you coffee in bed this morning." Her grin reminded Amber of Cruella de Vil in *101 Dalmatians*. The maid stopped advancing.

Amber, still on her knees, pressed the book against her thundering chest.

"My goodness, have we lost something?" Marie hurried to set the tray on the nightstand. "I can help you look." Her bright red lips turned up into a broader, evil smile. "What are we searching for?"

Amber rose. She ran a hand through her hair, knowing

how disheveled it must appear. "Nothing." She held out the book. "This fell on the floor. You startled me. Perhaps next time you could knock?"

"I heard you moving around. Figured you were up. It's my pleasure to serve you," she said, a little too brightly. "Besides, when my boss asks me to do something, I do it. If there's nothing further, I'll be off." She didn't wait for an answer, but strolled from the room.

Amber heard the maid snicker before the door shut with a resounding click. She plopped on the bed, clutching *The Last Honest Man*, and eyed her purse and the cup that had fallen to the floor.

Her purse? She threw the book down on the bed and grabbed her purse, noticing the zipper—wide open. She usually closed it.

Inside, the vial of pills and the paper lay on top.

Before she could ponder the reason why, someone tapped softly on her door. It opened again. Amber jammed everything back in her purse and dropped it to the floor. A head peeked around the door.

"Very good, Ms. Rockwell," James said. "I thought I heard movement inside. Everything all right? Mr. Lancaster wanted to make certain you were comfortable. I have brought you tea." The butler stepped into the room with another silver tray. His staunch façade boasted a bit of a smile.

When James glanced at the nightstand, his smile faltered. "What the..."

Amber caught a whiff of bitter caffeine. "Thank you, James, but Marie just brought me coffee."

The butler's thick eyebrows scrunched together. His mouth opened as if to speak, but he snapped it closed. He glided over and picked up the tray Marie had left. He set down his own. He retrieved the cup on the floor and placed it on the tray in his hand. "I am to bring you anything you need. It is not her job."

After sniffing the coffee, he inspected the tray. "I will speak to her about this. Enjoy your tea, Ms. Rockwell."

She blinked twice. *Talk about a control freak! That was creepy.* James did an about-face, and marched from the room. Amber zipped up her purse and put *The Last Honest Man* on the nightstand. She reached for the tea with the scent of lemons. *Before I drink this, I better use the bathroom.* Amber snatched her robe from the end of the bed and headed off, still wondering who and why someone would come into her room.

Was she being paranoid? *With that zombie dream, I must have flung my arms around, knocking everything to the floor. That would explain things. I've done that before.*

Amber pondered her dream idea while she trudged down the hall. She hated feeling out of control. This house and its people were getting on her nerves.

She could understand knocking things over, but how would the piece of paper and valium fall so perfectly into her purse? When she returned to her bedroom, the lemon tea aroma had disappeared. She held the cup. Cold. She set it back without taking a drink. Her watch read eight o'clock in the morning. She dug out the pill bottle and found the number for the doctor, who was listed on the vial, in the yellow pages.

After making an appointment with Dr. Madison, she went downstairs to eat. During breakfast, Amber told Lancaster, "Perry and I will be going downtown for lunch."

Perry set down his fork. "I look forward to that."

James, hovering behind Lancaster, inclined his head.

"Tired of the food, here?" Lancaster asked.

"No. I want to go through the antique stores," Amber said. "See if there's any Tiffany glass, rose quartz, or other objects suitable here to add to your collection. We should have the inventory list organized by then. We might as well look here first. If I don't find any specific item, I have a piece of amber from Perry's store that I think would work. I can have Tom ship it out."

"That is not necessary. I'm just glad you're here." Lancaster pushed his plate away and smiled. "I am thankful you are keeping busy. I feel guilty, but I do have plans again. This campaign takes up a lot of time and energy, which I am grateful for. I hope, though, we can have dinner tonight."

"Are you having more guests in?"

"No. I thought we would dine here this evening, while I try to convince you to stay longer."

Amber said to Perry, "Dining in sounds good. The food here beats restaurant cooking." Speaking to Lancaster, she continued, "We're scheduled to stay until next Saturday. You'll be ready for us to leave by then."

"No, that's too soon. We have not had much time together. James will have Hale prepare his specialty crab dish for you. Say, dinner at seven?"

"Perfect," Amber said.

"Very good, sir," James said. "I will see that everything is arranged."

"Of course you will. Now, if you'll excuse me, I am running late." Lancaster rushed off.

CHAPTER 21

Amber parked in front of a renovated brick house and climbed out of the car.

"Look at those rosebushes," Perry said.

Fragrant yellow, pink, and blood-red blossoms surrounded the place. Bees buzzed among the flowers, and hummingbirds darted about, gathering nectar. An engraved oak plaque with black lettering hung above the doorway, announcing the psychiatrist Dr. Vince Madison. Amber pushed the door open and a bell tinkled, announcing their arrival.

"I haven't seen one of those brass bells in a long time," Perry said.

"My dad said all the Carsonville businesses had them when he was a kid." The young receptionist wore a bright yellow dress. Her red hair cascaded down her shoulders. *Why can't my hair look like that?* Amber's was unruly. The receptionist smiled. "May I help you?"

"I'm Amber Rockwell. I have an eleven o'clock appointment with Dr. Madison."

The receptionist scanned her appointment book. "I

don't see you down, but let me check with the doctor. Sometimes he makes his own appointments."

"I telephoned this morning about eight. He said he had a cancellation and could fit me in."

"Just one moment." The young woman used the telephone, jabbing a button. She announced Amber's presence and hung up. "Dr. Madison will see you in about five minutes."

"Thank you." Amber and Perry sat on the floral couch.

The inner door opened a few minutes later. A lean man dressed in a red-checkered cotton shirt, sleeves rolled up to his elbows, sauntered out. He reminded Amber of a construction worker, with muscular arms, calloused hands, and a mustache. She wondered what he had to see the doctor about.

In three strides, the man stepped in front of her, extending his hand. "Ms. Rockwell. Nice to meet you. I'm Dr. Madison."

Amber put down her magazine and pushed up off the couch. She shook the doctor's hand. "Thank you for seeing me, Doctor. This is my friend Perry Cole. I hope it's all right for him to come in, too."

"Fine. Fine. Right this way."

After entering his inner office, Dr. Madison walked around a large mahogany desk and picked up his wire-rimmed glasses. "Please, have a seat."

Amber avoided the brown leather couch. It made her feel too much like she needed counseling. Instead, she chose a comfortable wing-backed chair. Perry dropped into a straight-backed chair next to her. One side of the office wall held leather-bound books. Did the doctor have a system similar to Lancaster's? She yearned again for a look at the logbook in his study.

"Now, how may I help you?" Dr. Madison asked.

Amber, drawn back to the doctor, said, "As I told you on the phone, I'd like to talk with you about Sarah Hudson. Because of patient confidentiality, you might be reluctant to discuss her, but Sarah is dead. Her parents will give you permission to talk with me." She handed Dr. Madison a yellow Post-It. "Here's their number, if you want to call them. I'm afraid we can't accept the fact her death was ruled a suicide."

The psychiatrist pushed his glasses up on his nose. "I've spoken with Sarah's parents. Most relatives and close friends find the taking of one's own life difficult to accept. Especially if there's no explanation."

Dr. Madison put the paper on his desk and sat back in his chair, fixing his gaze on Amber. "I find it hard to believe myself. Sarah was moody, but kept busy with charity dinners, gave to the homeless on the street, and raised ten thousand dollars for children with cancer. The woman I saw a year ago would never have committed suicide."

"Did you tell that to the police?" Amber leaned forward with renewed hope.

"I did, but a year had passed. A lot can happen in a year. I had to admit to that when Dr. Mayhill brought it up."

"Why did you fill Sarah's prescription without seeing her first?" Amber waited for the doctor's answer.

Dr. Madison pulled off his glasses and rubbed the bridge of his nose. "You knew Sarah. How did you perceive her?"

"I didn't know her well," Perry said, "but she had energy like a top that never quit spinning. While rotating, she was up, but it felt like if the spinning stopped, she'd topple over."

"Good analogy, Mr. Cole," Dr. Madison said. "But being with Mr. Lancaster, Sarah didn't have an outlet to unleash that vigor as when she worked as a model. Oh, she had her projects and Cash's dinner parties to keep her busy, but it was not the same."

"I remember after graduation," Amber said, "we traveled for fifteen days through Boston, New York, Washington D.C. non-stop. Exhausted me so much. I could hardly move, but not Sarah. She kept going like the Energizer Bunny."

Dr. Madison rested his chin on his steepled fingers. "Sounds like her. The Valium calmed Sarah from the stress of that constant energy."

"As I recall," Perry said, "she was easily frustrated. I assume the pills made life in Carsonville easier for her to accept."

"That's true," Dr. Madison said. "However, after a year, she didn't approve of the way she felt. She'd gained a few pounds, blamed it on the pills. She swore she'd quit taking them. She also halted her appointments with me. Said Cash didn't think she needed to see a shrink. It would look bad for Henry Longreen."

"What did Sarah have to do with him?" Amber asked.

"She believed Henry would make a good Congressman, so she threw herself into helping him win the election. Sarah never came to see me after that. She really didn't need me."

"Didn't you think it odd she wanted to begin the Valium again?"

"Odd?" Dr. Madison stared at the ceiling. Still resting his chin on long, slender fingers, he scrutinized Amber. "I don't think that's the right word. During visits with me, she talked, I listened. I hardly ever said a word. One day she told me, 'I'm not going to take the pills'."

"That is so Sarah," Amber said. "Once she made up her mind on something, not much could deter her."

"True," Dr. Madison said. "When she stopped taking the

Valium, I didn't find it medically unsound. When she said she wanted to go back on, I figured something stressful had happened to her."

Amber squirmed under the doctor's piercing stare. "Would deciding to leave Lancaster be stressful?"

"If she contemplated that," Dr. Madison said, "I'd say it would have been very stressful for her. When she phoned, I told my secretary to make an appointment for her on Monday. Nancy said Sarah told her she couldn't make it until Monday without Valium. She said she really needed those pills." Dr. Madison hesitated. "I'd understand her need if she were making that big a decision."

"When did you see her last?" Amber asked.

"Professionally, over a year before her death. However, I'd seen her socially. She hadn't changed that much. Perhaps a little quieter, but still very responsible."

"Had you seen her in the last few weeks before her death?" Amber waited expectantly for the answer.

"No, I'm afraid I'd been rather busy on a case here in Carsonville. I consult with the police department as well. The police work took all my free time. I haven't socialized much in the last month, though we did resolve the issue."

"Could this decision Sarah tried to make have changed her that much in one month?" Amber asked.

"You're asking me to speculate. I can't do that for you. I understand her suicide is hard to accept. Dr. Mayhill is an excellent coroner investigator and explored every avenue—"

"But doctor," Amber interrupted, "what if the police led her down the wrong path?"

"I'm afraid I don't quite follow you." Dr. Madison sat back in his chair.

"Perry?" Amber questioned.

He nodded, and said, "Why don't you at least confide in

the doctor? After all, he works with the police. We need to tell someone."

Dr. Madison asked, "What?"

Amber told the doctor what she'd been doing for the last couple of days. She reached in her purse and handed him the piece of paper she found in *The Last Honest Man*.

The psychiatrist put his glasses on and read. "Interesting."

"I believe someone wrote this over and over to get Sarah's handwriting down pat, so they could write that suicide note."

"You don't believe Sarah wrote it?" Dr. Madison questioned.

"No. As I said before, she always referred to me as Rocky, and her note was addressed to Amber."

Perry interrupted. "We discussed this with Detective Burns and decided that whenever Sarah wanted your attention, she addressed the letters with your legal name."

Amber ignored Perry, focusing on her idea. "Would your best friend suddenly switch names when she was about to kill herself? Wouldn't she use the more familiar?"

"Another guess," Dr. Madison said. "I can't say for certain, especially not having talked with Sarah."

"Dr. Madison, Sarah was murdered." Amber wanted to tell the doctor about their suicide pact, hoping it would give him a stronger picture of Sarah. But she couldn't tell him this in front of Perry. If she had too, she'd ask her boss to leave the room.

"Detective Burns knew us in high school," Amber said. "He thought Sarah would marry him. She came with me to New York and he was furious. They met again here a few weeks ago. Now Sarah is dead. Burns may have borrowed *The Last Honest Man* and this torn paper fell out of that book. I haven't been able to get a look at the logbook

Lancaster keeps to see who had the book last. I do know Lancaster recently read it. Detective Burns had access to it, and, for that matter, probably anybody in the house. Somebody tried practicing Sarah's handwriting."

Dr. Madison sat quietly and listened.

After several seconds ticked by and he didn't speak, Amber switched tactics. "Who's the young woman out front?"

The doctor blinked a couple of times and furrowed his brow. "Why?"

"You said Nancy talked with Sarah?"

"Indeed," Dr. Madison said. "Caroline, my receptionist, is out front. My office manager, Nancy, is on vacation. She takes calls when I'm unavailable. Helps calm my patients. Caroline works part-time."

"Nancy's on vacation?" Amber asked.

"She won a two week cruise. Funny, though, she didn't remember entering any contest." Dr. Madison moved some papers aside. "Legit, though. All expenses paid for, including the airfare to Florida to catch the cruise ship."

"Well, if Nancy talked to Sarah, then I want to hear what she has to say."

"Nancy did speak with Sarah, because I had a patient at the time. My office manager checked with me about the pills and I phoned in the prescription to the pharmacy."

"Which one?"

"I believe Sarah used CVS Drugs."

Amber retrieved the old bottle of pills she found in the bathroom and handed them across the desk.

Dr. Madison opened the bottle and poured out the remaining pills. He studied the label. "I don't understand. If she had these, why'd she call and want more?"

"These were in the back of the medicine cabinet behind Cash Lancaster's other medicine," Amber said, "but I'm wondering the same thing. What if it wasn't Sarah on the phone at all? And that's why your office manager is out of town. When did she leave?"

"Friday." Dr. Madison drummed his fingers on the metal desk.

"The day Sarah died. Did you know Detective Burns attended a party next door that day?" Amber asked.

"I did," Dr. Madison said. "I was there, too. I know Detective Burns and can't believe he'd kill Sarah for some slight she pulled years ago. He's had several women friends that I know of. He appears very happy with his life. If he harbored a grudge, I think I'd have had a clue."

"You two are friends?" Amber wondered if she'd just made a mistake.

"I do the psych evaluations for the police department, and I've seen him at some of the campaign functions for Henry Longreen."

Dr. Madison opened a desk drawer and withdrew what appeared to be some sort of schedule. "I have Nancy's itinerary here. Let me see if I can reach her, talk with her more about that telephone conversation. I do believe you've unearthed an oddity."

Before Amber could utter a word, he said, "I'm not saying someone murdered Sarah. I'm just saying you've brought up some interesting facts that should be explored. Let me talk with Nancy and I'll get back to you. How long will you be staying?"

Amber waited for Perry to speak. When he didn't, she said, "As long as it takes to get to the bottom of this."

"And you're staying with Cash?"

"We are," Perry answered. "As you said, he's quite generous. I have the feeling he'd do almost anything to keep Amber at the house."

"What?" Amber gazed at Perry with her eyes wide and mouth open.

"Haven't you noticed the looks he keeps giving you?" Perry crossed his arms.

"No." Amber shivered. "Why would he?"

"Cash is a virile man," Dr. Madison said. "He loves beautiful things around him, including women. I don't see him wasting his life on mourning, and I bet he'd replace Sarah as soon as possible."

Amber gaped. "You mean with me? That's crazy."

"Quite possible."

Amber embraced herself. She didn't like that thought at all.

CHAPTER 22

From the second floor hallway, Amber watched Lancaster. He strode past the staircase toward the study with James dogging his steps. Amber rushed downstairs and sidled up to the open study door. She peeked around the corner. Lancaster unlocked the roll-top desk and removed something. After he sat, she could see his head tipped down. She heard pages flipping. Was he reading the logbook?

"Sir, is everything all right?" James asked.

Lancaster eyed the butler standing next to him and then slowly faced the door. Amber snapped her head back so he wouldn't spot her. "Why would she want to see this logbook?" Lancaster asked.

"Ms. Rockwell is curious about everything to do with you," James answered. "Where you were born, how you run things. If I did not know better...Well, those are personal questions... She seems quite interested in you."

"She feels Sarah's death is my fault and is trying to find a reason for it, other than suicide."

"Perhaps that is why she is asking all those questions."

James' voice sounded perplexed. "She cannot see how affected you are by all of this. If you would permit me, I will converse with Ms. Rockwell, make sure that she is apprised of how much you loved her friend. It is irritating that she suspects you of foul play."

"Thank you, James. I'm not certain it's just me though. You'd better watch yourself, and keep an eye on Marie. I think Amber suspects all of us."

"That is preposterous." The way the butler said it... Amber pictured the scraggly line of murderous zombies scraping toward her. Was James angry?

"Well, I guess there's no reason not to review this binder with her. By the way, why didn't you show it to her the other day, or even let her borrow a book?"

"That is not my place, sir." James' voice deepened. "I believe that should be your duty. Therefore, I pretended not to know where you kept the key. What book did she borrow?"

Was James trying to set her up with Lancaster? Suddenly, Amber felt as if someone ran an ice cube up and down her arm. In the distance a chainsaw bit into wood and screamed.

She peered around the door jamb. The men perused the logbook. Lancaster tapped a page. "These are the two books. You think one of us left anything inside that could have interested her?"

"I have no idea what that might have been."

"I'm not going to worry about it. I'm not in the habit of leaving incriminating evidence around. Anyway, James, I know you mean well, and have only my best interest at heart. But, it's too soon to have someone new in my life, don't you think?"

"Any time is a good time to have beautiful women around you. If it makes you happy..."

"Thank you. I'll keep that in mind. However, I'm surprised. I always thought of you as the old-fashioned type. Figured you'd think I should let some time pass."

Lancaster let out a low chuckle. "But why do the beautiful women in my life have to die? Oh, I know sometimes they're a pain, but..."

"I am sorry, sir. Perhaps Ms. Rockwell is the one you are searching for."

Amber put her hand to her mouth and stifled a gasp. *My, God, James is matchmaking. He's so much more than a butler. Zombies my ass; more like psycho.*

Lancaster didn't speak, but Amber envisioned his "politician grin." She hugged herself and tried to stop shivering.

"Since I have to cancel dinner with her tonight, I should placate her by showing her the log book. When you see Amber, have her come to the study. I'll impress her with your brilliant technique on cataloguing books."

"A good idea, sir. Will you inform her of the reason we do this?"

"If she asks."

"I will direct Ms. Rockwell to you here as soon as I come across her."

Amber hurried back down the hall toward the stairs. She reversed direction and sauntered back the way she'd come.

James stepped into the hallway. "There you are, Ms. Rockwell. Mr. Lancaster would like you to go to the study. He is waiting there for you."

"Thank you, James. That's where I'm heading." The butler walked on down the hall.

Before entering, Lancaster laughed, a sound that made Amber cringe. What was he thinking about?

She took a deep breath and entered the room. Lancaster's head was down. A constant sound of drumming fingers ceased when he glanced up. The grin she was growing to detest appeared. He beckoned to her.

She strolled to the desk, thinking about the binder. Her heart thumped in her chest. Could Lancaster hear it? The muffled sound of a pocket watch wrapped in cotton, just like the old man's tell tale heart—surely he planned to retaliate.

The room was stifling. She had waited for this moment for what seemed an eternity. She reminded herself to breathe. "Is that the logbook?"

"It is. But, before I show it to you I must apologize. I have to cancel our dinner tonight due to an emergency meeting with Henry regarding his campaign. Hope you will forgive me?"

"Of course. Business comes first."

"Come stand behind me, and I'll explain the system to you."

Amber leaned over his shoulder, quickly glancing at him, disturbed by the smirk on his face. He wasn't stupid. They both understood the real reason she wanted to see the binder, but acted as if they didn't.

Maybe if she distracted him. "That's a good photograph of Sarah on top of this desk. Who are the other two women?"

"Just other friends." Lancaster opened the binder to the front sheet. "The system is nothing miraculous." He tapped the first entry. "I write the date, the person's name, and the title of the book. When they bring it back, I enter the return date. A simple way to keep track of my books."

Amber didn't push the photos. She'd find out later. She was disappointed that he began at the front of the log book, and asked, "May I get a closer look?"

"Of course." Lancaster handed it to her.

She flipped the first page, skimming up and down. Then

she went to the next, and it took willpower not to grab all of them and flip to the last entries.

As the last sheet of paper appeared, she ran her finger slowly down the listings. "Here's my name from the other night."

He perused the lowered binder. "Just like all the rest. After you return those books, I'll enter them in the return date column."

"Do you have a listing of all the books you own?"

"I do. The original inventory is kept in the safe. There are two: one by author, the other by title." Lancaster pointed to the wall behind them. "I keep the valuable books on the top shelves. Those I don't lend out."

"Technically, all of your books, especially the expensive ones, should be added to the collections inventory I made for you. What if I wanted to know if you have a particular book—"

"We could look in this copy." He pulled out another binder. "The books on the shelves are arranged by author. By running down the logbook's return date column, you can identify which books are borrowed and haven't been returned yet."

"By the way, why do you have such an elaborate system?"

Lancaster chuckled. "I had a few more valuable books than what's on the top shelf. Unfortunately, before this system, they disappeared. That can't happen again."

"I see." Amber scoured the top of the page and found the entry for *The Last Honest Man*. "Even your name is entered whenever you read one of your own books." She placed her fingertip on his name.

"James suggested I should keep track of each book, even if I read it, or I should say, removed it from the study."

Sarah's name appeared below Lancaster's. Amber learned what she was trying to discover, unsure whether it helped or baffled her more. The last person to check out *The Last Honest Man*, which held the torn piece of paper, had been Sarah the night before she died. However, the book had been returned the day of her death. But by whom?

"Oh, look." Amber put her finger on a line of the logbook. "Sarah read the book I have. Did she return it?"

"I don't know for certain," Lancaster said.

"Could she have left it in her room, and someone else brought it back? Whose writing is this?"

Lancaster frowned. "Technically, if a book is left in a room, then the log shows it's out, but—"

"What if, say, Marie puts the book back on the shelf?" Amber asked in frustration. *Was that what happened with Sarah's book?* She feared the answer. If wrong, she'd have to give up. She couldn't do that.

"My staff and everyone who stays in this house know my rules, especially Marie. They're allowed to borrow books, but whenever they return them, they must tell James or me, or at least leave a note on the desk so one of us can enter the return date. So far, there have been no exceptions. Marie might have done that. Why would it be so important?"

"No reason. Just curious." Amber still wondered who had returned Sarah's book. Who practiced that signature? She bit her lip. Could someone have tampered with the logbook?

CHAPTER 23

Steve reached for the phone and, for the hundredth time, withdrew his hand without touching the receiver. He could not decide whether to share information with Amber. The tiniest twinge of doubt about Sarah's death formed in his gut. Telling Amber would be like giving a vampire a virgin neck... and, more unsettling, would give his doubt a life of its own. Soon that doubt would begin nagging him, pestering him with unanswerable questions—questions he was going to answer and jeopardize his career over.

Great, now he thought like Amber with her sci-fi fantasies. In high school, the three of them always went to the shows together to watch science fiction movies.

Thoughts of Sarah brought to mind Cash. Lancaster did have inexplicable deaths in his past. What if Amber was right?

Steve gazed at Debbie's photo on his desk. His sister would have asked: 'What's with your doubts? You don't think you're smart enough to figure this out? Quit waffling!' If he'd been more decisive when she was alive, she'd still be here to tell him so.

Why did Rocky have to look so much better than she did in high school? It made his job so much more difficult. The weight loss, longer hair, and contacts transformed her from a plain-Jane to a real beauty. He used to tease her mercilessly, just to watch her blush. She got flustered whenever a boy talked to her. Kids joked that she was Sarah's shadow, the quiet, ugly duckling that never spoke. Kids could be so cruel.

Steve reached for the telephone again. When it rang, his hand jerked. Then, his fingertips tingled with warmth as if stroking Amber's smooth cheek.

He grinned, appreciating caller ID. Lifting the receiver, he took a chance. "Dinner in an hour. Meet me at the Samoa Cookhouse."

After a hesitation, Amber's voice came over the line. "Why would I have dinner with you?"

Steve let out his breath when he heard her voice. "For the same reason that you telephoned. See you at five-thirty."

He disconnected and sat back. He gazed heavenward, feeling an unmistakable stirring. The blob of doubt pricked up its ears.

CHAPTER 24

Amber drove across Humboldt Bay. At five-thirty, she sat outside the last surviving cookhouse in the old West and surveyed the area. No sign of Burns anywhere. Had he led her on another of his wild goose chases like he'd done in high school?

A black Camaro slid in and parked alongside her rental. Burns stepped out dressed in a black suit.

After locking the Mustang, Amber tugged down her yellow blouse and smoothed her black slacks. "You're here."

"Yeah, not like that time I left you at the park standing in the rain. Sarah stayed ticked at me for a week over that prank. Why don't we forget the past? I'm starved."

"Okay." Amber faced the front of the Samoa Cookhouse. "Let's grab a seat." She pushed through the doors and surveyed the restaurant. It hadn't changed a whit. She swung into the familiar dining room.

"I haven't been here in years. Remember when the gang came here to chow down? They served us this huge bowl of salad with three different dressings, and if we wanted more, they brought it."

"They still do that. There's two choices of meat, like chicken and steak."

"I think that time we had pork and fish. They also dished out mashed potatoes, two different veggies." Amber's salivary glands watered. Thinking of all that food made her feel fatter.

"Yep. Still serves all its meals lumber camp style."

Amber examined the in-house museum. A two-man cross-cut saw from the mid-1800s hung on the wall, along with smaller one-man saws and various-sized wood wedges, sledge hammers, and felling and limbing axes. She swallowed bile that rose to her throat and remembered why they were there.

"You still with me?" Burns asked.

"The place looks the same." Amber inhaled deeply. "Still smells wonderful, too. After dinner I'll buy some of their fresh-baked bread."

"Sarah loved that bread," Burns said.

"But it never put weight on her. Me, I puffed up like Casper the Ghost's spook friends when they tried to scare someone."

The wood floors squeaked in protest as the hostess guided them to a long table. Burns cracked a smile. Amber remembered he'd laughed in high school when they'd come in and the floor made noises. The detective and Amber joined six others seated on long wooden benches at the table covered with a red and white checkered oil cloth.

Amber leaned across toward Burns. "Tell me about—"

"Not, now." His gaze darted around the table. "Later."

"Eating here wasn't such a good idea." Amber bit her lip.

He grinned. "I think it's great."

Amber quit chewing on her lip. "You suggested this place on purpose."

Before Burns could comment, their server set down the salad, with a turntable of three different dressings. The detective, with a sardonic grin, asked, "How did you manage to get out of dinner with Cash?"

"He hadn't returned yet." The aromas in the restaurant made Amber's stomach grumble. She resigned herself to enjoy the food. "He told me earlier about an emergency meeting with Henry Longreen and canceled our crab dinner. Perry wanted a quiet evening to call Tom."

"The guy at his store, right?"

"Correct. He'll run by my place and pick up my mail. Hopefully the letter Sarah sent me will be there and he'll mail it out. Also, we're having a gift sent out for Cash."

"A letter Sarah wrote you?"

"When I talked with her on the phone Friday, she told me she'd written me a letter. I'm hoping it will give me some information to go on."

"Might explain her depression. Why she did what she did."

"We'll see." Amber hoped the letter gave a clue to the killer.

The server brought out a pork roast and fried chicken with all the side dishes. Amber bit into the chicken, savoring the taste. The butter she'd spread onto the warm bread melted. Delicious. She closed her eyes for a moment to savor the tastes, but Sarah's image rose unbidden. The food lost some of its flavor.

Later, after the waitress served two pies, steam still rising from the slits at their centers, Amber moaned. "It's been a long time since I've eaten like this."

Burns looked across the table at her after he'd helped

himself to a piece of both berry and apple pie. "You diet all the time now?"

"I never diet. Diet is just 'die' with a 't.' No, I keep track of my food intake, try to eat lots of fruits and vegetables, and still go to Weight Watchers."

"Weight Watchers?"

"That's how I lost my weight. But, these smells and flavors here are just too good to pass up."

"Sarah loved this place."

"She did." Amber stared across the table. "Tell me, were you still in love with her?"

Burns balked with the fork halfway to his mouth. "Not in the way you mean."

"Oh, you really believe that?" Amber asked.

"Wait a minute, is that why you think I... you suspect me because you think I still loved her? That's ridiculous. After all these years, I never would have hurt Sarah." He set his fork down. "You're way off base."

Amber thought about her conversation with Dr. Madison. She hoped the doctor was right when he'd told her Burns wouldn't be a part of this.

After most of the people departed, she asked, "What did you have to tell me about Lancaster?"

"Not here." Burns finished his pie and picked up the bill. He left a tip. "Come on. We'll talk where it's more private."

Amber snatched the ticket out of his hand. "Sure. But, I pay for my own meal."

Outside, standing next to the cars, Amber said, "We're not on some date here. The Samoa Cookhouse—a bad idea. Too crowded to talk privately."

"Food's good though. Get in my car."

"Excuse me?"

"We'll talk inside."

Amber glanced around. "I'm comfortable standing. There's no one around."

"Just get in."

"Why don't we sit in my car?"

"Because I know mine's not bugged."

Amber widened her eyes. "Bugged?"

"One never knows." Burns shrugged.

Amber stared at her car, then climbed into the Camaro. Burns had to be paranoid. She half expected him to run a wand over her, checking for bugs. What did he have to hide?

A file lay on the passenger seat. He grabbed it before she sat down.

"Is that information for me?"

"Might be."

"Oh, come on. That's how you used to answer in high school."

"Sorry. You bring out the best in me."

"We weren't very nice to each other back then." Heat rose to Amber's cheeks. She swallowed. "I was jealous."

"You? Jealous? But—"

"I was afraid you'd take Sarah away from me. Shocked me when she came with me to New York. I figured you two would get married."

"So did I."

"You were pretty furious about that."

"It was a long time ago." Burns raised one shoulder. "I was young. I moved on. So did Sarah."

"You never married?"

"Haven't found the right woman." His gaze bored into her. "How about you? Have you found the right guy?"

"Too busy." Amber dated, but no one caught her interest. "Anyway, back to Lancaster."

"I still don't believe this has anything to do with Sarah's death, mind you." Burns opened the file. "However, to satisfy some of your questions, here goes." He glanced at a sheet of paper. "I checked on Cash's past from Boston. Keep in mind I did this way before you even arrived in Carsonville."

Amber said nothing.

The detective continued. "As you discovered, Cash was born in Boston. Not from a wealthy family at all. His mother worked for the Fullerton's as a housekeeper. She didn't live there, but cleaned twice a week, more if needed."

"Lancaster said he hasn't always been rich." Amber shifted in the seat and faced Burns. "How did his fiancée die?"

"You're not going to like the answer."

"Tell me."

"According to this report, R. Harriet Fullerton committed suicide."

Amber's mouth dropped open as she stared wide-eyed at Burns. "What?"

"Nothing similar to Sarah's death, I assure you. A car accident, but they think she drove off the cliff on purpose."

"How did they arrive at that conclusion?"

Burns flipped a page and read. "No skid marks, a high blood alcohol content, and she left a note." He rushed on. "A more detailed note than Sarah's."

"Do you know what it said?"

"It's very different from Sarah's."

"May I read it?"

"Not going to happen." Burns placed the page at the back of the folder. "You're not a cop, I am. Trust me on this. The report indicates Cash had an air-tight alibi—he was with her parents. Also, her death devastated him, and her family. As you said, she was an only child. They took

Cash in after her death and treated him like a son. So, it wasn't surprising for him to inherit when they passed."

"Do I dare ask how they died?"

"Airplane crash. According to the newspaper article, the three of them were supposed to fly to Martha's Vineyard together."

"How soon after their daughter died?"

"Three weeks."

"Why wasn't Lancaster with them?"

"He had to back out at the last minute to attend some meeting. He was supposed to join them later, by car."

"What caused the crash?" Amber chewed on a strand of hair.

"Small plane crashes are usually due to pilot error. The plane was so badly burned, it was hard to tell."

Amber spat out the wet hair. "Could it have been sabotaged?"

"Who knows? The FAA didn't think so at the time. Evidently, fog rolled in unexpectedly."

Amber thought a moment. "Did Cash go to the meeting?"

"That was confirmed."

"What else do you know?"

"I can tell you this because it's public record. After the inheritance, Cash stayed in Boston for awhile. I heard his parents didn't get along with him after he inherited. Maybe they were too poor for him. I don't know. Anyway, he moved everything and the staff out West."

"I knew he brought James with him. Who else would there be, if Lancaster's mother was the housekeeper?"

"The cook came with him," Burns said. "That explains why Hale makes the best Boston clam chowder, although that's not the mystery we're trying to solve. Also, a young maid came out with him."

Amber, caught in her musings, didn't realize at first what Burns said. "You mean to tell me Marie was a maid at the Fullerton's?"

"It appears so." Burns ran a hand through his hair. "If she's the same one from Boston."

"You don't think that's a little strange?"

"No."

"Two suicides, and that flaunty little creature, and you're not suspicious?"

"I had some, but came to a decision after Dr. Mayhill ruled it a suicide, not an accident. I respect her work. Why can't you just accept it?"

Amber considered telling Burns about her parents. *No,* she thought. *That doesn't need to be brought up.* The shock and all the unanswered questions. She couldn't tell him about her suicide attempt back in high school either.

A little nagging doubt assaulted her. Burns said something about Harriet, Lancaster's fiancée. What was Amber missing? She couldn't put her finger on it.

"Anybody else come out west with him?"

"Other than his best friend Henry Longreen, no one else. Why?"

"He's known Henry for a long time?"

"I guess so."

Dr. Madison might be right about the detective. After a moment, she decided to trust the good doctor's judgment.

Taking a deep breath, she plunged in, relating the discovery of the pills and talking with Dr. Madison. She omitted the handwriting sample.

Burns furrowed his brows. "What's the doc say?"

"He can't believe she took her own life either. Dr. Mayhill didn't give it much credence, because Madison hadn't seen Sarah professionally for over a year. But Max had. He couldn't believe it either."

"Max?" Burns asked.

"You know, Max and Wally?"

"You mean Kazinsky from the Old Town Carriage Company?"

Amber nodded.

"What's he have to do with this?"

"Sarah visited him the day she died. Remember how she loved to go for a ride, feed the horse apples and carrots? Well, some things never change."

"I forgot about that." Burns gazed out the front windshield. Amber watched people come in and out of the restaurant.

Burns ran a hand through his hair. "We talked to everyone, except Max Kazinsky. Cash must not have known about him either."

"Max didn't say nice things about you."

"We've had our run-ins before." Burns frowned. "In high school, whenever I'd see him and his horse... used to spook them both. Not very nice to either one. Don't like horses. If Sarah talked with Max, he knew more about me than I'd care to have him know."

"He says you're pretty tight with Lancaster." *I can't believe I'm telling him this.*

Burns sat back in his seat, both hands gripping the steering wheel. "I like Cash, and Longreen, too. I admire success. I knew Dr. Madison didn't believe in Sarah's suicide, but not that strongly. He told me he could have been way off base because she was no longer his patient."

"Maybe he changed his mind because of the piece of paper I found." Amber bit her lip.

"What paper?"

Amber dug in her purse. She took a deep breath. *He can't be all that bad, or Sarah wouldn't have cared for him and the doc did trust him. Guess I should try.* She handed over the torn paper. "This."

He studied the progression of handwriting for a long time. "Where did you uncover this?"

"In one of Lancaster's books."

"Ah." Burns cocked his head. "Now I understand. One that I'd borrowed, right?"

Amber grabbed a strand of hair and placed it in her mouth. Heat rose to her cheeks.

"The pills would pique Dr. Madison's interest, but this..." Burns tapped the note. "This would get his dander up. He's worked with our department for many years. Now *I* have concerns. Perhaps you and Mr. Cole should move to a hotel."

Amber pulled the hair out of her mouth. "Not now. I'm making progress."

"Who else checked out the book?"

"It's really popular. I think everyone has read it, including Lancaster. However, the last one to have *The Last Honest Man* was Sarah. The book had been logged back into the study on the day of her death. Lancaster or James does the logging. The way his system works, one of the staff could have put it back. They're allowed to borrow books, but check in and out by leaving notes on his desk. Anyone could check it out and say someone else had."

"You don't think Sarah read the book or returned it?"

"Sarah *was* the last one to have it. But, with this proof that someone could write like her, anyone could have checked *The Last Honest Man* out, or put it back, other than Sarah."

"What difference does it make?" Burns pounded the steering wheel. "Sarah's dead, so it would only be unusual if no one had brought it back. Sarah *might* have been murdered."

"I've been trying to steer you to this idea."

"I know." Burns held up his hand to ward off any further comments. "You've aroused my curiosity. I'll talk with Dr. Madison. Dig a little deeper. I can't believe Cash is a killer. God, poor Henry Longreen. If this turns out to be true, his campaign chances slide down the ruler to almost zero."

"We're talking about a possible murder," Amber said.

"I know that. Longreen won't keep me from detecting the truth, but I will proceed cautiously. You need to get out of it, though."

Amber laughed. "Told you you wouldn't like it when I dug up the truth."

"You haven't unearthed the truth. You might be way off. There could be any number of explanations. I'll keep this piece of paper. Run fingerprints, although you possibly obliterated any. How many people have handled this?"

"Oh, gosh. I'm sorry. I didn't think. Perry, Dr. Madison, me. And hopefully, the killer."

"Let's not get ahead of ourselves. I'll have to get fingerprints from you and Perry to rule those out."

"Okay. I better go. Perry's probably concerned about me. He wanted me to tell you all of this when we were in your office, but I didn't want to. I'm still not convinced it was a good idea."

"For once in your life, have faith in me. Sarah did. Give me a chance."

"I'll try." Amber climbed out of his car. *Maybe he's okay, after all.* Then she remembered what her nagging thought had been about earlier. She leaned her head in through the open door. "Hey, what did the 'R' stand for?"

"What?"

"Lancaster's fiancée," Amber said. "R. Harriet Fullerton."

Burns scanned through his notes. "Rose. Why?"

"Just curious. Keep in touch." Amber got chills as she pictured the rose quartz necklace and other pieces, but none in the master bedroom.

CHAPTER 25

I arrive at the house in time to see the prize pull out from the driveway. I follow Amber, parking a few spaces away, and watch what unfolds at the Samoa Cookhouse.

Detective Steve Burns steps out of his shiny muscle car. Whatever he drives, he's still a loser. Why is Amber meeting with him? Does she have feelings for Steve? Granted, he is handsome, but not as handsome... Never mind, there are other things to think about. My plan to make Amber part of the collections needs to get back on track. She asks too many questions for her own good. Perhaps this isn't a good idea. Maybe bringing her into the group is too soon after Sarah's death.

Amber is different from the others. She possesses more than beauty. Her endless questions to everything... Well, no matter. Even though I'm not prepared for this new development, it can be rectified. At least I have taken care of that letter.

I cannot follow them inside. Too risky. No cover at those long community tables. Perilous waiting in the car.

But necessary. Is this meeting between Steve and Amber business, or pleasure?

I tap my fingers on the steering wheel and bang my foot on the floor. What are they conversing about? Will they be smart enough to figure it out? I feel the fear bubble inside me. I hate unanswered questions.

People come and go from the restaurant. Each time the door opens, I hold my breath, and then expel it loudly. Can't they eat faster? I shift from one side of my buttocks to the other.

While they're inside the restaurant, I close my eyes and let my eyelashes rest on my cheek. Pictures of the others run through my mind. Harriet, the first one. So in love and so willing to please. I even endured going shopping with her. Carrying her packages. But then she changed. Using contacts, going to salons, calling herself Rose. Started paying more attention to herself than others. Vanity!

My hands glow white in the foggy gloom from strangling the steering wheel. I inhale and exhale slowly, and let loose of the wheel, one finger at a time.

More images flash through my mind like a picture show. Tampering with the car, making certain the salon gave her alcohol. Writing the suicide note. Too bad I had to end her life, but Harriet should not have changed.

The other murders—necessary, too.

I wish Steve and Amber would hurry up and come out of the restaurant.

It's a full hour and a half before the door opens and they stroll away from the Samoa Cookhouse, smiling and chatting like old friends. I'm stiff and cold. They should not have made me wait so long. They will find out why.

Hunching down in my seat, I watch. Amber ignores her own car and eases into the front seat of the detective's Camaro. They turn toward each other and talk. Did they not do enough of that at dinner? Are they discussing Sarah, or something else? Perhaps they suspect Sarah *was* murdered.

Ah, that kill. Another stroke of genius. Too bad she changed as the others. Vanity! If only... stop! What is done is done. Hopefully, Amber will be better.

Glaring through the darkened windows, I pound on my steering wheel, cursing. I can't hear. Why didn't they sit in her car? Then perhaps...

Finally, Amber opens the door of the detective's car and climbs out. She gets into the red Mustang. After Steve leaves, she drives away. I pace her a couple of car lengths behind.

CHAPTER 26

Steve gripped the steering wheel and squirmed. Frowning, he decided to check out a few things. Instead of going home, he headed for the station. Had he let money lead him astray? God, he desired to be rich. Could he have overlooked something because he got too close to Cash and all that money?

Marching into the office, he sat in his seat. He slammed his fist onto the desk. The other officers eyed him warily before returning to their work.

As he contemplated Lancaster's file one more time, he gazed at his sister's picture. He might not have noticed her problems, but hadn't he learned from that mistake?

Amber's questions echoed in his mind. Man, she'd make a good detective. But he was good, too. Had he covered all the possibilities? Dr. Mayhill would discuss her conclusion with him if he phoned her. But, she'd never let him live it down if he asked her for advice. They seemed always at odds. The smart coroner investigator kept him on his toes.

His hand hovered over the telephone. He snatched the

receiver and dialed Dr. Vince Madison. After the second ring, a man said, "Hello, this is Dr. Madison."

"Hello, Doc. I'm impressed you answered the phone this late. Detective Steve Burns here. Do you have a few minutes to speak with me about a case?"

"I'm working late. If it's not an emergency, may I call you back in about fifteen minutes?"

"How about I see you at your office to discuss this?"

"If it's important. Sit in the waiting room until I come out."

"Thanks, Doc." Steve hung up, wishing Amber had come to him sooner. If he'd not been so miserably cruel to her in high school, she might have trusted him.

Twenty minutes later, Steve sat in Dr. Madison's inner office. "I'm sorry for the late hour, but Amber Rockwell and I just talked. She's unearthed a couple of inconsistencies about Sarah Hudson's death."

"We discussed them. She even suspects you. I told her she shouldn't."

"Thanks, Doc. She and I go back a long way." Steve hesitated, debating whether to tell the doctor about their past. He decided it wasn't relevant. "Anyway, she said you have doubts about Sarah's suicide?"

"I have questions that need answers. Did Miss Rockwell show you that torn paper with the different handwriting on it?"

"Yep, I'm having it analyzed. Told me about the Valium she found, too."

"I've tried getting in touch with my office manager," Dr. Madison said. "Nancy and her husband are on a cruise. She enters every contest that comes in the mail. Even has a thick folder with photocopies of entry forms. Odd though, she couldn't find any information on this particular one. Should you check it out? Everything was paid for, so we figured it must be legit. But, now I'm having doubts. Anyway, I left a message on the cruise ship for her to phone me. She and her husband took a tour away from the ship. She hasn't returned my call yet. I thought when you phoned, it might be her."

"If it's all right with you, I'll stick around a bit. See if she returns your phone call. In the meantime, can I use your computer to check out the cruise?"

"By all means, have a seat." Dr. Madison gave Steve his chair behind the desk. As the doctor fed him information on Nancy's cruise, Steve punched it into the computer. The screen filled with text. They both craned to see what appeared.

Steve banged on the side of the computer. Couldn't they be faster? After searching all the information available, he found no record of the described contest. He dug further, thinking how Amber was never satisfied with the first answer.

"Look." Dr. Madison pointed at the screen as information came up about Nancy's cruise. "Does that mean what I think it means?"

"She never won any contest. But, someone paid for her entire package." Steve wrote down a name that was on the screen. "Do you recognize this corporation?"

"I don't. Nancy deals with the salesmen. I hate talking with them. And, of course, bills are paid by a service."

"With some digging, I'll uncover the person behind the corporation." Steve hit keys with rapid determination. The blob of doubt began to take shape. Did this have anything to do with Sarah's death?

While Steve worked at the computer, Dr. Madison walked around the desk toward the door. "I'm starved. Care for something to eat?"

"No, thanks. I've already eaten."

Dr. Madison's office was a converted Victorian house with a kitchen. "I'm going to fix a sandwich. Be right back."

The doctor sauntered back into the room and pulled out some patient files. He sat across the desk, reading and munching on his sandwich. Dr. Madison finished his food, yawned, and soon his head dropped. Steve heard soft snores.

Twenty minutes later, when the telephone rang, the doctor jerked his head up and reached out for the phone. He knocked the receiver off the cradle, nabbing it before it bounced on the floor.

"Hello?" Dr. Madison cleared the huskiness from his throat. "Nancy? Sorry." He motioned to the doorway. Steve hurried into the other room as the doctor said, "Guess I fell asleep."

Steve picked up the extension in time to hear Nancy's reply. "Sorry I woke you, but the note said to call ASAP."

"No, no, I've been waiting here with Detective Steve Burns, who's on the line, too," Dr. Madison said. "Nancy, do you remember the conversation you had with Sarah Hudson?"

"Miss Hudson? I... I guess so."

"The day you flew out, she committed suicide."

"What's that have to do—"

"Some things have come to my attention, and I wanted to clarify that conversation with you."

"I'm so... so sorry. Like... like what?" Nancy stammered through the scratchy connection.

"Is something bothering you?" Dr. Madison asked.

"Oh, boy. When I called the office Monday after we left, Caroline told me about Miss Hudson's death. I should have talked with you then. I felt bad about not discussing my concerns with you, but from what Caroline said, the coroner ruled her death a suicide, so I put it at the back of my mind."

"What did you have a problem with?"

"Well, thinking back, I'm not positive it was Sarah on the phone."

"You didn't say anything back then."

"Dr. Madison, I'm sorry. It was a very busy day. I had a cold. Also, I'd found out about the cruise the same day. In my excitement and hurrying to pack to be ready by Friday night, I forgot to mention anything to you."

"And?"

"I can't put my finger on the reason or why I doubt it now," Nancy said, "but I couldn't swear that it *was* Miss Hudson on the phone. Call it one of those little things that pricks at the back of your mind or makes the hair stand up on the bottom of your neck, and you can't figure out why."

"Was it even a woman on the phone?"

"I couldn't swear to it."

"Nancy, your instincts are usually correct," Dr. Madison said. "I appreciate you telling me."

"Do you think it was my fault she killed herself?"

"Absolutely not, Nancy. Even if Sarah did call, it was not your fault. If anyone is to blame, it's me. I should have talked with her before prescribing more pills."

"Nancy, this is Detective Steve Burns. I'm listening in here. You're not in any trouble, but I do have a couple of questions."

"Of course, Detective, I'll answer if I can."

"We've been checking into your cruise."

"It's so wonderful. My husband and I are—"

"Nancy." Steve interrupted her. "You didn't win any contest."

"What? I don't understand."

"Neither do we. There's no contest attached to your

tickets. A corporation by the name of BeauCollec, Inc. paid for your trip." Steve spelled the company name for her. "I'm still digging for who is behind the corporation. Do you recognize that company, or know of anyone who might have sent you on this cruise?"

"No. I'm stunned," Nancy said. "Is the corporation a medical firm?"

"Just says, sales and investments," Steve said.

"I thought I'd won a contest since I'm always entering things. But, I don't remember one for a cruise."

"You don't know anyone who might have sent you? A grateful patient? Rich relative? Anyone?"

"No, Detective, no one."

"Nancy, don't worry about it," Dr. Madison interjected. "Enjoy your good fortune. We'll figure it out when you get back."

"Thanks, Doctor. If I think of anything else, I'll call you."

Steve hung up and rejoined the doctor in the other room. "I don't like this. I haven't been able to trace a name associated with this company. Lots of sub-corporations."

"No. This isn't good," Dr. Madison said. "We need to keep digging."

"Do you know of anyone who might have sent her on that cruise?"

"No," Dr. Madison said.

"It sounds crazy, but—"

"Detective, she understands this is too important to fool with. I'm positive she would have reported over the phone if she knew someone was interested enough in her to send her on a cruise. She would have let us know somehow, even if her husband was standing next to her."

"All right, Doc. We'll work on this, but there's another

problem. I have Lancaster's file in my car and I want you to look at it. See what your take is. Do you have the time?"

"I'll make the time," Dr. Madison said.

"Be right back."

CHAPTER 27

Amber parked the Mustang, and hurried into Lancaster's house. She found Perry sitting in the parlor reading a magazine. "Hi. Did you have a good evening?"

"God, Amber, I was getting worried." Perry put the magazine on the coffee table. "Where've you been?"

"With the police. Where is everybody?"

"Have no clue. Cash still isn't back. James and Marie disappeared about the same time you left."

"Weird. Did you call Tom?"

"Yes. Umm..."

"What's the problem?" Amber stood in front of the coffee table, gazing down at Perry.

"Er, none at the store." Perry patted the couch. "Come sit by me."

Amber plopped next to him. "Well?"

"Everything's fine. Tom says stay as long as we have to. I think he's enjoying running the shop by himself."

"What about the letter?"

"Oh, Amber. There's nothing you can do now."

"About what?"

"Tom swung by your apartment. The door jamb was broken. He pushed the door open."

"Oh, my God."

"Tom says your stereo, T.V.—all there. He wasn't positive anything was missing. Mail scattered all over the floor, papers from your desk strewn about, your refrigerator had been gone through. Also, it appears your bed was slept in. Police think a homeless person broke in for a place to sleep and eat."

"I've never had trouble before."

"Police say there've been a couple break-ins similar to yours in the area. Tom watered the Creeping Charlie you always forget about, and gathered your mail. Why don't you have a mail box? I did away with my door slot. Anyway, no letter from Sarah. Tom said he'd stop by every day, turn off and on a light, and overnight the letter the minute it arrives."

"Someone wanted to steal Sarah's letter ."

"A bit paranoid, are we?" Perry asked. "No one here has flown to New York and back. Besides, as I told you, cops said the neighborhood has had similar break-ins."

"So this is how it feels... the violations." Amber shivered. "Someone broke into my apartment."

"We can go home if you want, but Tom said he'd keep watch."

"I should have Sarah's letter by now. The thief stole it."

"You know how mail is these days"

"I guess. I feel bad Tom has to keep watch over his place and mine."

"He's fine. Said your place wasn't any trouble to clean up." He put his arm around her. "I'm so sorry. What did Detective Burns have to say?"

"Finally, we've grabbed his interest." Amber leaned her head on Perry's shoulder. She refused to give into the defeat she felt. "He'd already checked out Lancaster." Amber told Perry the story of Lancaster's fiancée and her parents. "And, Marie might have come out with James and Lancaster. She might have worked with the butler before they met Lancaster. If she did, she's known Lancaster for a long time."

"So?"

Amber stood and paced. "Don't you think it odd that the flirty maid might have come with him?"

"Possibly. I'm glad you're getting along with Burns," Perry said. "What's he think?"

"I'm not sure about him yet."

"Oh, come on, Amber."

She stopped pacing and placed her hands on her hips. "He didn't think much about Marie, but his curiosity piqued when I showed him the different handwritings. Said he'd go talk with Dr. Madison."

"About time." Perry shifted on the couch, gazing into Amber's eyes. "Now we can bow out of this. Let him handle it. I would like to get back to the shop. Don't you need to check out your apartment?"

"I've faith in Tom. We have until next Saturday."

"But—"

"You can fly back." Amber sank back onto the cushion next to Perry. "I'll call Tom about the break-in. I'm staying 'til this is finished."

"Then I'll be right here with you."

CHAPTER 28

I maintain my two car-lengths behind as Amber heads in the direction of the house. She parks out front and goes inside. I drive up the driveway, parking in my usual spot. I sneak around, and peer into the front parlor window, I see Amber's silhouette meet up with Perry's.

After a few minutes pass, I slip inside unnoticed. Parts of their conversation drift through the parlor doors. She tells Perry he can go back to New York. My heart rate increases. That's perfect. Wait. Her boss refuses. No matter. At least the apartment break-in isn't sending her east.

None of this changes my plans. However, I must be more vigilant with every move. I don't make mistakes. Not before, and I cannot afford any now.

Vanity is not tolerated. Having long flowing hair, perfect bone structure and a figure is one thing—flaunting beauty in someone's face is another. It has been drilled into me: all beautiful things must be appreciated and admired. That includes innocence. A woman should not realize how gorgeous she is. Does a vase know it's pleasing to the eye?

Of course not. Women should be totally unaware of their looks.

I shudder at how vain the women become. Their vanity contaminates them. Contamination must be destroyed.

I cannot allow it to happen to Amber. She's too refreshing after the others. I have to convince her that Sarah took her own life. Hopefully, the new letter I write from Sarah will do the trick. It needs to work, or else…

CHAPTER 29

"Good evening, Ms. Rockwell. May I get you anything?"

Amber spun her head toward the butler. She hadn't known he'd walked into the parlor. "No,... no thank you," she stammered. Had he heard any of their conversation?

Marie sauntered in behind James. "Your beds are turned down. Is there anything else I can do for either of you?"

"No... no. Not for me." Amber plastered on a smile. "Thank you."

Perry shook his head.

James spoke to Marie, "That will be all."

Amber thought it sounded like a rude dismissal. Marie's eyes darkened to an even deeper brown and narrowed down to what Amber considered a "pin-prick" stare toward James, which chilled Amber. Marie's right hand, with long, red fingernails, curled into a fist. The maid took a deep breath. Amber waited for the erupting volcano. Instead, Marie spiraled on her heels and marched out of the room. She brushed by Lancaster and Henry Longreen as the two men entered.

"Ah, Mr. Lancaster, Mr. Longreen, may I get you

something?" James asked. The men shook their heads. "Well, if there is nothing further... Good night." The butler strolled over to the parlor doors and started to close them.

"James," Amber called.

He stopped and looked up. "You require something, Ms. Rockwell?"

"Since you do most of the posting, do you remember when you mailed Sarah's letter to me? I haven't received it yet."

"I am sorry, Ms. Rockwell. With all that has happened, I do not recall. I am not even positive I mailed a letter to you. Ms. Hudson went out Friday. Perhaps she sent it then."

"Okay. Thanks anyway." Amber knew it took about five days from coast to coast. The letter should have arrived by now, but considering snail mail, she'd give it a few more days. *I bet the letter had something to do with the break-in, but why would it be so important?*

After the butler shut the doors behind him, Lancaster said to Amber, "You look confused. Everything all right?"

"All good," Amber said. "How was your evening?"

"A bit of a mix-up, but now that Henry and I have finally gotten together, we've some work to do. Have to make a few phone calls. If you'll excuse us, we'll be in the study."

They left, closing the doors again.

"Odd," Perry said. "Where did everybody come from all of a sudden?"

"You haven't seen any of them until now?"

"No, I haven't."

Amber stared at the doors. "I'm kind of glad I told Steve."

"So, Detective Burns is totally off your suspect list now?"

Amber lifted an eyebrow. Steve, she said to herself, and wondered when she'd started thinking of him as "Steve" and not Burns? "I didn't say that, but Dr. Madison thinks there is something very wrong here, too."

"What's your next move?"

"Wish I knew."

CHAPTER 30

Amber went to the dining room on Sunday morning and found Perry pouring a cup of coffee. She fixed her tea and sat down.

"Hello, Miss Rockwell, Mr. Cole," Marie said, smiling as she walked in. "Anything you need?"

The maid bustled about the room. "No, thank you, Marie." Amber wondered why the maid was grinning. "So, how long have you worked for Mr. Lancaster?"

Marie smiled broader and her eyes twinkled. "A long time. He's a pleasure to work for."

"Were you in Boston with him?"

The young woman paused and glanced at the open dining room doors. "You bet. I've been with him as long as James."

"Did you know Harriet?" Amber asked.

"Harriet?" Marie questioned. "Oh, you mean Rose. Her parents always called her Harriet. Poor thing. With a name like that... I knew her." The maid's gaze darted toward the doorway and back again. She lowered her voice. "That girl blossomed when people started calling her Rose. And, I knew Tiffany in Los Angeles, and Sarah, too. None of them were good enough for Cash. No one is." She glared at Amber as if to say, "So there," and hurried from the room.

"Tiffany?" Amber asked Perry. "Who's Tiffany?"

"I don't know. You better call Detective Burns. See what he knows about Cash when he lived in Los Angeles."

"Rose?" Amber pondered aloud. "How come that name makes me think about all the rose quartz? Come to think of it, Lancaster has a lot of Tiffany glass around, too."

"And he has a lot of amber, among other things," Perry muttered.

"What?"

"He has several types of collections, but where does Sarah fit in?"

"I have no idea."

"It's all probably a coincidence anyway."

"I don't believe that. I better contact Steve."

"Contact Steve about what?" Lancaster asked, as he sauntered into the room.

"Good morning." Amber hadn't heard him out in the hallway.

"It certainly is," Lancaster said. "I assume you mean Detective Burns. I thought you didn't care for him. What do you need to contact him about?"

Amber swallowed and tried to come up with what to say.

The telephone rang.

Lancaster picked it up on the second ring. "Thanks, James, I have it in the dining room. Hello? Why, she's right here, Steve." Lancaster drew out the detective's name and frowned. Then he handed Amber the telephone.

Amber took the receiver. Lancaster held onto it a fraction of a second longer than necessary. She tugged it from his hand. "Hello. Detective Burns, what can I do for you?"

"You sound funny. Are you all right?" Burns asked.

"Lunch. Well, as a matter of fact, Perry and I were just discussing that. We wanted to take you out to lunch to thank you for being so understanding. It'll be our treat."

"Okay," Burns said. "I take it Cash stayed right next to you?"

"That's correct. One o'clock would be fine," Amber said.

"Where?"

"We can pick you up at the station if that's better for you?"

"Okay, see you at one o'clock." Burns hung up.

The dial tone buzzed in her hear, but Amber said, "Bye. Thanks for calling." She hung up. "Looks as if we don't have to contact him. He must be psychic. We were both thinking of lunch."

"How nice for you," Lancaster said, with slight irritation in his voice.

"Is there a problem?"

"No, I hoped we could spend some time together today."

"How about dinner?"

"Of course. I have a meeting with Henry Longreen at one anyway. I'm going to church this morning. You're welcome to join me."

"Thank you. Henry wasn't too talkative last night. How's his campaign coming along?" Amber asked.

"We were late getting together last night, but barring any scandal, I think we have it made."

Amber cringed inwardly at the word "scandal." She liked Mr. Longreen and didn't want to ruin his chances, but if Lancaster killed Sarah, Henry Longreen's career wouldn't stop Amber from exposing the crime. She hoped it wouldn't keep Steve from investigating either.

~~~~

Amber and Perry entered the detective's room and walked over to Steve's desk. He was all business, and she needed to get back on track. *I have to think of him as 'Burns' and not Steve.* "Do you have any information about Lancaster's life in L.A.?"

"Hello to you, too, Rocky. Why don't you at least sit down?" He waited while they settled into the two metal chairs. "If you mean, did I do a complete check on Cash Lancaster's past, no. I knew he lived in that area before moving to Northern California. He said the rat race got to him. Why?"

"Marie said something this morning about a Tiffany in Los Angeles. Also Harriet Fullerton was known as Rose by everyone, except her parents."

"That's interesting." He grabbed a pad and wrote in it.

"Don't you find it odd Lancaster has a collection of rose quartz and Rose is dead? He also has a Tiffany glass collection."

"You trying to say that this Tiffany in Los Angeles is dead?"

"I don't know. Maybe you could check it out."

Burns opened his mouth to speak, but Perry asked, "Was Amber inquisitive in high school?"

"Kind of," Burns said.

"Well, she knows the answers to a lot of questions my clients ask, and what she doesn't know, she keeps after until she finds out." Perry scratched his chin. "It's a big help in our business. Might work for you, too."

"Rocky." Burns ran a hand through his hair. "You'd make a good detective, but your cases would take too long to close. Brass wouldn't appreciate it."

Amber grinned. "Does this mean you'll check it out?"

"If I don't, you won't give me any peace." The detective pushed his chair back and winced. "But, what's this have to do with Sarah? Does Cash have a 'Sarah' collection somewhere in his house?"

"Really funny." Burns acted like he did back in high school which annoyed Amber. "How should I know? I just ask the questions, remember?"

"If you're trying to establish some sort of pattern," Burns said, "it appears Sarah doesn't fit."

"Or we just haven't figured out how yet. But since we're here to go to lunch, we should head out to a restaurant. We can investigate this when we come back."

On the walk down to the deli, Perry asked, "By the way, Amber, did you call Tom about your apartment break-in?"

"What break-in?" Burns almost stumbled.

Amber could have kicked Perry. Why did he have to bring that up? "Tom and I talked. My apartment—the police think a homeless person broke in. Food littered the kitchen, bed mussed, papers strewn about. Nothing big is missing. The police and Tom think some poor soul tried to get in out of the weather. The air-conditioning was on full blast. Tom will now go over to turn on and off a light. Police will cruise the area because of other break-ins."

"Seems odd. Who was the officer in charge?" Burns asked.

"Officer Carl Drake. Why?"

"You should return to New York. See for yourself about this break-in," Burns said.

"Nice try. You're not going to get rid of me. Finding out about Sarah is more important. Let's just order our lunch and enjoy the food."

CHAPTER 31

Steve sat at his work computer, punching up Cassius Robert Lancaster. *Thank God I talked Amber into leaving the office. Convincing her it would take a long time was a stroke of genius.* He entered "Los Angeles, California," and "Tiffany," and then leaned back in his chair with his hands clasped behind his head. He waited to see if any information popped up.

The computer "pinged" and he threw himself forward. The chair banged and the other officers glanced up. He slapped both hands down on the desk. "I don't believe this."

"What's up?" Red asked.

"Too many coincidences," Steve said, glancing over his shoulder.

Red went back to studying a file.

A missing person's report showed up on the screen filed by Lancaster. He'd filed it for a Tiffany L. Baintree a few days after she'd disappeared. The report noted that her own parents weren't concerned—said she often left the area and never contacted them for days at a time. She liked getting away.

The report led Steve to believe Cash must have put up a big stink. Insisted the police search for her. A note in the report stated the police had contacted other friends who said she "often split for awhile." The police decided that's what she'd done this time. No one searched for her.

Steve found the L.A. police number and dialed. He searched for the lead investigator on the Baintree case to talk with. Sometimes pertinent information was held back.

After several transfers, he reached the last officer to work on the case. The woman informed Steve she wasn't the initial investigator. He'd retired. Further discussion disclosed he'd moved to Florida.

Steve decided to track him down. Otherwise he would have to listen to Amber's incessant questions. Besides, there were too many inconsistencies popping up that made his gut roil with acid. He grabbed a Tums.

It also bothered him about Amber's break-in. Something wasn't right there. While Steve worked on the computer, he searched for the number of the New York P.D. and after several calls, located Officer Drake. He made sure all was okay with Amber's apartment. This break-in was too co-incidental, and Steve didn't like coincidences.

The telephone registry revealed no number for the retired officer—not unusual, since many cops, both retired and active, didn't list their numbers. Steve dug deeper and came up with a registered vehicle giving the man's address.

He dialed the Punta Gorda, Florida P.D. and asked if one of the police officers would go out and deliver a message asking the man to return his call.

An hour and a half later, about to leave for the day, Steve gathered up some papers and pushed his desk chair in. His telephone rang. He snatched up the receiver. "Detective Burns."

"Yep, this is Trask MacFee, the ex-cop in Punta Gorda, Florida you wanted to talk to."

"I do, Mr. MacFee. Sorry to bother you on a Sunday. Thank you for returning my call."

"Call me Trask. What's this about?"

"Just a second." Steve sat in his chair and opened his briefcase. He grabbed the file and flipped to the report. "Do you remember a missing person named Tiffany L. Baintree? Cassius Robert Lancaster filed the report in L.A. about three years ago?"

"That's one case I'll never forget. Mister Lancaster sent me to an early retirement. So arrogant and vain, he 'bout drove me nuts."

"Can you tell me the details?" Steve held his pen ready to write.

"Over the phone? It's a long story. Is it important?"

"Did you ever find the girl?"

"No! Did you?"

Steve heard anger in MacFee's voice. "No. Anyone else? Any idea what happened?"

"What's going on? You read the report?"

"But sometimes we don't write everything we know, especially our gut feelings."

"I have a gut feelin', but I ain't sayin' over no phone. Think that's why I got early retirement. Man had power back then. Does he have it now?"

"Some."

"Then I suggest you don't ask no more questions. You want answers? We get together."

"Can you write it out and mail it to me?"

"I'm retired. I fish a lot. That's all I do. Don't even

write cards to my kids. Tired of writin'." Trask MacFee hung up.

"What the heck?" Steve muttered. *Does Lancaster instill that much fear in the man from this great distance?* Or was MacFee a bad cop? Perhaps this Baintree did run away from Lancaster. Could he be involved in killing several women?

As the detective looked up from his desk, Cash Lancaster walked through the office door.

He stepped over to the desk. "Have a minute?"

Steve threw the file in his briefcase and closed the lid, not wanting to tip Lancaster off yet, if there was anything to this. The detective pointed to a chair.

Lancaster sat down and glared.

"So, is something wrong?" Steve asked.

"Why are you showing so much attention to Amber?" Lancaster folded his arms across his chest.

"Excuse me?"

"Dinner last night, lunch today. Why the interest?"

Steve cocked his head. Why would Lancaster care whether he ate with Amber? "So I can answer her questions about Sarah's death."

"But you phoned her for a lunch date."

"So what's it to you?" Steve eyed the man sitting before him. Lancaster's behavior reminded the detective of the way Lancaster acted with Sarah. *Damn, could Amber be right?*

"You have history with this woman, just like with Sarah," Lancaster said.

"So? Why's that important?"

"Full of 'so's' this morning, aren't you. Nervous?" Lancaster crossed his legs and glowered at Steve.

No wonder MacFee's afraid. The detective came around and sat on his desk in front of Lancaster. "More like curious."

"I came in here to give some friendly advice." Lancaster

uncrossed his legs and lowered his arms. "Not a good idea to get involved with her." He inclined his head. "She's quite obsessed with Sarah's death. Don't you agree?"

"She has some valid questions. I've tried to provide her with answers. Is there any reason why I shouldn't?"

"No. What kind of questions?"

"Good ones," the detective said.

"Answer them during regular working hours. Not lunch or dinner."

Steve thought about telling Lancaster to mind his own business, but remembered MacFee's fear, and wondered what that was all about. The detective kept his anger under control. "Keep it professional, all the way?"

Lancaster nodded. "As far as she's concerned."

"Don't want me to get to know her?"

"You already do, just like Sarah." Lancaster waved his hand in the air. He lowered his voice so Steve had to strain to hear. "Besides, I'd say it was in your best interest, say even financially, to stay away from her in that respect."

Steve scooted off the corner of the desk, went around and sat down in his chair. "Financially, huh?"

Lancaster tipped his head slightly in acknowledgment.

Anger churned in Steve's gut. He reached for another Tums and chewed on it for a minute. He did not want to let Lancaster have any idea about the suspicions rolling around his mind. "I think you're pushing our *friendship* a bit far. I don't appreciate what you just said. And, I know for a fact, Rocky would be ticked off. I won't mention this little conversation to her. I'll forget you ever tried to bribe a police officer."

Lancaster glared. Steve felt cold waves beat against him. He'd never seen this side of Cash Lancaster before. The detective thought about Sarah, Rose, and Tiffany. He should take a quick trip to Punta Gorda, Florida.

CHAPTER 32

Steve hated going to his captain this morning. Cap always came in every Monday in a bad mood. *Was it because he had to spend the weekend going to concerts with his wife?* But Steve had to give it a shot, so he stepped into the captain's office. "I need some time off. Gotta talk to a retired cop in Florida."

"On a case?"

"Not opened. I'm checking into something. Not quite ready to say."

"If it's not an open case, I can't let you go. Do it over the phone, or by fax. We're shorthanded. Sorry."

"But, Cap—"

"No, Detective Burns. You scheduled vacation time for fall, and that's when you can go."

Steve marched out and sat down. He banged his knuckles on the desk. He couldn't wait until fall. What if he was wrong and Rocky was in some sort of danger? The trail was cold already.

Maybe I should ask Henry Longreen about Lancaster. Get his opinion of him. That might shed some light. But, if Steve were wrong, and caused any problems for Lancaster, Henry, the man in real power, would end Steve's career.

Steve clicked on the print button on his computer. The printer spewed out a long list of corporations and sub-corporations. Someone must have sent Dr. Madison's secretary on that cruise, but who? And why? Did it really pertain to this case? His gut told him it did.

The phone rang. He grabbed it. "Detective Burns."

"Steve, Dr. Madison here. Have you discovered who sent Nancy on that trip yet?"

"No." Steve had not found the Board of Directors or anyone responsible. "I'll call you if I get some new information."

"Sorry to bother you."

"Hey, Doc, what do you make of this?" Steve told Dr. Madison about Lancaster's visit.

"That is odd," Dr. Madison said. "Let me consider it. I'll work up a profile and get back to you. I'll have to do it on the Q-T."

"Hurry, Doc. I'm worried." Steve hung up. He drummed his fingers on the desk.

A man, who resembled a linebacker from the Oakland Raiders, walked into the room. The man hollered, "I'm looking for a Detective Steve Burns."

"Over here." Steve rose and waved the man over.

The linebacker wannabe came to the desk and extended a weathered hand. "Trask MacFee at your service. Decided Carsonville has some excellent fishin' off its coast, so I might as well kill two birds with one stone. Besides, I hate leavin' business unfinished."

"Trask MacFee." Steve shook the man's beefy hands. "You're here. But... Please, have a seat." He disengaged his hand from the man's bear-claw grip and motioned to the seat in front of the desk. He grabbed the armrests of his own chair and eased back down.

The big man sank into the chair and set his brown cowhide briefcase beside it. "There's always one case that gets under your skin. And, my nephew says there's some great ling cod and salmon fishin' off this coast. I figured you'd never get to fly to Florida. Am I right?"

"Right on the money," Steve said.

MacFee grinned. "From the expression on your face, my timin' is perfect. Want to fill me in on why you're so interested in Tiffany L. Baintree?"

"Detective MacFee, is she dead?"

"Call me Trask. I think so. No proof though. What's the catch?"

Steve filled the retired cop in on Sarah's death, Amber, and what he knew so far.

"So, because this here little gal can't believe her friend offed herself, you're diggin' deeper into one of my old missin' person's cases. Connection?"

"Not positive there is one," Steve said. "Lancaster was engaged to a woman named Rose. She's dead. He knew Rose's family. Now they're dead, and he inherited. Lancaster dated Tiffany. And she might be dead."

"And Mister Lancaster was close to this Sarah person and she's dead." Trask shifted in his seat. "So?"

"Explaining this to you sounds ridiculous. But, Lancaster collects beautiful stuff: rose quartz, Tiffany glass, amber—"

"Sarah have a middle name?"

"Yeah. Anne."

"Anne. Don't know nothin' you could collect by the name of Anne or Sarah for that matter. Nice theory, but it seems to break the pattern with her."

"I know," Steve said. "But worth a shot. You don't understand how pushy this Amber Rockwell is."

"Sounds as if she'd make a good detective. I'm curious. Why can't she let her friend's suicide alone?"

"I'm not certain it's a suicide any more. And, I don't have a clue what's driving her."

"Might be wantin' to find that out. Theory is good, especially if this Sarah does have a connection. Maybe it's not in her name, but what she did, had, ate, drank... Who knows? Did Mister Lancaster have a nickname for her?"

"That's an idea," Steve said. "As far as I know, Lancaster called her Sarah. She and I were friends. I'll give what you said some thought, and ask Amber to think about it, too." Steve studied the man before him. "Why are you here on your own dime?"

Trask glanced around. Steve followed his gaze. One detective was at the coffee table pouring a thick liquid from the pot into a 49er mug. Red's desk was empty. Trask leaned forward, glaring. "I enjoy fishin'. But, I loved bein' a cop. Mister Lancaster ruined all that."

"How?" Steve wondered if what befell Trask could happen to him.

"Mister Lancaster must have had some friends in high places. Lots of pressure."

"Over Tiffany Baintree? What can you tell me about her?"

Trask shifted his mass and snorted. "You goin' to set me up on a fishin' boat out here?"

Steve laughed. "I better if I want any info. I'll arrange a fishing trip."

Trask grinned. "Fine. Do that, and I'll fill you in on what I didn't write in the official report. Deal?"

Steve made a quick call to a boat captain friend of his. "Mr. MacFee, you're all set for tomorrow at seven-thirty in the morning."

"I said call me Trask." He picked up his briefcase and

opened it. Pulling out some papers, he shoved them across the desk. "These are copies of my reports—my copies and my own notes. Unofficially, I've never given up lookin' for that gal. I think she's dead, but I can't quit hopin' she'll show up. From what I've heard here, I can quit hopin'.."

"Why?"

"You're not stupid. Too many coincidences. You and I don't believe in them. If Mister Lancaster didn't murder those women, he had somethin' to do with their deaths— or someone close to him did."

"Everyone who was with him back east, and in L.A., is here."

"You checked them all out?"

Before Steve could say "yes," Trask continued. "Anyway, back to Tiffany. A real looker. Everyone liked her. Not one bad word ever said about that gal, except from her parents. Both alcoholics. She didn't spend much time with them. After I had the pleasure of interviewin' them, can't say I blame her."

"Your report stated they weren't too concerned about her disappearance," Steve said.

"She hardly ever contacted them. Nothin' unusual there."

"Anyone she saw regularly?"

"After Tiffany met up with Mister Lancaster, he sort of became her entire world—his showpiece. He made her host formal dinners, attend charity functions, and demanded most of her time. The only ones concerned besides Mister Lancaster were a couple that had foster children. She stopped by often. Spent time with their kids. Hardly ever let a week go by that she didn't visit them. That's why I think the gal is dead. She may have split from Mister Lancaster, but she would have contacted those kids to at least say 'Good-bye.'"

"Any clues as to what happened to her?"

"A note that she started. Said, 'I'm leavin'.' It was never finished."

"How do you know?"

"No signature and no period at the end."

"She ever write notes like that before?" *Another controversial note. How many are there?*

Trask shifted in his seat. Steve wasn't sure if the folding chair could handle the man's bulk if he didn't quit fidgeting. The man rubbed his chin. "I interviewed the entire household. They all said no."

"All?" Steve asked.

"Yep, Mister Lancaster, James the butler, Hale the cook, and Marie the maid."

"You have a good memory. Exact same staff he has now, plus I think a housekeeper. I never quite figured out what he used Marie for, since she doesn't seem to keep house."

Trask chuckled. "Another good looker from what I remember. You say they were with him from the beginnin'?"

"Worked for the Fullerton's back in Boston." Steve explained the relationship. "They left everything to him."

"Includin' the staff?"

"Well, I guess they elected to stay with Lancaster. He must pay well."

Trask tapped the folder. "Wish I could be of more help. I think Mister Lancaster has a lot of power and tends to abuse it. He put me on that case then wouldn't let me be. When I went in another direction, got me off it."

"You're positive about that?"

"Minute I started makin' noises towards a homicide, the captain discovered I had a bad back. Doc said a job injury caused it and made me unfit for duty. Gave me a disability retirement. Hell, a man my size—who doesn't have a bad back? Told me someone else would handle the case. Tiffany's still a missin' person. No mention of suspected death."

"Any clues other than the note?" Steve asked.

The big man's stomach grumbled. "They don't feed you much on those planes anymore. And this chair's a bitch. Where can we go to grab a bite to eat?" Trask patted his overextended belly. "I can smell the ocean. Where can we get some scallops?"

"I know just the place."

Half-hour later, they sat at a booth in Spoons, Steve's favorite deli, on 5th and L. The cops hung out here because it was close to the department. The black and white booths were comfortable and the music from the old fashioned carousals on each table covered conversation so other patrons didn't overhear. Steve played B15, "Your Cheating Heart."

Trask stuffed a bite of his scallop patty sandwich into his mouth. Melted garlic butter dripped down his chin.

"This's the place for me. Your friend goin' to feed me on that fishin' boat?"

"I'll warn him to stock the galley. He'll treat you right."

"Anyway, now we're away from your office, I'll finish about Tiffany. A year or so passed. While visitin' some relatives in L.A., I checked in to see the boys in my old squad. Not many left I knew, but one of 'em told me the Baintree case had been dropped the minute I so-called *retired*. They stuck it in the file drawer and never thought about it again."

"Why?"

"Pressure. I think Mister Lancaster knew someone high up in the department or had a friend in office somewhere. Anyway, I decided to do some checkin' on my own. Since I was no longer official, Tiffany's best friend opened up to me a little after I swore I'd never mention it to Mister Lancaster."

Steve polished off his peach pie while Trask devoured his. The detective waited.

Trask sipped his coffee. "This gal told me Tiffany was quite unhappy with Mister Lancaster. He was against her goin' into modelin'. Seems Tiffany decided she was so pretty—a shame to hide herself away. Felt she'd make a fortune in that modelin' business. Must have thought a lot of herself. Anyway, the friend said Tiffany never used to think about her looks. Guess she changed when she connected with Mister Lancaster."

Steve wondered if Lancaster's money had anything to do with Tiffany's behavior. After all, it affected his own.

"This young woman also told me," Trask said, "Tiffany wanted to get away from Mister Lancaster, but didn't know if he'd let her go."

"Let her go?" Steve asked.

"Those were her exact words. I know, surprised me, too. Had the same reaction." Trask shook his head, staring at Steve. "Boy, you remind me of me.

"Anyway, a day after Tiffany told her best friend she was goin' to tell Mister Lancaster about leavin' him, Tiffany disappeared. Friend said she's the one that went to him and asked him where Tiffany was. Told him she would contact the police. Mister Lancaster told the woman not to report it, that he would. He insisted she not go to the police, and to keep her mouth shut.

"Seems durin' the investigation, Mister Lancaster sent Tiffany's friend off on a wild goose chase, so she'd be out of town. She came into the department when she returned, and they informed her Tiffany L. Baintree was an open, cold missin' person's case." Trask held up his hand to prevent Steve from interrupting.

"The same day the young woman had wanted to go to the police, she'd found Mister Lancaster comin' in from his sailboat. Said he'd been out all night in it, alone."

"You call him '*Mr.* Lancaster.'"

"I say it with the most disrespect, but the man's still got clout, doesn't he? Has dinner parties with your Police Chief, congressman, and others?"

Steve kept an eye on the restaurant door. Spoons was almost empty and no other officers were in sight. Trask might be a tad paranoid, but he did have a point. He thought about Henry Longreen who'd been in L.A., too. "And, was he out all night?"

"Yep, verified. Nobody noticed Tiffany anywhere near that boat the day before, or after. No one saw the poor thing again. I called to the foster couple after you phoned. In all these years, they've never heard from her. I reached her parents, too and they haven't either."

"Sounds like she's fish food," Steve said.

"I'm afraid so. Now what are you goin' to do?"

"Keep digging. The more I learn, the more concerned I get. You said Tiffany was about to tell Lancaster she was leaving. So was Sarah."

"That don't sound good."

"No," Steve said. "And, I'm worried about Rocky."

"Rocky?"

"Sorry, Amber Rockwell. Sarah nicknamed her 'Rocky'."

"From the sound of it, she'll be okay as long as she don't think she's too beautiful."

"What do you mean?" Steve frowned.

"I believe it's the real beauties that are missin' and dead."

"But Amber is a beauty too and is staying at his place. She isn't heading east until Saturday."

"That might not be good."

"My thoughts, too," Steve said.

"Well, if I can't be of further use to you, if you'd drive me back to my hotel, I'll rest up for that fishin' tomorrow. Sure do appreciate that trip you arranged."

"Not as much as I appreciate you coming out. Thanks." Steve grabbed the check and went over to the cashier. Trask followed. "If I learn anything, I'll let you know."

Trask handed Steve a card. "Here's where I'm stayin'. Might stick around for a few days. See what you come up with, especially if the fishin' is as good as my nephew says. Also, my home phone and cell number's on the back of that card. Figure it's safe with you, 'cause I'm sure you won't mention this to Mister Lancaster until this is resolved. Keep in touch."

CHAPTER 33

Amber felt as if she'd been tested last night, but had she passed, or failed? The big question—what was the test?

She finished her morning shower and reached around the curtain, fumbling for the towel. A shuffling sound near the door caught her attention. "Is somebody there? Marie?" Amber listened. Nothing.

She snatched the towel from the rack, wrapped it around herself and stepped onto the tiled floor. No Norman Bates. No hacking daggers. She was alone.

She dried off then wrapped the towel turban-fashion around her head. She grabbed her panties and bra. *Didn't I leave those on the other side of the sink?* This house was making her paranoid.

She hiccupped a tiny chuckle and dressed, wondering whether Sarah's death would drive her insane. It dredged up all the memories from her parents' murder. *I barely survived that catastrophe,* she thought as she swiped mascara on her lashes.

Amber finished getting ready and headed downstairs, carrying one of the books from the study. At the bottom,

she caught a glimpse of a blonde exiting through the front
door. Lancaster stood by James, who held the mahogany
doors open.

"Cash, wait." Amber hurried toward him.

Without turning, he stepped over the threshold to the
outside. James closed the massive doors with a resounding
thud. "Good morning, Ms. Rockwell," the butler said as he
faced her. "I trust you had a pleasant night's sleep?"

"I did." She tried to pass him to reach the door handle.
"But, I—"

"Now is not the time, Ms Rockwell." James folded his
arms across his chest.

A car raced off. "What's his problem?" Amber asked.

Through hooded eyes, James watched her.

"Was that Henry with Cash this morning?"

The butler didn't say a word.

Did he have to look so creepy? Amber wouldn't get any
answers from James. His agenda never included helping
her. *Why had Henry been here so early?* Reviewing last night's
dinner, she decided that she hadn't said anything to offend
someone, or upset Lancaster. As she chewed on a strand of
hair, she wondered what had caused his foul mood.

Amber withdrew the wet hair strand and tucked it
behind her ear. She held up the book she'd borrowed.
"May I return this, James?"

Without saying a word, the butler walked down the hall.
He removed a key from his pocket and unlocked the study
door—the one room in the house kept locked, day and
night.

James moved aside for her to enter. "If you cannot
return it to the proper shelf, just leave it on the desk."

As she passed him, she got goose bumps. There were
answers in this room, and she would discover them. "Did I
say something wrong last night?"

"No, Ms. Rockwell. Mr. Lancaster has Mr. Longreen's welfare on his mind. Things are not going as planned." James followed her into the room. With a long, old-fashioned skeleton key, he unlocked the desk drawer. Pulling it open, he removed the logbook. With fluid writing, he marked down the date.

As she peered over the top of the desk, he shut the binder, but not before she noted the script. The brief glimpse reminded her of Lancaster's handwriting. She opened her mouth, but snapped it closed. She didn't want to bring attention to the fact she saw the different writing, yet.

"Is that all, or do you care to borrow another book?"

"No... no, I still have one, thanks."

Amber forgot Lancaster's actions, the departing blonde, and the way Longreen's campaign wasn't going as planned. She now possessed a clue that reinforced her belief Sarah didn't write her suicide note.

"Is Perry at breakfast? I'm starved."

An hour later, Amber watched the road as Perry drove toward Henry Longreen's office. "I don't understand why James would use Lancaster's handwriting to record the entry in the logbook."

"Are you positive it was the same?" Perry asked.

"My brief glimpse was upside down, but the writing for both dates looked alike. Lancaster wrote the date when I checked out the book."

"So James can copy Cash's handwriting. It doesn't prove anything. But you do have a valid point."

"Wonder who else's handwriting he can copy?"

Perry parallel-parked in front of Longreen's campaign headquarters. They entered. Three pretty twenty-something's: a redhead, a blonde, and a brunette, staffed the office. Two stuffed envelopes. One typed, but all three answered the telephones. Piles of buttons and stickers littered the tables, chairs, and floor.

The brunette acknowledged them. "Hi! I'm Robin. May I help you?"

"We wish to speak with Henry Longreen, if he's in?"

Robin gaped for a brief moment. "Like, you mean, you want to speak with him, now?"

Amber shared an amused glance with Perry. "If that's possible. Is he here?"

The young woman glanced back toward a closed door. "Well, but, like I believe he's with someone. Perhaps if you'd come back later."

"When will he be free?" Amber asked.

"Free?" Robin asked as she stuffed and licked another envelope.

Amber got the impression she was in a science fiction movie where the people's brains had been eaten out of their heads. Robin could stuff envelopes with a vengeance, but her verbal skills needed improvement. Her long, red-painted nails hadn't quit moving the entire time she talked. Speaking slowly, as if talking with a small child, Amber stated, "Finished with the person who is in Mr. Longreen's office with him."

"Oh, yeah, right. I don't think he has any other appointments, but, like, this one might take a while. I don't think you should wait."

"Strange way to run a campaign office."

Perry surveyed the room. "He might not be comfortable talking with his constituents."

"Oh, like, are you voters here?" Robin asked.

"No," Amber said, "but we are his friends."

"Well, why didn't you say so? He's with Franny."

Robin licked another envelope. "You know that can take, like, awhile before he's through."

Amber smiled, pretending she understood. Obviously, anyone who knew Henry knew Franny. "Well, maybe it would be better if we came back."

With an all-knowing smile, Robin winked. "Good thinking. You know, like, Franny and him could be in there another hour or so. I could have him call you, if it's important."

"No, we'll catch him later."

Outside the office, Amber reached for Perry's arm. "What did that sound like to you?"

"Not a clue, but it sounds as if Franny keeps Henry tied up for some reason. Is he married?" A taxicab whizzed past with a sign on the side, advertising, 'Henry Longreen for Congress.' Perry glanced knowingly at Amber. "I don't recall meeting a wife at Cash's party, nor do I remember hearing of one."

"This might be important." A dog barked at a bicyclist racing by, drowning her words. "What do you guess he thinks of his campaign manager?"

The blonde came out of the campaign office carrying a bundle of mail. She started to walk by them, but stopped. "I couldn't help hearing you're friends of Mr. Longreen's." She spoke to Perry. "I noticed you have an eastern accent. Did you know my boss when he lived in Boston?"

"No," Perry said. "We're new friends. I didn't know Henry came from Boston."

"Oh, Mr. Longreen and his campaign manager were both raised in Charlestown, a suburb just outside of Boston." The woman smiled. "Well, nice chatting with you." She hurried off down the street, avoiding the still barking dog.

"Boston?" both Perry and Amber stated in unison.

"I wonder if Steve knows about this," Amber said.

"We should go in and see if Henry has a biography sheet? Wait here." Perry rushed into the office. In a few minutes, he stepped back out, grinning.

"Well?" Amber asked.

"Robin chatted on the phone, but the other girl—a very accommodating redhead." Perry waved a piece of paper. "Seems Henry has a history of being in power, starting clear back in Boston."

Amber grabbed the sheet away from him. "No! Let me see that." After studying the biography, she said, "A state representative of Massachusetts living in Boston. Then he moved to Los Angeles, same time as Lancaster. In politics there, too. Think this has anything to do with Sarah?"

"Who knows? The more we discover," Perry said, "the more confused I get."

CHAPTER 34

Steve looked up from his paperwork as the sergeant waved Perry and Amber in. *Oh, no, here she comes again.* She marched over to his desk and tossed a piece of paper toward him. Perry eased into one of the chairs, while Amber remained standing.

Steve picked up the paper; Henry Longreen's bio. "So? What about this?"

"I'm not sure." Amber gripped the back of the chair. "Henry and Lancaster have been in the same towns together, and wherever they go, beautiful women die."

"I bet wherever I go, beautiful women die. But…" Steve laughed and held up a hand to ward off any comment, "… I have to admit, this is strange."

"Finally, you see what I mean." Amber crossed her arms over her chest.

Steve closed his eyes. He wished Rocky would just disappear. Unfortunately, he did see what she meant. He wanted her out of here, out of Carsonville, back home in New York where she would be safe.

But, was that true? He'd talked with Officer Drake about

Amber's apartment break-in. The official version—a homeless person—but, the young cop had some reservations. The papers pulled from desk drawers and file cabinets seemed odd. That hadn't happened in the similar break-ins. Also, no other apartments in Amber's building had been broken into. Drake said he'd keep an eye on the building.

Steve frowned at the bio. He'd lost Sarah for a second time. He wasn't about to lose Rocky. Complications piled up. If she knew that he presumed Tiffany dead, Amber would really be in for Lancaster. Or, now, Henry Longreen.

She clenched her fists and put them on her hips. "Why don't you just sit and stare off into space. Ignore all of these coincidences?"

Steve pointed to the chair. "Sit! Don't stand over my desk glaring at me."

She inhaled so loudly, he thought she'd swallowed her tongue. Then her face softened. *Here it comes. She wants something.*

"What did you learn about Tiffany?" Amber asked softly. She plopped onto the chair across from his desk.

"You bring up some interesting points," Steve said. "Your ideas are good, but I need more evidence to barge into the captain's office. I can't spend time on closed cases. The open ones are more important."

"What about Sarah's murder?" Amber asked. "Would he just let that go?"

"We don't know it was murder." Steve spoke to Perry. "Can't you talk some sense into her? Get her to leave. I promise I'll keep working on my own time. If there was a murder, then it's dangerous living under Cash's roof. Go home. Get back to your antiques."

"That would be nice," Perry said.

"We don't have to head out 'til Saturday," Amber stated.

Steve was glad her green-eyed, dagger-stare was directed at Perry, not him.

"I've tried to get her out of here," Perry said. "You ever try to strip layers of paint off a chair without paint remover?"

"I need to know what really happened," Amber said. "Is that so hard to understand?"

Perry went silent.

"I know you." Steve tilted his head. "There's more happening here than you being best friends with Sarah."

Amber stared into her lap. "I don't know what you're talking about."

"Don't play games, Rocky." Steve banged on his desk to get her attention. "It doesn't suit you. What is it you're not telling me?"

Amber flinched and eyed Perry.

Steve waited. They needed to tell him the truth. The whole story.

Perry nodded to Amber, and she spoke, barely above a whisper. "My parents moved back to Wisconsin after I graduated from high school."

"Yeah, so?"

"I think they're both dead."

Steve wasn't prepared for that. "You're not sure?"

"Somebody brutally murdered my mother about a year ago. They've never found my father. His blood, but no body."

"I'm so sorry. What happened?" Steve relaxed his frown and half-smiled.

"The police's theory: Dad murdered my mother, and during the struggle, she injured him. He ran off. Of course, I don't... can't believe that. I dug on my own and I hired an investigator."

"What did he uncover?"

"Nothing. He told me to give up about a month ago. I've never heard from my father, and, we were close. I think he's dead. But I don't know for sure. I still have many unanswered questions. I can't go through it again. I need to have all the answers for Sarah."

"Were your folks into something dangerous? Involved with some past criminal?"

Amber wiped a tear from the corner of her eye. "Of course not... at least I haven't come across anything or anyone."

Steve's gaze shifted to his sister's photograph. He picked up the gold frame and his hand caressed the smooth glass. "I understand why this is so hard for you. Believe me, I can relate."

"I doubt that."

Still holding his sister's picture, Steve took a deep breath. "Look, Rocky—"

Her hand flew to her mouth. "Oh, God, I'm sorry. I forgot, you said Debbie was murdered, didn't you?"

"Yeah. She married a guy from the Police Academy. We were buddies. He became a sergeant. Someone stalked her, and none of us could figure out who."

"I bet you did everything you could." Amber's voice sounded sincere to Steve.

"As I said before, I didn't have a clue. Too young then, too inexperienced and naïve to the horrors people can dream up. If it hadn't been for a passing paper boy, Nick would never have been caught."

"Nick?" Amber asked.

"My brother-in-law, the Sergeant. He'd been harassing his own wife, my sister, for some time. He killed her cat, and then the dog. Left them for her to find. She loved animals. He ran her off the road, put her in the hospital. Finally killed Debbie. That's how I can relate."

"I guess you can."

"We could..." Steve hesitated.

"What?" Amber asked, sharply.

Steve set the picture down. "You have a good theory working here. Something is going on with these people, but I don't know who's responsible."

"Did you locate Tiffany?"

Steve weighed the pros and cons. Amber was too smart. She'd never let go. Better to work with her. "No, and I don't expect to. Tiffany Baintree has been missing for two and a half years."

"Dead?"

"Not officially. However, I have a problem with Sarah. What's her connection to Cash's collections? Do you know of a pet name he had for her?"

"No." Amber shook her head. "You were around them. Do you?"

"I never heard one. Sarah just doesn't fit the pattern, if there *is* one."

"I could ask James if Lancaster had a nickname for her," Amber said.

"No, don't do that."

The phone rang. Steve grabbed it. "Detective Burns." He listened a few seconds and said, "Tell Mr. Lancaster, I'll be there. Thank you." Steve hung up.

"Why can't I—"

"Hold it," Steve interrupted. "I have an invitation to Lancaster's for dinner tonight. Between the three of us, we might discover a connection. If we don't, we'll have to back off—figure out another angle."

"But—"

"No buts." Steve had to get Rocky to quit. He had to find answers, but he wanted her out of the picture. "If Sarah has no nickname, or anything connecting her to

Cash's collection, then I can't work on it any further. And I won't allow you to." Steve shook his finger at her. "You'll just have to accept the fact that Sarah committed suicide. Clear?"

CHAPTER 35

A cool breeze blew through the open bay windows. The parlor buzzed with stimulating evening conversation. Amber, Perry, and Burns stood to one side, listening to Henry Longreen discuss his campaign. Henry, in a blue suit, appeared more like a model than a politician, although the premature gray in his hair made him appear older than his years.

After Amber spotted James, she thought of a military general, not a butler. Dressed in his usual black-tie attire, he stood ramrod straight, looking around from his corner as if to anticipate everyone's desires.

The maid wove among the guests, serving caviar and crackers in her suggestive black-and-white uniform. She wore that sickening-sweet smile. She stopped near Amber and asked, "Hors d'oeuvres, miss?"

After Amber declined refreshment, Marie hustled over to Lancaster leaving her heavy perfume trailing behind her. Cash conversed with a tall, muscular blonde woman who had just entered the room.

Amber leaned closer to Burns. "Who's Lancaster talking to?"

Henry quit speaking in mid-sentence to stare at Amber. "I couldn't help overhearing. You two haven't met yet?" He waved. "Franny, come over here and meet Amber." Henry snapped his fingers. "Of course, that's right. Franny left town the evening after Sarah's funeral. She's been in and out regularly since."

The tall woman and Lancaster strolled over. "Franny Longreen," Cash said, before Henry could say a word, "this is Amber Rockwell and her friend Perry Cole. Franny is Henry's sister."

"Henry's sister?" Amber shook Franny's hand. She glanced at Henry, noticing his scowl. "Nice to meet you. You don't live in Carsonville, too, do you?"

"No, dear, I run our family business in Boston. However, I spend quite a bit of time with my baby brother."

Amber expected the woman to reach out and ruffle Henry's hair. He even took a step back. Franny reminded Amber of a football player with her strong upper body, seemingly no neck, and short page-boy hairdo. She seemed more like a brother than a sister for Longreen, especially with her deep-throated voice. However, the woman's posture and manner resembled James', except for the wonderful smile that spread to her blue eyes. Her frilly black-lace blouse and long black skirt suited her. The firm handshake hurt Amber's hand.

Franny squeezed once more, and then released her grip. "This is about time. These two can*not* stop talking about you."

"Where are you staying?"

"Here, of course."

"Here? At the house?" Amber couldn't believe she'd missed this woman. "How have we not met, then?"

"I sleep late. Fly back and forth."

Could this be the blonde I saw leaving the other day? "Flying?" Amber questioned. "Don't you get tired of it?"

"Never," Franny said. "I fly myself to the San Francisco airport. Then, hop a 747 to Boston. I love to fly, and Cash lets me borrow his plane."

Amber couldn't believe what she'd just heard. "You're a pilot?"

"I don't fly too often anymore," Cash said.

"Oh, dear, do *not* be so modest." Franny punched Cash's arm. "He flies, he does most of his own repairs, and he taught me and Henry all he knows. Of course, he learned from James. Anyway, enough about us, Cash tells me Sarah referred to you as, Rocky?"

Amber whirled with the change of subject. It was hard to keep up with Franny.

Burns smiled. "All through high school we called her Rocky. Don't you, your brother, and Lancaster have nicknames?"

"No," Franny said. "I guess Rocky is short for Rockwell. Amber is sweet and fluffy. Rocky is a tough name. Powerful, like your red hair."

Amber's cheeks burned. Perry and Burns laughed. But she noticed Henry hadn't said a word and was frowning.

"You know," Perry said, "I think she's right,"

Franny's face turned pink. She grinned at Perry and entwined her arm around his. "You are a cute one. Just my luck you're gay. But you will do as an escort. Come along. There are some people I think you should meet. You sell antiques?" The two of them strolled off arm in arm, chatting away.

"I like your sister." Amber watched her drag Perry through the guests. "She says what she thinks."

Henry snorted. "She does at that."

Amber caught the sarcasm in his voice. "I wished I had a sister, or any family for that matter."

Henry rolled his eyes and muttered something.

Wow, did I hear—too damn confident and not beautiful enough? "What did you say?" Amber asked.

Lancaster slapped Henry on the shoulder. "He loves his sister, but she's a bit loud at times. He wishes she'd find a husband. Too bad Perry's... Even though he's much older, they make a cute couple."

Henry glared at Lancaster for a brief moment. Then he said, "If you'll excuse me, there's someone I need to speak with."

They watched him walk away. Lancaster leaned over, and in a hushed voice said, "I apologize for Henry. Normally, he's not so uptight. However, when his older sister's in town..." He hesitated, then cleared his throat. "Henry will be this way until she leaves."

"She doesn't stay with Henry?" *Boy, what an odd family.*

"She and I get along better." Lancaster smiled. "Besides, I have lots of room. I guess you're up and running too early for Franny. She's a night owl."

"I thought I'd noticed another guestroom in use, but no one said anything." Amber wondered how she'd missed this. "Too bad she can't stay with her brother. Families are important." *Wish I had mine back, including Sarah.*

"Unfortunately, Henry has this thing... let's just say it's too bad she's not a beauty. Henry could accept her better then."

"What does being beautiful have to do with how he feels about her?"

"Not certain. But, Henry gets along better with them

when he thinks the women around him are beautiful. He once had a secretary who reminded him of Franny. He couldn't function until after he fired the poor woman. Too bad—an excellent secretary."

"That's a shame." Amber thought, *Why is he telling me all this?*

From behind them, James came up with a tray of champagne. "Mr. Longreen happens to love beautiful things like paintings and women around him, just as Mr. Lancaster does. I see nothing wrong with that. By the way, we are nearly out of champagne."

"Thank you, James," Lancaster said. "Why don't you go to the cellar, pick out a bottle from my collection. Make it a Krug. I feel like celebrating tonight."

There's that awful grin. Amber furrowed her brows. "You have a champagne collection?"

"Along with my wines. Oh, I guess we forgot about that. Should those be on your inventory list?"

"They should. May I see the cellar?" Amber asked.

"Let's all see it." Clapping his hands, Lancaster yelled, "Attention, everyone, we're heading for the cellar to pick out a bottle of my best champagne. Anyone care to join us?"

The fifteen hundred square foot cellar, located through the kitchen and then down a flight of stairs, smelled damp. Amber shivered at the change in temperature. Perry, who had escaped Franny's grasp, wrapped his arm around Amber, and whispered in her ear, "How come we didn't know about this?"

"I thought this door was just a pantry. Never looked inside," Amber mumbled.

Standing just behind them, Burns said softly, "I didn't know about this either."

Oak bottle racks were stacked in rows, floor to low-ceiling, filled with wine. Labels stated red, white, rose, and sparkling; and champagne—all dated from the vintage to present, inexpensive to very expensive. The champagne and some of the wine bottles appeared clean, but dust caked several other wine bottles, as if they'd been sitting for a long time.

Champagne bottles lay in the front racks but several slots were empty. Amber thought about the champagne bottle in the car, the one she'd bought for Sarah. Musing aloud, Amber muttered, "Sarah loved champagne. Said it tickled her nose."

"Her favorite beverage," Lancaster said. "We began this champagne collection together." He caressed some of the bottles. "I haven't been down here since... I'm certain she'd love sharing a bottle with her best friend." He raised his voice. "All her friends."

He grabbed a bottle of Moët and gently stroked it. "This was the very first we purchased. I think it's fitting we drink this, don't you?" Lancaster's dark eyes almost challenged Amber to say otherwise.

She ignored his reminder. Sarah had died from Valium mixed with champagne. "It's your collection."

"That's true. And, Sarah would want this. We have to move on. Don't you agree?"

Amber wanted to throw something at him and storm out, but she bit her lower lip and tilted her head slightly forward in acknowledgement. She had to keep control like Burns. They'd agreed that they would not let Lancaster have any inclination now that they both suspected him of foul play. Otherwise the detective would pull her out of the house.

Burns laughed, and Amber felt some of the tension leave

the room. "Sarah loved that drink so much," the detective said, "you could almost nickname her champagne."

"My pet name for her," Lancaster said, smiling, "—Miss Champagne."

When he walked away, Amber elbowed Burns in the ribs. She glanced over her shoulder and mouthed, "Connection!"

CHAPTER 36

In the morning, Amber followed James down the hall to the study. She'd arrived in Carsonville last Tuesday in time for Sarah's funeral. Was she any closer to answers? She still didn't know who killed Sarah, but she knew someone inside this house committed murder.

Could James be the killer? She watched him open the roll-top desk and retrieve the binder. He'd mark off that she returned *The Last Honest Man*. Three yellow Post-It notes lay on the desk. All were written in the same handwriting, but with different initials on each one.

"Is something wrong, Ms. Rockwell?" James asked.

She blushed. "Are those notes all from the same person?" Why did she have to blush. She wasn't doing anything wrong, but she felt as if she'd been caught.

For the first time since she'd been in the house, a twinkle came into the butler's usually sinister eyes. He let forth a deep belly laugh. "Does it matter?"

Okay, that laugh is creepy, and so out of character for him. Amber held back a shudder.

239

Marie trounced in with a book in her hand and another Post-It note. She dropped the note in front of James.

"Does what matter?" the maid asked innocently.

Amber recognized the note's handwriting was similar to the others. "Did you write that?"

Strolling over to a shelf, Marie shoved the book into place. "Of course. Who else would have written it?"

James chuckled.

Amber wondered what he found so funny. "I can't help noticing that each yellow note has the same handwriting, with different initials. Is that a code?"

"No, nothing so secretive." James' smile resembled a sneer, the kind one sees in films just before a body emerges from the alien's chest.

Marie and James exchanged glances. He shook his head. The maid winked and then laughed.

Amber figured they were communicating in a language she didn't understand.

The maid said, "Back in high school—"

"Now, Marie, you can run along." James motioned her toward the doorway.

Before Marie went through the door, she spun around and finished her sentence. "James taught me his gift."

"Gift?" Amber looked from her to the butler.

James glared at Marie. "That is enough."

"Don't be so modest," the maid said. "James can mimic people."

"He can sound like others?" Amber reached out and laid her hand on the desk to keep her balance. *What was going on here?*

"No." Marie rolled her eyes. "He can copy people's handwriting. He showed all of us how. But if we leave a note, we write down our own initials."

Amber furrowed her brows. "Why?"

"Why does she continue to do it?" James asked. "I have no idea."

"Old habits are hard to break," Marie said. "Besides, I think Cash's handwriting should be copied. It's gorgeous, just like him." She glared at Amber, and then hurried from the den.

"When younger," James said, "she wrote notes, forging her parents' signatures. Not a good trick to teach her back then, or any of the others, for that matter. Would you care to peruse any more books?"

"What? No, not now, thanks." Amber rushed from the room, searching for Perry.

She found him in the dining room, munching on dry toast in between sips of black coffee. His bloodshot eyes drooped in his pale face. "Are you through eating?" Amber leaned over and placed her hands on the table. "We need to get downtown, now."

"Please don't shout," Perry whispered. "Boy, can Franny pack the champagne away. Why'd I try to drink glass per glass with her? What's the rush anyway? Is the house on fire?"

"No, I have to see Steve. Come on, let's go to the car."

Amber managed to rush Perry out to the car and as she drove out of the driveway, Perry asked, "What's up?"

"You'll never guess what I just discovered."

Perry held his head. "Whisper it to me."

"James taught everyone his parlor trick."

Amber hurried over to Burns' desk with Perry trailing behind. "Are you busy?"

The detective looked up from a stack of paperwork. "Of course not. I've nothing better to do than be at your beck and call." He pushed back from the desk.

"You're bright and chipper," Amber said.

"Sit." Burns waved his hand toward a chair. "I can't find a name I'm looking for. And, now that we know Sarah had a nickname tying her to Cash's collections, like the others—"

"There's more."

He eyed Amber, then Perry.

"Don't look at me." Perry slumped into a chair. "It's something about parlor tricks."

Amber eased into the leather-cushioned folding chair. It belched its usual satisfaction. "All right you two." She told them about James and the Post-It notes.

Burns' jaw dropped open. "He what?"

"You heard me. Marie says he has this gift, as she called it, of being able to forge people's handwriting. And he's taught everyone he knows."

"Forgery?" Burns asked. "Do you know how hard that is?"

"No, but evidently he and the others can do it."

"There's four ways to forge a signature: traced, simulation, freehand, and lifted. Traced and lifts are the easiest to detect, but the identity of the forger cannot be determined. But James has a lot of confidence and that's what forgery takes, as well as lots of practice to do freehand. Great, this narrows the suspects down."

"And all of them have had lots of time to practice." Amber crossed her arms over her chest. "Now what do you think of Sarah's so-called suicide note? Do we have enough to re-open the case?"

"I talked with the captain this morning about how we discovered the champagne collection. He was angry, but said there were valid questions. This will clinch it."

"So?" Amber asked.

"So, nothing. You stay out of that house and go home.

I take over the investigation." Burns said to Perry, "Now it's more dangerous."

Perry nodded in agreement. "He has a point."

"The good detective said that before." Amber's anger rose. The nerve of him to tell her what to do. He tried that in high school.

"I'm not leaving." She wanted to add: and get that through your thick skull, but kept that to herself. Instead Amber said, "I'm on the inside. I can help. Tell me what to do, or I'll do it myself."

"Give her a job to do." Perry rubbed his temples. "Or she'll go out on her own. I don't think you want that."

Burns' gaze went to his sister's picture. He ran a hand through his hair. "If something happens..."

Amber placed one leg over the other and tapped her foot to an invisible beat. "Don't worry. Nothing will happen to me, but I am waiting for an answer."

"Let me run some things by the captain," Burns said. "I'll get back to you."

"No way. Run them by me."

"You're not a police officer! This plays by the book, or we could blow the case. Do you want him to get away with murder?"

"He, or she, has already gotten away with it."

Burns raised an eyebrow. "You think Marie—"

"I don't know who. Could have been any one of four suspects. What do you think?"

"Lancaster's at the top of my list."

CHAPTER 37

Amber is refreshing, but is she too much? I sit in my car staring at the gray building. What are they doing in there again? Did Amber figure everything out? How? I squeeze the steering wheel and growl.

I nudge the car slowly out into traffic. What shall I do next? Why can't she leave Sarah's death alone? It's been ruled a suicide. All settled.

To calm my nerves, I drive around Carsonville. I stop the car downtown in front of the Eureka Mansion. Those tall spires and beautiful lines ease my pain. Every time I see the mansion, tension drains. It's so beautiful. I appreciate beauty. Why can women not just enjoy being admired? What makes them turn inward and decide their beauty for themselves? Then they get to thinking they know best, and desire more. I hate vanity.

Vanity killed those other women. It is my job to destroy that type of woman. They cannot get away with being vain. They spend hours making certain their hair is the right color and not a strand out of place. Make certain their lipstick matches the color of their nails. And if they don't like their friend's way of fashion, they suggest something different, mocking them. They constantly check themselves in mirrors and hardly listen to anyone when they talk, making certain they look perfect. Looking at themselves with admiration is totally unacceptable. No—vanity kills!

This is unbelievable. It's happening again.

Harriet—Rose—the first to die. No one suspects her death is anything but a suicide. Well, not until her mother receives that letter. But the Fullertons are deceased and no one suspects foul play there either. Then comes Tiffany. Thought she's the one—but no—she turns. And, she's no longer a problem.

Then Sarah—perfect for a time. But she decides she's leaving. I have to get rid of her, too.

I do not plan to kill. Circumstances come along and I have to take care of them.

It's just not fair.

I don't want to change my plans. Perhaps I should not have such high expectations. Do I set the bar too high? Each woman disappoints me. And yet, I still hope for—a completeness. Amber? Will she disappoint me, too?

I pull away from the curb and drive on. Time to make my decision. Will I kill her?

CHAPTER 38

Amber's head hurt from thinking so much.

"May I make a suggestion?" Perry asked.

"No." The detective paced behind his desk.

Perry leaned his head on one hand. "It's simple."

"What is?" Amber felt sorry for Perry who must have a splitting headache from the alcohol he'd imbibed at the party. Before he could answer, a phone rang and then another one. Those two calls sent the other detectives out of the office.

Perry massaged his temples. "The course of action."

Burns stopped walking. "What the hell are you talking about?"

"Please don't shout," Perry said. "Just sit down. If you two will give me a minute, I'll explain. Just don't yell."

The detective dropped into his chair.

Amber knew Perry had to get his thoughts together. She laid a hand on his arm. "Franny kept you quite occupied last night."

Perry continued rubbing his temples. "She wanted to

know everything about me and you, a detailed news report."

"Would you like another cup of coffee?"

"Thank you, Amber. Would you mind getting it for me?"

"If you promise not to discuss anything while I'm gone."

Amber filled a Styrofoam cup with black, acrid-smelling coffee. She thought about Burns. She wouldn't let him, or anyone else, change either her mind, or what she'd do.

Returning with the cup, she handed it to Perry. After blowing on the coffee, he took a gulp. "I don't like saying this, but you should work together. We all should."

Burns shifted in his chair. "How does this help?"

"Hear me out." Perry sipped his coffee. "Do we agree that someone killed Sarah?"

Amber nodded.

Perry glared at the detective and waited.

"Oh, all right, yeah, it's looking more like that all the time," Burns agreed.

"Sorry. I know that was hard to say." Perry shrugged one shoulder. "Anyway, let's assume all the women around Cash have been murdered. Why?"

"Good question," Burns said.

Amber wished Perry would hurry up and get to his point, but knew that he took his time piecing things together. In the end, he'd have a brilliant solution. "Steve, give Perry a minute. He's working with a handicap this morning. Besides, I trust him."

"With antiques. What about solving murders?"

"If you're hunting for something..." Perry tapped his finger on the Styrofoam cup. "You use the same deductive reasoning to locate it, whether it be antiques, or a motive for murder."

"I'll grant you that." Burns squirmed in his chair. "What's your idea?"

Perry stated the obvious. "Amber's in the house and so am I. We've snooped around, discovering a few things. We put all the pieces together—they fit and we have a list of suspects."

"Yeah, a big one," the detective said. "Anyone James knew, and taught his parlor trick to. What's the motive?"

"You're the one with the expertise. I don't have all the answers, so you'll have to help out a little here."

"Right, Perry." Burns leaned back in his chair. "Money, power—they're the usual motives for murder."

"Crime of passion."

"That too, Amber. But which one?" Burns stood.

"I need to see this on paper," Perry said.

"Oh, all right. Come on." Burns glanced around.

"You have a problem?" Amber asked.

"Just making certain no one sees you enter the room I'm taking you to. Follow me." The detective led them back to a room where a big white board was set up. Pictures of Harriet/Rose, Tiffany, and Sarah were pasted up with their names underneath each photo. Dates were written beside each one. "I haven't been idle."

Amber and Perry scanned the board. "You've been busy this morning." Perry reached out and touched Sarah's picture.

The board listed nicknames by each woman, along with rose quartz, tiffany, and champagne linking each one to Cash's collection. A line ran from all of them to Cash, with more lines connecting to his friends and staff.

Perry traced a red line from Sarah to Lancaster. "Looks like you've covered each woman."

"Yeah, but our biggest problem—what's the M.O.?

They all know Cash and his retinue, they were beauties, and their names relate to Cash's collection."

The three of them sat perusing the board. Each wrote ideas on a yellow legal pad. After updating them on Nancy winning her supposed cruise and that she was Dr. Madison's office manager, Burns went over to the computer in the room.

Amber followed and peered over his shoulder at the screen. "BeauCollec?"

"That's the company that paid for the cruise Nancy won. Doc didn't know what kind of company, but assumed it had something to do with medical. I can't discover the names of the owners. Too many subsidiaries."

Amber scribbled on her pad. "Break it down."

"Into what?" Burns asked.

"Different names using the first couple of letters and the last," Amber said.

The detective typed the information into the computer. It came up with a list faster than Amber could write on her notepad. "I hate computers, but they do come in handy. Aren't you afraid they'll replace your brain?"

Burns laughed.

Oddly, Amber found it re-assuring.

They reviewed the list on the computer screen. Burns pointed at two names. "Bingo."

"Beauty and collection?" Amber asked.

"Cash has a collection of beautiful things."

Perry wandered over. "He does, and Henry and James are obsessed with beauty."

"This is getting us nowhere," Amber said.

"Welcome to police work."

After running Lancaster's name and the names of those close to him through databases, Burns finally came up with the board members for BeauCollec.

"This is a big help." Amber looked over the list. "We're right back to where we started."

The detective pushed print and made two copies. "Let's go back out to my desk. We've been back here long enough."

The front office was still empty.

At his desk, Burns ran his finger down the list of printed names.

Amber repeated them aloud. "Cash, Henry, Franny, James, and Marie. Even Hale the cook is listed."

"Why would the maid, butler, and cook be board members?" Perry shifted in his seat.

"Another good question." Burns rubbed the back of his neck.

"But I'm finding out," Amber said, "police work is filled with good questions and not many answers. We could go ask?"

"I don't want anyone to know what we're thinking. Hey, Red," Burns called out to the detective who walked through the door. "I could use your help."

The detective with the flaming red hair came over. Amber remembered he'd given Burns Sarah's "closed file" the other day.

"Red, can you take these names? See how many business or financial connections you come up with." With a copy of the printout, the officer went over to his computer and typed in the information.

Amber asked Burns, "So, one of these people sent Dr. Madison's office manager off on a cruise about the same time Sarah, or someone, wanted more Valium?" Not expecting an answer, she continued, "One of them must have killed Sarah."

"Again, I have to ask, what's the motive? Why?"

"Haven't a clue." Amber frowned. "How do you stand this line of work?"

Burns leaned back in his chair. "I know parts of it can be frustrating, but it's like any good mystery: drives me crazy; but figuring out 'who-done-it' is worth it. Gets my adrenaline pumping, especially when you put the scumbag behind bars. I'm doing good work. Kind of like when I threw a touchdown pass. I completed my task and did it well."

"But with this, there's no applause from adoring fans," Amber said.

"True. But there are people who appreciate what I do for them."

"You're right about that." Perry crossed his arms over his chest. "I'd be happier, for Amber's sake, if you'd do it faster, though."

"From now on, we'll have to proceed with caution." Burns tapped the list lying on his desk. "Someone kills beautiful women for no reason we've come up with, other than that they seem to tie in with Cash's collection. And, Amber, you correlate quite well with his 'amber' collection."

"But there's a flaw. I'm not beautiful, and he's not my boyfriend."

"You are beautiful." Burns smiled. "You may still see yourself as that chubby high school girl, but the woman I see before me out-rivals her best friend."

Heat rose to Amber's cheeks. "Thank you, but I'm still not Lancaster's girlfriend."

"You can't be that blind." Perry let his arms drop to his sides. "Haven't you noticed the way Cash looks at you? The way he talks about you to others? He's at least smitten with you."

"Which is weird, and too close to Sarah's death. And it's not the same." Amber shuddered not liking that idea.

Burns stood and leaned over the desk, glaring at Amber. "Might be to the killer."

CHAPTER 39

I don't want to have to kill her. But, my God, they are still in the police station. What are they looking at? They're too ignorant to figure anything out. The sound of my fingernails drumming on the steering wheel vibrates through the car. Traffic noise is muffled through the rolled-up windows, but the sudden bark of a horn honking startles me.

I have to concentrate. Murder brings the death penalty, although they are so liberal in California, I'll be on death row until I die. Only if I get caught. Which I won't

Amber—too smart for her own good. Why did I pick her as Sarah's successor? Oh, beautiful, all right. Refreshing after the others. Perhaps too much of a challenge. The girl doesn't even realize she is beautiful. That *is* why she's so appealing.

Two police officers drive up and park in front of the building. As they exit the car, they look at me, and then gaze past my vehicle.

Time to go.

As I pull away from the curb, I glance in the rearview

mirror. A cop car follows. No way. They're not that smart, or fast. My heart races, my hands feel damp on the steering wheel. I slow down.

The lights on the patrol car flash. The siren erupts for one solid burst. It's so loud. I pull over to the curb, holding my breath.

The vehicle races past.

I exhale, and check my mirrors. No more police cars. I drive back toward the Eureka Mansion downtown, where I can park to think without being noticed. It is time to put a new plan in motion.

CHAPTER 40

Amber rose and leaned over the desk, glaring. *God, can I make this work and get Burns to help. I have to solve this.* "Well, are you ever going to say anything?"

Burns stared back. "I'm thinking."

"Amber, please sit down, and don't talk so loud," Perry pleaded.

Amber flopped into a chair. "Sorry, forgot about your hangover. Now that we know Sarah was definitely murdered, what are we going to do about it?"

"We don't *know*." Burns sat down in his chair. "We just *suspect*. Until we have proof, that's all we have—suspicions."

"*You* may not *know*." Amber crossed her arms. "But *I* do. I knew it all along."

Burns lifted one eyebrow.

Amber knew he wondered why she couldn't let things drop, but she had to go all the way. Since childhood, she'd been inquisitive, always asking "why." After her folks... well, she just wouldn't take, "I don't know," for an answer any more.

The detective remained silent.

Perry cleared his throat, but didn't comment.

"Someone say something." Amber studied one man, then the other. "All right, you two. You know I'm right. The only way to discover who did this is to set me up as bait."

"No! Absolutely not." Burns banged his fist on the desk. "You're not trained for it. The department would never sanction using you."

"I must admit you're both right." Perry massaged his temples again. "Detective, Amber won't rest until the murderer is discovered. The way I see it, there *is* only one way to figure out who did it. You may not appreciate Amber's suggestion, but I think she could flush out the killer. She's already involved. At the very least, Lancaster is infatuated with her."

"So?" Burns sat straighter in his chair.

Perry shifted in his seat. "We believe Lancaster being in love with these women has something to do with their deaths. As you said earlier, Detective, being obsessed might be the same thing as being in love to the killer. I don't have all the answers."

"I've made as many connections as I can." Amber leaned forward and placed her hands on the desk with her palms up. "It's time to take it further. I know you, Steve. You can't sit on your hands. For Sarah's sake, let me help put the murderer behind bars."

"What if you get hurt, or worse?" Burns asked.

Amber's voice softened. She clasped her hands. "You and Perry won't let it."

"Too many unknowns," Burns said. "It's too risky. Plus, my boss won't allow it."

"So, you'd try and insert some policewoman? That would take too long, and I bet it would never work."

"Amber's right, Detective. We could make a plan, only the three of us in on it. I'll be there to keep an eye on her. We have to try."

Burns perused the printed list of the BeauCollec's Board of Director's names.

Red walked over and dropped his copy on the desk. "I found no other connections with these names. Except this one corporation. Other than they either work for or with Lancaster." He pointed to a name on the printout.

"Thanks, Red," Burns said to the detective sauntering out of the office. He turned the list so Amber could see. "If I don't agree, you'll make a plan without me. I could lose my job. You truly want me to lose it?"

"I doubt you will, especially if you end up catching a killer. Can't you risk it to solve Sarah's murder?"

"And if there isn't one?"

Amber crossed her arms, holding her elbows. "There is, and you know it, Steve."

"Okay, I can see we'll just go around and around on this. And, you'll do it anyway. I'll help. This better not get you killed, too."

"It won't. Thanks for caring." Inwardly, Amber wrestled with herself. She came to a conclusion. "If Sarah trusted you, so can I."

Burns sat back in his chair and blinked. "Really?"

Amber lowered her lashes. "I don't have a choice."

They reviewed what information they had.

"Looks like when women are around Cash, they change." Burns stroked his chin. "In Sarah's case, she became vain. She wasn't like that before. She was beautiful, but never full of herself."

"Got that right." Amber nodded. "Cash's fiancée, Rose, changed, according to Marie, from an ugly duckling to a swan. Maybe she was vain, too?"

"And," Burns said, "I heard that Tiffany became like Sarah. Vanity must be involved."

Perry laughed. "Oh, great. Amber is supposed to get Lancaster to fall in love with her. That doesn't seem to be a reach. But, I don't think she can pull the vanity bit off."

"I did some acting in school."

"Yeah, high school." Burns came around the desk and sat in front of her. "And, if I remember right, they were one-liners."

Amber grimaced. "I can do this."

"You think so? But Perry's right. You don't even know you're beautiful. You've got a knock-out figure, you're caring, you're smart, and you're a funny woman."

Amber felt the childhood blush she'd tried so hard to overcome. She hated her habit, but grabbed a strand of hair and chewed.

"See what I mean?" Burns touched her hand with his fingertips. "A vain woman wouldn't blush when told she's beautiful."

"Nor would she chew on her hair," Perry said.

Amber ignored the tingle inside when Steve brushed her skin. She blew out the strand of hair. She hadn't felt like this in a long time. *Get a grip. Concentrate on the murder, nothing else.* "I was not in acting mode. You have to give me a chance. There's no other way."

"She has a valid point." Perry raised an eyebrow. "A dangerous, risky one."

"Oh, all right." Burns pointed a finger at Amber. "But you will wear a wire at all times. No exceptions. I want to hear everything that goes on with you, no matter where you are."

She smirked and wagged her finger at the detective. "Can I take it off in the bathroom, if I'm alone?"

CHAPTER 41

After the meeting with Burns, Perry and Amber rushed back to Lancaster's house with enough time to dress for the Tuesday night dinner party. Amber re-taped the one-way microphone to her chest, concealing it under her black dress exactly as Burns showed her. Where the tape attached, her skin itched. She tried ignoring the mechanism, but imagined X-ray eyes boring into her, people pointing fingers, and saying "Ah, hah!"

At Lancaster's dinner table, Perry leaned over and whispered in her ear, "You look fine. Nothing shows. Relax."

Amber sipped some water. The guests included the Martins, Henry Longreen and his sister Franny. James hovered, while Marie scurried in and out with shrimp cocktails, endive salad, filet mignon, and asparagus, all cooked and prepared by Hale the cook. The talk centered on Henry's campaign. Sarah's name—never mentioned.

An urge to fidget with the wire overwhelmed Amber. She fought it down. At first, when she talked with someone, she'd lean close. Three times she received looks as if she'd invaded their personal space, so she backed off, hoping Steve could still pick up the conversation. No, she had to stop thinking of him as Steve. It made it too personal. She couldn't get involved, not with him. And definitely not now.

Sweat ran between her breasts. Since her underarms were drenched, she kept her elbows close to her sides. What if the wire shorted out? She pictured smoke billowing out from her bodice.

"Is something the matter?" Lancaster asked. "You're not yourself tonight. If I didn't know better, I'd say you were hiding a secret."

Franny piped up from the other end of the table. "Did I hear the word secret? Oh, dear, that's not a word a campaign manager should say. Could start all kinds of scandals."

Everyone laughed.

Amber squirmed.

"All right," Perry said. "You've found us out."

The people at the table stared at him, including Amber.

"Oh, honey." Perry reached over and patted Amber's hand. "Let's face it; he's too smart for us. We might as well give it to him now."

Amber blinked several times and gaped.

"Give what to whom?" Lancaster asked.

"We weren't going to give the piece to you, yet," Perry said. "But, since Amber isn't too good with surprises, and all your friends are here..." Perry pushed back his chair. "If you'll excuse me, I'll be right back."

Amber forgot earlier Perry whispered to her that Tom sent some stuff out. At the time, she wondered if Sarah's letter came, but didn't find out, needing to be at the dinner table? She smiled. "Perry's right. I'm sorry I gave our surprise away."

"Darling, whatever are you talking about?" Mrs. Martin asked.

"Yes, don't keep us in suspense," Henry said.

"You know we've been inventorying Cash's collections for him, including some beautiful pieces of amber. For his hospitality and kindness, we've found an item we think he'll like very much."

"I told you that wasn't necessary." Lancaster clasped her hand.

"I know." It took all of her courage, but Amber left her hand in Lancaster's. "You've been so good, so understanding of how difficult this has been. I wanted to repay you."

Lancaster squeezed her fingers with that 'politician grin' on his face. "It's the least I could do. This has been upsetting for both of us."

Amber fought the urge to pull back. She felt like a boa constrictor had entwined her body—squeezing the life out of her, but kept smiling. Her face hurt and she wondered how much longer she could keep this up.

A minute later Perry entered with a small wrapped package.

"Our store manager sent that." Amber pointed toward the gift.

"He also sent your mail." Perry sat in his seat next to Amber. "I stacked it neatly on the dresser in your room."

"Thanks." Amber removed her hands from Lancaster and took the package from Perry. She handed the gift to Lancaster. "Go ahead, open it."

Lancaster grinned broader. He hesitated, looking around the table.

"Come on, Dear," Franny said. "Open the woman's present. I bet it is as beautiful as she."

Lancaster ripped the paper off like a three-year-old at

Christmas. He lifted the box lid and searched inside. "Did it have to be wrapped in tissue paper, too?"

Amber laughed. "I had to keep you in suspense as long as possible."

Everyone leaned forward to get a better look. Even James stepped closer to the table. Marie huddled near the butler, glaring. If the maid had a dagger, Amber figured it would be plunged into her chest. Marie was jealous.

Reaching inside, Lancaster pulled out the paper. With slow deliberation, he unwrapped the prize within. "Oh, Amber, it's beautiful." He held up a piece of amber with a scorpion trapped inside. The brownish, yellow rock almost looked like a heart. The scorpion had its claws raised, as if it would attack any moment. "It's perfect. Thank you." Lancaster leaned over and kissed her cheek.

Amber almost shuddered, as his lips stayed too long. She fought the bile rising in her throat.

"Come on, Cash, pass it around so we can admire its beauty, too," Henry said.

The gift went from person to person, each commenting on the exquisite object.

Amber beamed at Perry. He winked. The wire she wore was temporarily forgotten.

CHAPTER 42

Steve sat inside a black van parked down the street from Lancaster's home. One side was filled with electronic equipment, screens and knobs. While the detective listened in, the equipment recorded all that was said. "Nice save, Perry."

Trask MacFee, sitting alongside on a stool that looked too small to hold his weight, also wore headphones. "I thought your gal was goin' to blow it there. How'd you let her talk you into this?"

"She's persistent." Steve adjusted a dial to hear clearer. "Thanks for helping me. The captain wasn't too thrilled. He hesitated to give me any manpower. Said if I insisted on going through with my idea, it was my butt in a sling."

Why did I go out on a limb for Amber? He knew the answer. He owed it to Sarah and Amber. He had loved Sarah and wanted to marry her. He'd always been fond of Amber, even if she took Sarah away. But seeing her now, especially the beauty she'd become, he had to be there for her.

Could he lose his job? Sarah was murdered, but whether they could prove it or not—

"If this leads to what happened to Tiffany, I won't mind helpin' a bit. I hate unsolved cases. Besides, the fishin' out here is good. Think I'll stay a spell. I just hope you and that gal know what you're doin'."

"So do I, Trask. I don't think I could live with myself if anything happened to her."

"She's special, a real beauty. Trouble is—she don't even know it. She goin' to be able to pull off this pretty-gal act?"

"Guess we'll have to wait and see." Steve checked the recorder to see it was doing its job.

"What's your plan?"

"From the sound of that kiss—at least I think that's what that 'smack' was—Cash is interested in Amber. Now, if she can be subtle about turning vain. I mean it's not in her character, and if she does it quickly—"

"What if this 'vanity' thing has nothin' to do with it? Might be the length of time he's with them, or somethin' else entirely." Trask shifted and the van rocked.

"You could be right." Steve wished the man would sit still. He didn't want people to notice movement in the van. "We don't have all the answers, but time's running out."

"What do ya mean?"

"Perry and Amber are supposed to head back to New York on Saturday morning."

"Lancaster might ask her to stay longer." Trask swiveled his bulk to stare at the detective.

"But Cash won't ask Perry, and her boss won't leave without her."

"That could create a problem," Trask agreed.

"We'll have to figure this out soon. I'm hoping the recorded conversations will give us some direction. I'll get Perry to hide a camera in her room."

"That way, you can keep an eye on the little gal."

"And, no one, including my captain, should know you're

helping me." Steve was lucky Trask had come out and was eager to help. Without the retired cop, he wouldn't be able to do this.

"You think there might be a leak?"

"You said Cash had a lot of power, and my captain didn't agree with this." Steve pushed one of the headphones tighter to his ear. The sound was scratchy, so he dialed it in clearer.

"True," Trask said. "What if nothin' happens and Amber heads back to New York?"

"Amber won't leave." No matter how hard Steve tried to push her, she'd dig in her heels. What if he lost Amber? How would he handle it? When Sarah wouldn't marry him, it took him a year and a half to get over her. Accepting Sarah's murder was hard. He shuddered at the thought of losing Amber.

"What if Lancaster heads back to New York with her?" Trask asked.

"I don't want to even think about that."

CHAPTER 43

The party ended and most of the guests left. Amber squeezed Perry's hand to say good night.

"Hey, you two," Franny said. "You both know so much and are so good about shopping, let's get together and go downtown soon. The three of us could come up with some interesting items."

"I'd love to," Amber said. "I look forward to it." She figured she'd glean some more information from Franny about Lancaster, Henry, and the staff.

"Okay, dear, see you tomorrow. Come on Perry, I'm bushed and you look like you might drop where you stand." Franny grabbed his hand and they headed upstairs, Amber knew to their separate rooms.

The Martins lingered in the parlor after Henry departed. Cash clutched Amber's hand, begging her to stay with him. She hated his touch, and poured herself a drink to avoid his grasp.

Half an hour later, when the Martins said their good-bye's, Amber said goodnight to Cash and rushed to her room. She wanted to check the mail Tom had sent out with the package. At the dresser, letters were not stacked neatly. Perry's Obsessive Compulsive Disorder drove him to have all things squared. One envelope was an inch off.

Odd. Amber read the top note from Tom saying, "Hope this is what Amber's waiting for."

She rifled through the envelopes: bills, client letters, nothing from Sarah.

"Anyone still listening?" she asked, speaking to her chest. "Someone's gone through my mail. There's no letter from Sarah. How would anyone know it was here? Oh, that's right, Perry blabbed it at the table. This is awful."

Amber yanked off the one-way listening wire, realizing no one would answer her. She stuffed it in the bottom of her purse.

"Oh, Sarah," she muttered. "What am I doing?" With the flub at dinner, could she actually catch a killer? Steve was right, she couldn't act. *They'll never believe I fell for Lancaster and then became vain.*

Then Amber remembered the expression on Lancaster's face when he opened the box, and the lingering kiss on her cheek afterward. *I think he's attracted to me. At least the first part of this charade is working. Even if I can't stand it when he touches me, I don't think he knows.* Amber wanted to take a shower. She felt unclean.

But where was Sarah's letter? "Concentrate," she told herself. The maid had been in her room and turned down the bed for the evening. A carafe of tea sat on the nightstand. Had James brought the refreshment? Why would someone take Sarah's letter? If they'd already broken into her apartment in New York to take it, why now?

CHAPTER 44

The smell of bacon, eggs, and maple donuts assaulted Amber as she walked into the dining room. She stopped in her tracks. "Why are you all here for breakfast?"

Perry, Franny, Henry, and Cash chorused, "Good morning."

"Something up I don't know about?" Amber asked.

"There is, Ms. Rockwell." James pulled out a chair next to Cash.

The table was set with fine crystal goblets, Noritake China, and linen napkins. An elegant breakfast. What were they up too?

"Would you care for your usual tea this morning?" the butler asked.

"Please." Amber sat and smiled. "What's going on?"

Perry grinned. "Since we're leaving Saturday morning—"

"Unless I can convince you to stay longer." Cash put his hand over Amber's and squeezed gently.

Her first reaction was to jerk her hand away. Instead,

she kept it under his. She fought the bile down—she could do this. She had to, for Sarah. But, it took all her courage.

"Which would be great," Franny said, "because we must go shopping before you leave."

"We will." Perry smiled at Franny. "Amber, they're throwing us a party Friday night. Mrs. Martin insisted on having it at her house. Doesn't that sound like fun?"

Amber caught Perry's sarcastic tone. She was too stunned to say a word. Sarah had died on Friday two weeks ago, while everyone partied next door.

"I just love parties," Henry said. "And Mrs. Martin knows so many beautiful women. Cash, think we can do some campaigning, too?"

"Don't we always?" Lancaster's mouth twisted into that famous grin.

Amber thought of Sarah, then dug deep within herself. "Well, if you're having a party for us," she said, sliding her hand out from under Lancaster's and reached up, patting her hair, "I'll have to get my hair done."

Lancaster scrunched his eyebrows together. "Your hair done?"

"Why bother? Your hair looks fine."

"Franny, your hair is perfect. Mine, not so much. But, as you know, we girls must appear great at all times." Amber gazed down at her hands. She held them up for all to see. "My nails are a mess. I'll have to have them done, also. Does anyone know the name of the salon Sarah used?"

"She went to Headline International," the butler said. "It's down in Old Towne. However, if I may be bold, you do not need them."

"Oh, James, every woman *needs* a salon. It's time to get my makeover again, anyway." She was glad she hadn't choked on those words as she spoke. Maybe she was a good actress.

"Makeover?" Franny asked.

Amber smiled. "I couldn't look this good without help." She prayed she wouldn't blush. "I'll need to call for an appointment."

"Shall I phone and make one for you?" James asked.

"No thanks, I can do that. I think I'll skip breakfast, and go see what I can arrange."

"But, Amber," Henry said, "we got up early. I rushed over to have breakfast with you."

"Oh, darling." Amber almost gagged on the new voice she projected, "I do appreciate that—so really sweet of all of you. But if there's going to be a party for me, I have to look my sophisticated best for Cash." The coquettish smile she pasted on her face made her feel queasy. She hoped this performance was better than her high school days. "Besides, I can't add any pounds to my figure." She ran her hands down her hips. "Oh, Perry, this will be fun. I love New York parties. You know how I'm the center for those bashes. I'm sure this will be great, too."

Amber hurried from the dining room and dashed upstairs. It was all she could do to make it to her room. She closed the door and sat on the bed, clutching her chest. The expression on their faces. She laughed. This was so unlike her.

The bedroom door flew open, banging against the wall. Amber jumped up, her mouth gaped.

Marie strolled into the room. "I hear they're throwing a party for you. How nice. And you want to go to the salon, get your hair and nails done. You sound just like Sarah. Now Cash won't think so highly of you." Marie tossed towels on the end of the bed and left, not bothering to shut the door.

Amber walked to the threshold. Perry stood just outside. "Marie didn't seem too happy."

"No. What about the rest of them?"

"Stunned." Perry stepped inside and closed the door. In a hushed tone, he said, "If I hadn't been in on the plan, you would have seen my jaw drop. So unlike you. I'm proud of you." He hugged her.

"My heart raced so hard. I never get my hair and nails done. Now I have to call that salon. It's down in Old Towne, so Sarah, I bet, used it so she could see Max. I will, too."

"You scattered everybody." Perry followed Amber over to the bed and sat next to her.

She glanced up from the telephone directory, after finding the salon's number. "What do you mean?"

"Henry and Cash excused themselves right after you rushed out.

"Franny wanted to know when we'd go shopping. I told her I'd check with you, then she left. Of course, James disappeared as soon as Franny did. I guess I don't count."

"You do to me." Amber patted his hand. "Shall I make an appointment for you, too?" She pointed to the yellow pages. "Says here they have an artistic approach to hair. I need that. You could get a pedicure or a massage."

"No thanks. Maybe you should ask Franny to join you."

"I don't think so. Her hair is perfectly coiffed. Her nails look perfect. Plus she sounded appalled that I was going. She probably does that all herself and does a great job."

"You're most likely correct about that. What did Sarah write in her letter?"

"Perry, there wasn't one." Amber wondered what happened to it. "Didn't you say you put the mail over there?"

"Top right side of the dresser on the corner."

"When I came in last night, the mail wasn't stacked your

usual way. One letter stuck out. You always align envelopes in a perfect square. There was nothing from Sarah."

"Why would someone steal that letter?"

"I don't know." Amber stood and placed her fist on her hip. "But I'm going to find out."

CHAPTER 45

I'm glad I have a new plan. Wow! I can't believe Amber acts like that. What gets into these women? Could Amber be turning vain as the others did? This soon? Perhaps it's a ruse? She does suspect Sarah was murdered. No, she's not an actress. If it is true Amber is vain, then my decision is made. The woman must go. She is not the right one, either. I cannot believe I misjudged her. Another disappointment.

I'll have to perfect my plan and be very careful. Perry might be a problem. Easily handled though. How will she die? A car accident? Poison and a disappearance, or an overdose?

Rose—still hard to imagine her becoming vain. I never believed she would think she was too good for everyone. Toward the end, she could not pass a mirror without gazing into it. Then she decides she's too good for her fiancé and is going to call off the wedding. Well, that certainly could not happen. Fixing her car, getting her to drink at the salon. And then the call to upset her so she went for a drive—easy. She didn't make the curve. Now she's dead.

Who knew she'd write a letter telling her fiancé her feelings rather than talk with him in person? After her mother discovers the letter, and shows it to her husband, they might have changed the will. I have to take care of them quickly. I smile. A perfect plane crash.

Moving out West afterward—a wise decision. All the beautiful women. Tiffany comes along and fits in perfectly. The one.

Unfortunately, another disenchantment—all full of herself. Can women be just seen and not heard? Ha! The remark of a male chauvinist pig.

Getting rid of Tiffany—a tricky situation. Hard to convince that officer, but power has its privileges. A word put in someone's ear—later, the cop—no longer a problem.

I have fun in Carsonville with all its Victorian homes, antique shops. The shrimp, the crab—comparable to the East Coast. The Eureka Mansion—a real eye-pleaser, and calms my nerves. But I hate the fog.

Sarah—I enjoy her at first. Just like the others. But, I can't control her for long. Her unhappiness drives her to vanity. Miss Champagne, indeed. Lucky for me, it's her favorite indulgence. Never passes a bottle without taking a sip. A little Valium—or a lot—mixed in and "Good Night, Miss Champagne."

No one suspects a thing, except Amber. Why can't she just accept the suicide? A perfect plan, except she refuses to believe in Sarah's suicide.

One stupid mistake. The note. It should say, Dear Rocky. That little slip turns out to be my undoing. Like a dog with a T-bone, Amber cannot let it go.

Too late now. Rocky—what a nickname! Too inquisitive. Now, it seems, too vain. But, I will not make any more mistakes. I finalize my plan for 'Dear, Rocky.'

CHAPTER 46

Amber drove downtown with Perry. "I need to catch Max in Old Towne. I also want to see this salon I'm going to on Friday."

"What will Max tell you?" Perry asked. "To be careful. Why worry him?"

"I'm not going to worry him. Is anyone following us?"

Perry looked out the back window. "No, and if Detective Burns is any good, I don't expect to see anyone. You're wired, aren't you?"

"That was the deal. I'm wired all the time from here on. I bet he's not following us?"

"Burns or someone is."

"Oh, Perry." Amber spoke toward the microphone. "I know Steve's ego. He can't stand being told he's wrong," she said, a bit louder than she needed to. "You're too trusting. Steve still thinks Sarah took her own life, but I planted a little doubt. He has to check it out to prove me wrong."

"Steve?" Perry grinned. "Now you're calling him 'Steve?' Well, at least the detective is going along with us, and I think he's smarter than you give him credit for. He knows it's murder now. And, you know he believes that."

Amber blushed. *I must remember to call him Burns. This is too important. I have to stay focused.*

After parking the car, Perry and Amber walked up to the carriage by the curb. The old horse, Wally, had his head down, eyes closed. Max sat in the seat, reading the paper.

Amber rubbed the horse's velvety nose, waking him up. She fed him an apple. "Hello, Max." Wally's big lips curled around the fruit. The horse crunched the treat.

"Hi, Rocky. How would you like a carriage ride?" Max stored the paper under the seat.

"I'd love one, thank you." Smiling, Amber climbed aboard and extended her hand to help Perry in.

Max clicked his tongue and shifted the reins. Wally plodded off, horseshoes clacking on the pavement.

Amber scooted forward to the edge of her carriage seat, so Max could hear her. She gripped the back of his seat. "Did Sarah see you on the day she died?"

"I told you she stopped by. She'd been down to that hair place on First Street. In a hurry to get back to some party. A bit tipsy, but she took time to feed Wally an apple."

"Tipsy?"

"Seems the salon served her champagne while fixing her up."

"Did she say anything?" Amber asked.

"Like she was heading home to kill herself?" Max snorted. "No, afraid not. Unhappy? Yes. Did she kill herself? I doubt it. She talked about modeling again, and about waiting to hear from you with a reply to her letter."

"Did she mention the contents?"

"Rocky, she didn't stay all that long. Said something about returning to New York, soon."

"Did you tell Detective Burns?"

"He never came around to ask."

"I told him about you." Amber bit her lip. "He hasn't been by?"

"Haven't seen him."

"See, Perry, he's not totally into this."

The carriage slowed as it passed the Eureka Mansion. Amber scanned the area, looking back over her shoulder. She didn't see anyone following them.

"I can't believe Detective Burns hasn't spoken with you, Mr. Kazinsky," Perry said.

"Call me Max. I can. As I said earlier, Steve and I never got along."

"It's his job to question you," Amber said in a louder tone. "I'm coming down on Friday to Headline to get my hair done. I'll stop and see you after. By then the detective will have talked with you."

"I'll look forward to seeing you." Max pulled the carriage to the curb.

Amber chewed on the inside of her lip and wished she could pound some sense into Steve. Was Burns out there listening? Why did he act as if he didn't want to solve this case?

CHAPTER 47

Steve sat in the van listening to Amber's conversation. He'd given the retired cop a two-way listening/speaking device, so he knew Trask heard, as well.

"Are you catchin' this?" Trask broke into Steve's thoughts.

"I am. Where are you?"

"I'm followin' along on the street, pretendin' to window shop. I'm keepin' an eye on the carriage. The gal's right. You should have interviewed the carriage driver."

"But I've been focused on keeping Amber safe and delving into Cash's past." Steve knew he'd messed up, but wouldn't admit it out loud to Trask. "Anyone following Amber?" Steve wished he was on the street, but didn't want to be spotted.

"I haven't noticed anythin'," Trask said. "Wait. There's that same car I saw at the other end of Old Towne. Wonder if it's followin' the gal?"

"Can you get the license plate?"

"Too far away. It's a black sedan," Trask said. "The

carriage is turnin' around. Probably headin' back to the brick plaza."

Steve hated being in the dark. When Trask didn't say more, Steve fidgeted. He read Dr. Madison's profile on Lancaster. Not too much new information, other than the doc believed if Cash was pushed, he would be capable of murder. *Aren't we all,* Steve thought.

Was he doing the right thing? That nagging doubt itched at him. "What's happening?"

"Nothin'," Trask said. "I crossed the street and am window-shoppin' back. By usin' the reflection in the glass, I can see the driver's sittin' inside the sedan. I can't tell if it's a man or woman, or if even watching the carriage. Still too far away to catch any numbers."

Steve fiddled with a dial. The van didn't have any back windows. Second Street would be bustling with people visiting the antique stores, and watching the bay from the gazebo. The aromas of seafood would be wetting their appetites. His own stomach grumbled.

"Wait," Trask said. "The carriage is stoppin'! Now the parked car's drivin' away in the opposite direction."

"Sounds like nothing." Steve waited for Trask to say more.

"I hope so. Amber and Perry are headed for their car. I'll go talk with the carriage driver."

Steve couldn't see Amber's car, but heard them walking along the sidewalk. He also listened to Trask's conversation.

"Nice horse," Trask said.

"He and I've been pals for a long time. We don't miss much, neither. How come you're following the people I had in my carriage?"

"No." Trask chuckled. "You don't miss much. Notice anybody else following them? I didn't."

"Not that I could tell. You a cop?"

"Retired, but workin' with Detective Burns."

"Rocky know about you?"

"Rocky? Oh, you mean, Amber."

"As I asked before, is she working with you?"

"Yep. But she don't know I'm followin' her."

"No, she doesn't," Max said. "What's going on?"

"We're checkin' into Miss Hudson's death. Can you tell me anythin'?" Trask asked.

"If you were listening, just what I told Rocky."

"Her nickname. Is that what got her onto the scent?"

"Yep," Max stated. "The note was addressed to 'Amber' instead of 'Rocky'."

"Someone don't know about the nickname," Trask said.

"Or didn't choose to use it, trying to send a message."

Steve heard the horse snort. Then rattling, and he figured Wally must have shifted his weight, moving the harness.

"What do you mean, trying to send a message?" Trask asked.

"Keep an eye on your detective. Never did trust that boy. Why didn't he come to me and ask me about Sarah?"

"Good question. I'll check that out."

"If you're tailing Rocky and her boss, you best get after them."

"Thanks for your help," Trask said.

"Yep. You keep her safe."

Through the headset, Steve made out the sound of footsteps. Trask was on the move.

"Hey, there's a black sedan," Trask said. "Wonder if it's the same car I saw earlier? Still can't make out the driver or the license plate. Guess I need glasses. I'm gettin' too old for this. Should someone follow it?"

"Are you positive it's the same one?" Steve asked.

"It's black is all I can say."

"Let's stick with Amber," Steve said. "She's heading back to the house."

CHAPTER 48

Lancaster invited Henry and Franny, Detective Burns and the Martins to dinner. James poured wine into Amber's glass. Marie placed a salad in front of Lancaster. While the maid served the other guests, Amber chewed on her lip. Burns and she planned this next scene. She prayed she could be convincing.

Amber inhaled deeply. "Steve, did you ever find out about that woman's trip?"

He stopped in mid-bite. "Trip?"

"You know, the one who won a cruise, but she didn't remember the contest." Amber didn't fidget with the wire, but wondered why she had to wear it since Burns was sitting right across from her. "I forget her name. Nancy something or other. That psychiatrist's secretary."

Burns set down his fork and dabbed his lips with a linen napkin, appearing deep in thought. "Oh, right, Dr. Madison's office manager. Some company by the name of BeauCollec sent her on a vacation. Dr. Madison figured it came from some medical sales corporation that she dealt with through the office."

Franny dropped her fork, Henry choked on his food. Lancaster set down his wine a little too hard, spilling on the lace tablecloth.

When James hurried forward to clean up the mess, Lancaster waved him away. "What's this about, Steve? Someone won a trip? Why would you be interested?"

Burns glanced around the table. He nodded toward Amber. "She went to see the psychiatrist who gave Sarah the prescription of Valium. Dr. Madison mentioned his office manager had left on a vacation—all expenses paid, due to some contest she'd won."

"Only," Amber interrupted, "Steve learned the woman didn't remember entering a contest. He checked it out for the doctor. BeauCollec, Inc. paid for all the expenses: flight and ship. Dr. Madison said maybe some medical corporation. Must have been a salesperson signed her up for a drawing."

Henry, Cash, and Franny all exchanged confused looks, giving little shrugs. Amber couldn't tell if the name meant anything to any of them.

"Doctor Madison will ask his office manager about it." Burns picked up his wine glass. "I think she's due back Friday." He took a sip.

"What's that have to do with anything?" Henry asked.

"Don't know." The detective forked in a bite from his salad and crunched on a carrot. Then he swallowed. "Amber was curious. She's going to talk with the lady before she flies back to New York on Saturday. Me, I'm satisfied." Burns jabbed a tomato.

Amber eyed Perry. "I have a hair appointment Friday afternoon at Headline International. Want to come along?"

"I think not. I'll rest up for the party." Perry asked Lancaster, "What time does it start?"

"Six o'clock cocktails—"

"Oh, perfect," Amber interrupted. "My appointment is in the afternoon. I'll just make it back in time to change my clothes and look gorgeous." Those words stuck in her throat, but she managed to get them out. "I'll meet you all next door."

Perry chuckled. "I suppose you want to make one of your famous grand entrances."

Amber hadn't been staying here long, but she knew that everyone would think she was acting out of character. Using a throatier voice, she said, "Always. After all, I *must* make a great impression for these West Coast people. Oh, by the way, Cash, darling, if there's nothing on for Thursday, I thought I'd show Perry around the area."

Lancaster stared open-mouthed. A few seconds ticked off. Had she gone too far? Then he muttered, "That's fine. Henry and I have an appointment with our finance officer Thursday and another meeting in the evening."

"Great," Amber said. "I can do some clothes shopping, too, although I don't know what I could possibly find to fit me in this backwoods town."

"Well, dear, maybe I could show you a couple of dress shops I found here." Franny smiled.

Amber nodded. She'd forgotten she'd promised to go shopping with Franny. "Sounds like a plan. Perry and I could sightsee in the morning and then go shopping after."

"I look forward to it."

The news about the office manager flustered a few of them, but James, of course, gave nothing away. Amber wondered if they even knew they belonged to the BeauCollec Corporation? Why had none of them mentioned it? Burns pulled his part off, acting like the satisfied detective, making it sound as if she was the only problem.

Would it push the killer over the edge?

CHAPTER 49

Amber and Perry left early in the morning and toured the area. She showed him the Humboldt University campus and took him to a beach to see the Pacific Ocean. The wind blew and the salty air stiffened her skin. Perry dipped his toe in the cold water.

When they finished seeing the sites, they went back to Lancaster's.

"Franny, you ready to go shopping?"

"I can't wait, Perry. Where to?"

"I need a dress for the party." Amber drove downtown.

"I know just the dress shop." Franny walked them to a storefront. She pushed open the door. "I think you'll like this place."

The owner called out, "Ms. Longreen. So nice to see you again."

Franny admired herself in the mirror and pointed to Amber. "She requires a dress for a party. You have something as beautiful as she is?"

Amber blushed.

"You're blushing." Franny laughed. "How quaint."

While Amber tried on several dresses Franny handed her, Perry asked, "So, how long have you known Cash?"

"Henry, he and I go back a long time." Franny handed Amber a sleek, black dress.

"I like that one." Perry asked Franny, "You always stay at Cash's and not your brother's?"

"Cash has more room."

Perry kept asking more questions about Lancaster, Henry, and the staff.

Franny's answers didn't divulge anything detrimental about anyone. She punched Perry on the arm. "If I didn't know better, I'd say you were grilling me about marriage material for you." She laughed when Perry turned red.

Amber bought the black dress. Then they drove back to Lancaster's.

"Thanks for shopping with us Franny. I had fun. Come to New York and we'll have an adventure there."

"I'd love to do that, Amber. Of course, Perry has to join us."

"I wouldn't miss it." Perry grinned.

At dinner that night, Franny smiled. "We had a successful shopping trip today. Amber found a great party dress."

Cash took a bite. "Why didn't you buy a dress for yourself? You should where one once in awhile."

Franny chuckled. "You know I prefer pants. More comfortable."

The dinner conversation revealed nothing personal about any of them, or Sarah.

Later Amber shut the door to her bedroom. She removed her blouse and ripped the wire from between her breasts. "Lot of good this did me today." She threw the wire into her purse then shoved it under the bed.

All night long she tossed and turned, dreaming of shadowy figures laughing at her.

CHAPTER 50

Amber awoke tired and cranky Friday morning. After taping on the wire, she dressed in a blouse and pants.

Time dragged on. She snapped at Perry and wondered if she chased after phantoms.

At the salon appointment, she felt every tight muscle in her body. Instead of vamping, she'd rather be browsing through antiques. But, she'd agreed to do it. In fact, it had been her idea. *I sure hope this works.*

Amber wrinkled her nose at the smell of perms and nail lacquer. Women sat in swivel chairs, getting their hair done, receiving manicures and pedicures. They even entered private rooms to have facials. Amber dreaded the experience. There was nothing she hated more than being fussed over.

When an Asian woman called her name, Amber gritted her teeth and strolled into a room where the walls glowed a soft pink. She donned the terry robe and slouched into a padded leather chair. She angled her face up toward the esthetician who applied a lavender lotion to her face. It shocked Amber that the aromatherapy facial felt good. The muscles in her face relaxed. After the head and neck massage, her shoulder's tension loosened.

When finished, she went back out to the main room where a blonde stylist worked with her hair. The receptionist brought Amber a bottle of Brut champagne and poured a glass. "This is for you, with compliments."

Amber didn't want it, but knew Sarah had some, so took it. While the hairdresser named Cindy washed and styled her hair, Amber pretended to sip the bubbly. When no one watched, she tossed the contents into the ice bucket. Each time Amber emptied her glass, Cindy refilled it. *I wonder if this happened to Sarah?*

The stylist piled Amber's hair on top of her head—artistically done, as the ad in the phonebook said.

Amber moved to the pedicure chairs, where the back vibrated, massaging her muscles. A young Vietnamese girl with short dark hair placed Amber's feet in warm, blue-colored water. Amber now understood why Sarah enjoyed this treatment. Tension drained from her taut body.

The young girl painted Amber's toenails a cherry color, drawing flowers on her big toenails. Then she shaped and colored Amber's fingernails a matching red. Amber started to bite her nails, but stopped herself—she had to be perfect for the upcoming party.

She never pampered herself this way, and when she received the bill, she gasped. She'd never do this again.

Amber caught her image in a mirror. *My God, is that me?* Her wild red hair was tamed. Her nails were fancy and her face was relaxed. Amber thought about the differences between Sarah and her. Sarah was so vivacious, enjoying her beauty, while Amber was content with studying how things were so beautiful. Hard to believe the creature in the mirror was Amber—definitely not Rocky.

No charge was asked for the several glasses of

champagne that had been poured. Amber was able to dump the glasses, but she deliberately slurred her speech slightly and didn't walk in a straight line, as if she imbibed them.

After leaving the salon, she surveyed Old Towne. If Burns followed her, she couldn't spot him. No one else looked familiar. She figured that was a good sign. Amber staggered, hoping to fool anyone watching that she'd drunk too much champagne. She weaved toward the little brick plaza, hoping to catch Max and Wally before they had another fare for a carriage ride.

A man dressed like Max climbed into the carriage to take an older couple on a tour. She placed her hand above her eyebrows forming a visor and examined the person. Not Max. The man struck the reins, and Wally plodded off before she could reach the carriage. "Wait," she yelled, waving, but the driver didn't see her. Where was Max? Was he all right?

Amber reflected on those questions for a minute, and decided she might be paranoid. Why would anything happen to Max? After all, he did deserve a day off.

She hurried in a zigzag line for her car. Inside, she spoke into the space between her breasts. "Anyone out there listening? Max Kazinsky, the carriage driver, isn't around. It might be his day off, but could someone check it out? I talked with him on Wednesday, and told him I'd see him today. He said nothing about feeling ill or taking time off. I'm heading back to Lancaster's."

CHAPTER 51

Steve dreaded disappointment on Trask's face. The retired cop swiveled in his seat and the van rocked. "Didn't you ever follow up on the carriage driver?"

"Figured I had all the information I needed after you talked with him."

"You're getting pretty sloppy." Trask frowned and adjusted his headset. "You heard my brief chat. The old man is sharp. He spoke with Sarah the day she died."

"Sounded like he had no pertinent information." Steve ran a hand through his hair. What was the matter with him? He was better than this.

"He might have seen someone followin' her." Trask shook his head. "He knew about me followin' Miz Rockwell. I bet the old guy never misses work. I'd check it out if I were you."

"Guess I'm not myself." Steve looked down at the floor. "I'm too involved with Amber. If she's hurt, or—"

"She'll be fine."

Steve fiddled with a dial in the van. "But what if—"

"Quit worryin'." Trask slapped Steve on the back. "The killer won't succeed."

Steve didn't have time to check on the driver, but he used his cell phone to call the office. "Red, please check on a Max Kazinsky. If he's not at home, call Old Town Carriage Company. See if they know where he is. Get back to me as soon as you locate Kazinsky."

"That's more like it." Trask nodded his approval.

Steve drove to Lancaster's to get ready for what he hoped would be a revealing of the killer. If not, his career was over. Worse yet, Amber's life may be in jeopardy.

CHAPTER 52

Amber drove up the circular driveway to Lancaster's place, the back of her neck tingling. She didn't see Burns' van anywhere. She thought about Sarah. Déjà vu? Speaking to her breasts where she taped the wire, she said, "Testing one, two, three. Hope you can hear me?" God, she wished Burns had given her a two-way mike. She could have covered the earpiece with her hair.

Not seeing the van didn't mean anything. Burns might have parked around the corner. He informed her he'd stay out of sight. Maybe boredom set in while he listened to her at the beauty parlor. She smiled, remembering all that girl talk. Did it drive him crazy?

The lawn was freshly manicured. The Victorian sprawled above her and the curtains at the parlor window fluttered. A warm afternoon for Carsonville, but she felt cold. She wondered if Sarah felt this way on that fateful Friday, two weeks before.

After exiting the car, Amber took a deep breath, and muttered, "Here goes nothing." She slammed the door. As she zigzagged up the walkway, she patted her hair. Then she admired her nails.

After throwing open the mahogany front doors, she yelled, "James? James, are you here?" She knew there wouldn't be any answer. He would be next door, helping with the Martins' party. Mail lay on the sideboard. Drawn to it, she inspected the envelopes and shuffled through them. Nothing for her. She stacked the mail and then noticed her reflection in the mirror. Why would I expect any mail? Did Sarah look in this mirror, too? Did her friend really become so vain? Amber wondered if she would have recognized Sarah. She couldn't have changed that much. They were together a year ago at Amber's Mom's funeral. They talked on the phone, exchanged letters.

"Letter," Amber muttered. "Wonder what happened to Sarah's letter to me?"

Still gazing into the mirror, she leaned closer, rotating her head slowly from side to side. She never looked in mirrors at herself this long. An eyelash had fallen on her cheek. She flicked it off. Then she drew her gaze down to her nails. She made herself lift her hand and study the back. Then she rolled her hand over and dropped her fingers, staring at the painted nails. This was so uncomfortable she wanted to grab a strand of hair and chew, but bit her lip instead. Aloud, she said, "Headline International does a nice job. Sarah picked the best places to go." Amber drew her gaze away from the mirror and trudged up the stairs to change for the party.

Halfway up the steps, she heard a creak. She stopped. Turning around, she called out, "Is anyone there?"

Nothing.

She listened, and then asked, "James, is that you?"

No one answered her. She chewed on her lip and walked up the steps. She hesitated. "Marie, are you here?" No response. Her heart raced, but she continued climbing the stairs.

As she reached for the door handle of her bedroom, a door hinge squeaked. Peering down the hall, Amber yelled, "Perry, are you up here?"

Again, no answer. Perspiration ran from under her arms. Why had she agreed to do this? Her heartbeat thundered in her ears. She should take a hot shower to calm her nerves before going to the party. Of course that would ruin the hair job. She crossed the threshold into her bedroom, and swung the door back. She wanted to close it all the way, but left it open a crack as Steve told her to do.

On the dresser sat an arrangement of fresh, blood-red roses in a crystal vase. Their beauty took her breath away. But what caught her attention was what sat on top of the nightstand.

A silver tray held an ice bucket with a bottle and an etched crystal glass. She swallowed hard, thinking that this is what had been left on Sarah's nightstand. Now, Brut champagne waited for her. Amber didn't enjoy champagne as much as Sarah, but she'd tried to let everyone know that Brut was her favorite. Tingling sensations ran through her. She spun around. No one peeked through the crack in the doorway.

Instead of picking up the bottle and pouring a glass, she strolled to the window, staring straight out. The neighbors' backyard could barely be seen from here. Through the bushes she could see people standing around the pool, holding drinks and talking. Was Perry over there, or hiding out somewhere in the house? Where was Steve? Amber was cold.

Alone.

She had to believe someone was out there somewhere. Listening? Watching?

Were Burns and Perry in the house? She went to the closet and opened it. She whispered, "Anyone here?"

Of course, that was stupid. They weren't going to answer her. They couldn't. No one lurked behind her clothes. Rolling her eyes and feeling the heat in her cheeks, she pulled out the new black cocktail dress and laid it on the end of the bed. Why hadn't she made Steve go over this plan more thoroughly?

CHAPTER 53

My final plan is in motion. I stand behind a curtain and see her drive up. Amber's hair looks different. And those red fingernails... The color reminds me of spilled blood. How appropriate. She talks about how New York is more sophisticated than Carsonville. She *is* vain, just like the others. Unfair, but such is life. I realize she's predictable now, a final sin.

Amber talks to herself and seems to be focused, studying everything. Too curious for her own good. Great care will have to be taken to get away with this cleansing of vanity. But the risk is worth taking. The Lancaster house is empty. All the staff, and everyone else is at the Martins' except for me—just like last time.

It's easy to get away from the party. I excuse myself, slip into the Martins' house, and, while alone, sneak out a side door and rush next door. The side gate between the properties makes it simple. If anyone comes over to Lancaster's, I'll hold up a bottle of champagne—an excuse for being here. After Amber goes upstairs, I wait until she is out of sight. As I pass the hall mirror, I can't help but glance at me. I look good. I smile. Then I creep up the steps.

Will Amber drink the champagne in her room right away, like Sarah? I hope so. Time is important.

I peek through the open door. Amber stands at the window, the champagne untouched. Will she spot the letter poking out from under the tray? Not supposed to. It's the reason she kills herself. The excuse everyone will believe. Sarah's letter. Telling her how upset Sarah is, how desperate she is, how if Rocky didn't come to Carsonville, she'd kill herself.

This time, I address the letter to "Amber," but make certain the name "Rocky" appears several times within the contents. No more confusion as to who writes it.

Amber turns toward the crack in the door. I pull back. Can't be seen now. That will ruin everything. *Come on girl, drink the champagne.*

I spy through the crack again. That new black cocktail dress lies at the end of the bed. Amber is next to the nightstand, pouring champagne into a glass. She holds it up.

CHAPTER 54

Champagne flowed into the glass as Amber poured. Was it laced with Valium, like Sarah's must have been? Maybe a poison? She wanted to scream, "I can't do this!" but she kept filling her glass.

She set the bottle down and wandered to the dresser where the vase of roses rested. Her hand shook. The bubbles hissed, like the sound of a snake. She looked out the window. No one could see her from outside.

With her back to the bedroom door, she held the glass aloft and gazed at the liquid. Could she see toxins? "To Sarah. May you rest in peace."

Amber put her lips together and lowered the glass towards her mouth. "Hope you're ready out there," she whispered.

Keeping her mouth closed, she placed her lips on the glass and tilted her head slightly back. Some champagne dribbled down her chin. She made it look as if she took sip after sip, eventually drinking the entire glass.

With her back still to the door, she touched the roses, and then poured the liquid into the vase. Amber hoped if anyone peered in from behind, they couldn't see. "Mmm, tasty. Think I'll have another glass." She slurred her words.

Back at the nightstand, she filled her glass with more champagne.

She strolled to the flowers again, and caressed the petals. God, what if it *was* a corrosive agent this time? Would the tiny bit that dribbled onto her lips kill her? Had she screwed up? She controlled the urge to throw the glass and run. She lifted the glass. "Oh, Sarah, why did you do it?" Amber appeared to drink again, but dumped it into the vase. She walked back to the bottle to refill her glass.

If the champagne was laced with Valium, Amber had to act. Lying down on the bed, she curled into a fetal position, still holding the glass. She yawned and murmured, "I don't understand why I'm so tired all of a sudden."

Then, she spotted a corner of paper under the tray.

The glass fell from her hand. She attempted to reach out, but didn't make it to the paper. She whispered, "What's that under the tray?"

She allowed her eyelids to close.

CHAPTER 55

I'm happy she drinks so much more champagne. Smiling, I still spy through the doorway. Amber's head is resting on her arm. She looks so beautiful. What a shame, but I have to kill her. Headline assures me she drank the champagne bottle while getting her hair done. Two full glasses of champagne now will be more than enough. I push the door open and move to the bed.

Amber blinks. In slurred speech, she says, "Oh, it's you. What are *you* doing here?"

"It appears I'm cleaning up a little mess. That is my job. I clean up messes."

"I don't understand," Amber mumbles.

I reach out my gloved hand to brush a strand of her hair aside. "You had to become vain, didn't you? You, Amber, are so perfect. But then you all change, become full of yourselves. And, you could not accept Sarah's death as a suicide. You should have let it go. So what if she didn't call you Rocky. Did she call you Rocky *all* the time? I doubt it. She uses Amber in her letter to you."

"Letter?" Amber manages to say.

She's succumbing to the valium like Sarah. I pull the envelope from underneath the tray. "Yes, this one."

I remove the letter and place Amber's hand around it to get her fingerprints on the paper. "Sarah addresses her letter to you with 'Amber' and she says if you don't come to Carsonville, she'll kill herself. Of course, I say 'Rocky' in the body. You are so guilty over reading it, you do the same thing."

I grab the Valium bottle from my pocket and squeeze Amber's fingers around it. Then I let the vial and letter fall to the floor. With a fresh bottle of champagne, I pour two glassfuls into the unused glass. Then, I open the window and check to make certain no one is looking up this way. After throwing the liquid outside, I fill the glass part way with the unlaced bubbly and close the window.

"Well, dear, I have to get back to the party. Someone will wonder why you're not there and come searching for you. Probably Perry. Don't worry. I will console him for you. He'll have to learn to adjust. You should have stayed the same. Vanity killed you."

I clutch the tainted bottle of champagne and Amber's original valium-laced glass. After surveying the scene, I pat her on the head and walk to the door.

CHAPTER 56

Amber stayed curled on the bed, eyes closed, trying not to shake. Any movement and the killer would know she was faking. She couldn't believe that the person standing next to the bedside murdered Sarah.

Those listening now understood that Sarah hadn't overdosed herself. *Oh, my God, what if the electronics failed and Steve hadn't heard. If he did hear, did he recognize the voice?*

Vanity—what a motive. Amber couldn't believe it killed Sarah, and now, someone was trying to end her life.

Shuffling noises near the bed made her heart race. What if valium and champagne wasn't for her? Could a knife be about to plunge into her body? How had the others been slayed? Not all by valium. Amber wanted to scream, or run, but didn't dare move.

Why weren't Steve and Perry rushing in to arrest the murderer? Footsteps receded away from the bed. The door creaked open.

Nothing happened.

"Hey guys," Amber whispered, "where are you? The killer's getting away."

She stole a glance through one eye in time to see the door close. Thinking Steve would grab the killer outside to protect her, she waited.

No sounds of a scuffle.

Nothing.

She jumped up and ran to the door.

It flew open. Steve almost collided with her. "Rocky, are you all right?"

Amber shoved him aside and glanced up and down the hall. "Where's the—?"

"Shh, Rocky, let's get inside."

Steve guided her back to the bed. For a moment, she didn't say a word. She gazed up at him. "You called me Rocky?"

Steve reached out to caress her cheek. *The twinkle in his eyes... my God, he cares about me.* An electric tingle coursed through her body.

Before either could speak, Perry stepped inside the room, followed by a big man who appeared ready to tackle someone. "Amber, you did great," Perry said.

Steve drew his hand back and let it fall to his side.

"Thanks." Amber pointed to the champagne and glass. "I didn't drink any of that stuff, but some of the original spilled onto my lips. If it's poison... I poured it into the flower vase. Did you hear everything?"

"Every word," the big man said. "'Cause of Detective Burns and your friend here, we even have pictures."

"Pictures?"

"Movies, to be exact," Perry said. "Remember, I told you I'd install a surveillance camera in your room while you were out? And, because you gave the detective permission, it's legal."

Amber asked, "Really?"

"Since it's in your room," Steve said, "and you gave

permission, the pictures should hold up in court. Even though you're wired, we decided a video would be better than having someone hide in the closet. What was that 'Anybody here' stuff?"

Amber's cheeks burned. "I was so scared. I felt all alone."

"You weren't," said the big man. "We were in the next room, ready to rush right in."

"Who are you?" The man resembled a linebacker.

"Sorry," Steve said, "this is Trask MacFee. A retired L.A. cop now living in Florida. He worked on Tiffany Baintree's disappearance."

"Yep, and thanks to you," Trask said, "I now have a good idea what happened to her."

"You're welcome. Steve, why didn't you stop—?"

"I didn't want to take a chance you'd get hurt," Steve interrupted. "Besides, I need to see if any of the others are involved."

"You think there's more?" Amber asked.

"We'll find out." Steve strolled toward the door. "Now we get back to the Martins' party."

"Guess I better change." Amber picked up the black dress on the end of the bed.

"No, come dressed as you are. A few minutes ago, Perry sneaked out, ran to the Martins, and told Lancaster he was worried and would come over to check on you. Trask and I will go back. He'll cover an exit. I'll get close to our killer then you and Perry walk in. I'd like to see the expressions on some faces."

"You think that will tell you if they're involved?" Amber hung the dress in the closet.

"It's a start, but no proof," Steve said. "Let's go find out. Give me a minute to round everyone up."

At the nightstand, Amber reached for the fallen letter.

"No, don't touch it. Leave it on the floor."

"But I want to read it."

"Doesn't matter. That's not Sarah's original letter."

"How do you know?"

"Because of your apartment break-in. The killer stole the original and wrote this one."

"But—"

"Rocky, please. The crime lab guys are waiting in the hall. Let them do their work. Let's hope the killer made a mistake."

CHAPTER 57

Five minutes later, Amber and Perry hurried over to the Martins. They entered the front door and crossed through the room to a sliding glass door leading out to a patio. Amber surveyed the scene before opening the door.

It shocked her. The scene reminded her of the bash Lancaster had for Sarah's funeral. Men in suits and ties; women in cocktail dresses, jewelry glistening from their ears and necks, stood drinking from crystal glasses.

She blinked her eyes. Only difference—Tiki torches lined the pool. A table with a lace covering held china filled with crab cakes, salmon pate, and much more. A chocolate fountain with strawberries sat in the middle. Glass bowls filled with candles which flickered from bistro tables positioned around the patio. Revelers stood in clusters near the food or chatted in pairs and trios at the tables. Amber wished the party were real and Sarah were there to enjoy it with all these beautiful, smiling people. But it would all come to an end the minute she walked in.

From inside the house, she saw Steve standing with Lancaster, Henry and his sister Franny. Marie and James hovered nearby. Hale was next to the barbecue. Amber wondered if the big retired cop was pawing through the trash for the other champagne bottle.

Steve glanced toward the glass door. He gave a slight nod. She took her cue. Opening the door, and arm in arm with Perry, she strolled out into the fresh air. Amber observed all of their faces.

Lancaster spotted her first. He wore a pin-striped blue suit and a bright red tie. He put on his grin she detested then frowned, scrunching his eyebrows together. Maybe because she had on slacks and a shirt.

Henry, dressed in a black, silk suit, acknowledged her with a bow of his head.

Marie wore a black bolero jacket, white low-cut blouse and short black mini skirt—her idea of a maid's outfit. She turned one corner of her mouth down, and Amber knew if the maid could, she'd stomp her foot.

James, dressed in his usual butler's outfit, standing ramrod straight, noticed her and smiled.

Amber couldn't see Hale's face because he had his back to her as he flipped a filet mignon steak.

Franny almost dropped her wineglass, spilling wine down her silk pants. Her face paled. "It can't be."

"Hi, Franny. What can't be?" Amber asked as she and Perry joined the group.

"You are not..." Franny looked at the others. "You are not dressed, dear."

"No, Franny, I'm not," Amber said. "Anything else you want to add?"

"Me?" Franny knitted her brows together.

"Ah, you disappoint me." Amber patted her heart. "You just tried to kill me, and you don't want to gloat about it to the others?"

Lancaster choked, spewing the champagne he'd just sipped. "Kill you?"

Henry glared at his sister. "What have you done now?"

"Why didn't you succeed?" Marie asked.

James came to attention. "Are you all right, Ms. Rockwell?"

"I am, James. Thank you for asking." Amber eyed Franny, holding back the urge to slap her. "Why?"

Franny stood taller. "I don't have any idea what you're talking about."

Amber let go of Perry's arm. She stepped away from him, and ripped her blouse open, exposing the wire. "There was a camera, too." She blushed, glad she wore a lacy brown bra.

Franny threw her wine glass down and lunged at Amber. She spun her around. With her superior height, she wrapped one arm around Amber's neck in a chokehold. "You bitch," she hissed and pulled the two of them back a step from the group.

Henry's mouth dropped open. "Franny, what are you doing?"

Steve drew his gun. "Franny, it's all over. You can't get out of this."

"What's going on here?" Lancaster's eyes widened. "Franny, no—you wouldn't."

Perry stepped closer. Amber held out her hand, warning him to stop.

Steve grabbed Perry and kept him back. He mouthed, "Okay," to Amber. Was he telling her to trust him, that he had everything under control? Even so, she clawed at Franny's arm as the grip grew tighter around her throat.

Her fingernails raked the skin. Drops of blood beaded in the scrapes. Franny tightened her grip and yelled, "No one moves, or I will choke her to death."

She dragged Amber back toward the sliding glass door.

Steve stepped forward. Franny squeezed tighter. Amber's eyes bulged. Would they pop out of their sockets? Her heart raced. Franny was strong. Why didn't Steve jump in and help? All she could see was him staring, or was he staring past them?

People gaped, but no one moved. All conversation ceased. Amber knew it was a cliché, but they looked like deer caught in headlights, all staring wide-eyed, unmoving.

Franny hauled Amber backward. "Was it all an act?"

Amber tried to nod, but Franny tightened the chokehold. Amber's mouth opened and her tongue stuck out as she choked. Her vision grew fuzzy. Her body sagged with her arms dropping to her sides.

Suddenly, Franny's arm left her throat. Amber slumped to the patio cement, gasping.

Steve ran to her and lifted her up into a strong embrace. She sucked in great amounts of air.

Perry hurried over to her. "Take slow, deep breaths."

From behind her, she heard Trask say, "Stop strugglin'. You aren't gettin' away. I'm puttin' these here cuffs on you."

Still in Steve's arms, Amber turned to see dark sinister eyes boring into hers. She figured Franny didn't notice a tear streaming down the square-set jaw. In a way, Amber felt sorry for her, but hated her for killing Sarah, and the others.

Lancaster rushed toward Franny. "Why?"

"Franny," Steve interrupted, "you can talk all you want, but you have the right to remain silent." He recited the rest of her Miranda rights.

"Oh, Franny, you've ruined me." Henry slumped down in a chair with his head in his hands.

"I should have used 'Rocky' instead of 'Amber'," Franny said.

"What are you talking about?" Lancaster placed one hand on her shoulder.

"Oh, Cash." Franny gazed into Lancaster's face, looking like a hurt puppy. "I'm so sorry I have wrecked everything for you and Henry. If only I had long flowing hair and perfect cheek bones."

Franny's gaze glowed with love, even though she appeared angry that her plan failed. "Cash, you do understand? I wasn't beautiful enough for you. I've loved you so much."

"You love me like a brother." Cash ran a hand through his hair.

"That's what you think. Those women—they weren't for you. Only Henry and you were allowed to be full of yourselves. When the women became vain—well, that was unacceptable."

"Women?" Lancaster frowned.

"Yes." Franny blinked. "Rose, Tiffany, Sarah." She glared at Amber. "I should have known you wouldn't become vain. You were the perfect one. Not the others—you."

"Perfect for what?" Steve holstered his gun and held onto Amber while Trask kept a firm grip on Franny's arm.

"For Cash," Franny said. "I could never have him, so I had to find the perfect woman for him. Gorgeous; intelligent, like me; but not vain. Only he could be that way. James said so."

"Me?" James shoulder's sagged, as if he'd lost all the starch in his uniform. For the first time, Amber noticed how old he appeared.

"You always indulged the boys in their vanity," Franny said. "Beauty is to be admired and acquired."

"I am so sorry. You twisted all this." James bowed his head.

"It's all right." Franny lifted her chin high. "I learned a long time ago I would never have sexy long hair. Be model thin. I thought Harriet was like me. Then Marie helped her style her hair, use makeup, and changed her name to Rose. She was leaving Cash. I could not let that happen."

"Oh, my God." Lancaster took a step back and stared at her.

"I didn't know she'd written a letter. Her mother found it. They were going to cut you out of their will."

"No, not the Fullertons." James' eyes glistened and his stature diminished even further.

"What about Tiffany?" Lancaster asked.

"She attached to that stupid foster couple's kids. They were more important to her than you."

"Sarah?" Lancaster's face paled.

Amber's heart ached. She clung to Steve's arm. Franny didn't sound remorseful at all.

"She was deserting you, too. Going back to Amber in New York, work as a model. No one leaves you. I could not let that happen."

Steve removed Amber's hand and stepped away from her. "Franny, that's enough. Get moving. You're under arrest." He growled as he spun her around and shoved.

"Cash, I did it for you," Franny pleaded, craning around to see him.

Lancaster crossed his arms in front of him. "You've done a horrible thing." He wiped a tear from his eye. "Go with Steve. I'll… I'll make certain you get a lawyer."

Clutching her throat, Amber rasped, "Why'd you have to kill them if they were leaving?"

Franny stopped. She stared at Amber as if she were from an alien planet. "For Cash. They couldn't leave him. Only he could leave them. He's everything. He is the only one who treats me well. I have adored him all my life. He doesn't care if I have long flowing hair like Rose, or Tiffany's shapely legs, or Sarah's perfect posture, or even your grace. I'll never be beautiful to him. But he should be *mine*. He is my soul mate. I would do anything for him." She gazed at Lancaster. "You would do the same for me?"

CHAPTER 58

Amber fidgeted in Steve's office. Purple bruising showed on her neck and it hurt. She'd covered the bruises with a scarf. "Well, can't you say it?" Her voice sounded husky.

Steve looked from his sister's picture, to Perry, then back at Amber. "Okay. You were right. I was wrong. Happy?"

"No, I'll never be happy. Sarah's dead. But Dan and Linda were relieved to hear she hadn't committed suicide. At least I found answers to these questions."

"You did." Steve leaned back in his chair. "I'm sorry you may never know about your parents, though.

"I'll keep digging."

"I have no doubts. You might ask Trask to check into it for you."

Amber grinned. "I already have. Did you locate Max?"

"Red never did." Steve stood and sat on the corner of his desk. "But I did."

"You?"

"Yeah, don't sound so shocked. On our way back to the Martins' from Lancaster's, I spotted this old beat-up van and checked it out. Max was watching out for you. He didn't trust me. I advised him to go home. When I told him we'd found Sarah's killer, he was so thrilled he cried."

"Max cared for Sarah." Amber smiled.

"We all did," Steve said. "Cash is moving away from Carsonville. Henry Longreen's campaign is over. He doesn't believe he will survive the scandal. After giving his resignation speech tonight, he's heading east."

"Where?" Perry asked.

"He didn't say."

"Too bad Henry can't stay and support his sister." Amber crossed her legs. Steve was too close and she felt warm. "I feel sorry for her."

"Even after knowing she murdered Sarah?"

"Steve, I want her punished, but she's ill. She needs help."

"My sister's husband was ill, too, but I don't mind knowing he received the death penalty."

"And Franny might get that." Amber uncrossed her legs and pushed her chair back a little ways further from Steve. She needed breathing room.

"Cash is staying to help her out before he moves on," Steve stated.

Perry shifted in his seat. "How nice, since she did all the killing for him."

"He said he never had a clue." Steve glanced at Debbie's picture on his desk again. "Never even suspected Franny felt that way about him. She was always like a sister to him."

"Cash is more of a brother than Henry is," Perry said. "I can't believe Lancaster is supporting her."

Steve reached out and adjusted the picture frame. "I don't think James would let him do otherwise. The butler feels guilty."

"I imagine he probably does." Amber looked Steve in the eyes. "I have a question for you."

Steve raised an eyebrow. "Only one?"

"Really funny. Who brought the champagne into my room?"

"James. Franny told him the letter came and that he should take the bottle up, but place the letter under the tray. Said if it was bad news, you might not see and wouldn't read it until after the Martins' party."

"He bought that?"

"He never had reason to doubt Franny."

"And you believe it?"

Steve nodded and glanced at the clock. "You better get going or you'll miss your connecting flight."

"I'm anxious to get back to New York, where it's quiet." Perry stood, ready to leave.

Amber rose. "One more thing: what about the Fullertons' plane crash?"

"Franny was a good pilot and she also worked on her own plane. I believe she sabotaged their plane and fixed it so Cash wouldn't be on it."

"She tell you about Tiffany?" Amber asked.

"She's not talking to us about anything other than what she said at the Martins. I think I figured it out about the plane, but I have no idea where Tiffany is. So far, Franny's not saying."

"And the BeauCollec connection?" Amber asked. "How'd Dr. Madison's office manager fit in?"

"I knew you had more than one question." Steve smiled. "Franny admitted she'd sent Nancy on the cruise. She wanted her out of the way. Cash didn't have a clue about the corporation. Franny created it years ago. She'd forged everyone's signatures. No one knew about it."

"Think that's true?" Amber asked.

"So far no one's saying anything different." Steve stood and stepped closer to Amber.

She admired Steve for tying everything up and finally believing in her. She realized she'd miss him. Amber gazed up into his eyes. "Will I see you again?" She couldn't believe the little flutter in her chest and beads of perspiration forming at the nape of her neck as she waited for his answer.

His eyes twinkled. Her stomach rolled. "I have vacation time in the fall. Thought I might see the Statue of Liberty. Know anyone who could show me New York?"

Amber let out her breath, not realizing she'd held it in. She smiled. "I might be able to find someone." With her cheeks burning, she extended her hand. Steve clasped it and warmth spread through her body. "Thank you," she said, in a husky voice. "See you this fall, Detective."

The End

ABOUT THE AUTHOR

J. A. Winrich lives and writes in Ukiah, California and Green Valley, Arizona. J. A. Winrich has also written *Night Terror*, a psychological thriller, (available on Amazon both in print and e-book), and is working on another novel.

See website: www.writerjaw.com

www.ingramcontent.com/pod-product-compliance
Lightning Source LLC
Chambersburg PA
CBHW071241170626
46809CB00001B/43